About This Book

A new cozy mystery series from *USA Today* best-selling author Dale Mayer. Follow gardener and amateur sleuth Doreen Montgomery—and her amusing and mostly lovable cat, dog, and parrot—as they catch murderers and solve crimes in lovely Kelowna, British Columbia.

Riches to rags. … Hidden guns, … old but not forgotten wounds, … and a buried treasure!

Finding an Uzi in the urn at the shattered mausoleum is exciting and frustrating. Yet Doreen can't delve into the case, and Mack has been firm about that. She struggles to focus on other cases from her journalist files, in particular the Bob Small file. Only her plan goes off the rails when Nan and her cronies show up at her door, with the Rosemoor bus, intent on heading to the excitement happening at the cemetery.

When a grave is opened to reveal its shocking contents, the city is on high alert, as gang members arrive, circling around, looking for a rumored buried treasure, all connected to a man who died six months ago. Between crooked lawyers, greedy family members, changes of heart, and everyone else out looking for a buried treasure, Corporal Mack Moreau is on his toes. Especially as Doreen and her animal cohorts are in the middle once again.

But no one could possibly envision where this case ends up—right back in the cemetery where it all started …

USA Today Bestselling Author

DALE MAYER

Uzi in the Urn

Lovely Lethal Gardens 21

UZI IN THE URN: LOVELY LETHAL GARDENS, BOOK 21
Beverly Dale Mayer
Valley Publishing Ltd.

ISBN-13: 978-1-773367-62-0
Print Edition

Chapter 1

Midway into the Third Week of September

DOREEN WALKED ALONG the cemetery in Kelowna, Mack at her side, the animals roaming gently on leashes around them. Annabelle's funeral had been well attended by many of the locals. It did Doreen's heart good to see the large crowd, to see the people who loved Annabelle and who would miss her.

Doreen took a deep breath and stretched out her arms. "Life can be pretty good sometimes," she noted.

"At least you look a bit more relaxed, after taking a few days off from your bizarre hobby."

"I feel better too," she murmured, looking up at him with a bright smile. "That last one was a little scary."

"A little?" he quipped. "Remember how you weren't supposed to get attacked anymore?"

"Remember how you were supposed to jump in at the right time to save me?"

He sighed. "Yeah, believe me. I'm still not happy about that."

"What? The fact that you followed my instructions, or the fact that we solved this one?"

"It's not even a matter of having solved it. We did get the confession, on paper, and that makes it a heck of a lot easier for us," he noted, with a smile. "But thinking about how crazy it was will give me nightmares for weeks."

"Right? And then Nathan, he needs some counseling."

"His dad's there for him," Mack noted. "I can't imagine what that conversation looked like."

"No, I'm sure it wasn't easy. I have heard from both of them since though, and they're doing better. They will be fine."

He smiled, kissed her gently on the forehead, and said, "You're good people."

"I know I am. So are you."

He laughed. "Sometimes I wonder."

She looked over at the mausoleum full of tiny little locked drawers. "So these are full of those urns? I guess it's for people who have been cremated and who don't want to go in the ground."

He nodded. "People who don't want to be buried, and family members who want a place where they can come and visit their loved ones." He pointed to the beautiful plaques on the marble faces of each locked drawer.

She nodded. As they wandered up and down, she read off a bunch of the names. "Some of these are old."

"Sure," Mack said, "this practice is fairly common in a lot of places in the world."

"I haven't had a whole lot to do with death," she noted. "Outside of, …"

He nodded. "I know." He gave her a smile.

She laughed. "Kelowna has been good for me."

"Yeah, it has been—and for me too. And, yes, I did talk to my brother and my mother," he shared, with an eye roll.

She chuckled. "At least we know that they have your best interests at heart."

"Sure, but it's been a long time since I had to deal with my family checking in on my love life."

She smiled. "I never really had it at all, so I find it very cute."

"It's hardly cute," Mack argued. "Even my brother was in on this."

"I know, but think. Maybe my ex will finally divorce me, and we can get free of him."

"Maybe." Mack studied her. "You keep telling everybody that, until you're free and clear, you won't take the next step."

"Nope, I won't. You know that."

"I do."

She hesitated, a little bit of uncertainty entering her voice as she asked, "Or are you changing your mind?"

He stopped and glared at her. "Do I look as if I'm changing my mind? How many people do you know who wander cemeteries?"

"We were here for Annabelle, so it's not all that unusual."

"Maybe." He sighed. "But no. I'm not changing my mind. I'm waiting. Patiently."

"Sometimes patiently." She chuckled.

"Fine. … Impatiently."

She nodded. "And it's appreciated. I don't feel as if I can move forward until I take care of my past." He reached out, letting his hand slide down her arm to grasp her fingers in his. She gave a gentle squeeze back. "This is such a beautiful resting place," she murmured in quiet joy. "So much history." As she rounded the corner, she gasped. "Look."

And there, one of the tiles had been cracked open.

Mack frowned, as he dropped her hand and stepped forward. "Vandalism is another problem but not usually like this." He sighed.

"Yeah, but …" She stopped and looked into the opened-up area. "The urn's still here, or something is."

He opened up his phone and hit Flashlight and said, "Yeah, you can still see it there. That's something."

Peering closer, she pointed. "Something else is beside it. I can't really see it clearly."

He put on a pair of gloves, and, moving some of the marble out of the way, he managed to open up enough that his flashlight shone into the dark space, and they could see what it was.

"It's black," she noted. "What is that?"

He muttered a curse word.

"We really should work on your swearing."

He sighed. "Says you."

"What is it?" she queried.

He drew his phone closer and made a call.

She frowned at him. "What's the matter?"

He placed a finger against his lips, and he quickly answered the questions at the other end.

After he'd disconnected, she asked, "Uzi? Did you say an Uzi is in there?"

He glared at her. "No. No, I did not."

Her lips twitched. She'd heard him, and, once she'd heard him, there was no end to it. "In an urn," she cried out. "So there is … Wait for it, wait for it."

And he shook his head. "No, no, I'm not listening." And he clapped his hands over his ears.

She burst out laughing. "Doesn't matter," she declared.

"You can run, but you can't hide. My next case is the *Uzi in the Urn*."

And she burst out laughing because she had another case, and it rolled off her tongue. *Uzi in the Urn.*

Chapter 2

DOREEN SAT OUTSIDE on her patio, a notepad beside her, her laptop open, a cup of coffee at her side, but all she could do was stare out aimlessly at the world around her. She was focused on a gun—an Uzi at that. The gun had been dismantled, so a piece would fit in the cremation urn itself in the broken vault that she and Mack had found.

She understood men and their toys, but wasn't that carrying a favorite weapon a little over-the-top that he be buried with it? And not tossed into a grave and buried in the ground but hidden in a vault with an urn full of ashes? If they were ashes? She shook her head.

Mack had done an incredibly fast job of getting her out of there, against all her protests. She'd been pretty upset at the time, as this was something that she could really get into, but he didn't want her involved. Of course not. She kept inserting herself in his cases. She sighed at that, and, when her phone rang, she snatched it up. "Hello?"

Mathew, her soon-to-be ex-husband, and not who she had expected. She groaned, pinched the bridge of her nose. "What do you want? You realize now I'm in trouble for even answering."

Mathew sighed. “I don’t understand you.”

“What’s to understand?” she cried out. “I want this divorce mess over with.”

“That’s all I want too,” he roared.

“Then sign the dratted paperwork,” she muttered.

“I would have done so already,” he snapped, “if you weren’t such a greedy *B*. If you weren’t, none of this would be a problem.”

She stopped at that and glared at her phone. “Okay, so now that this conversation is degenerating, I’m hanging up.”

“Don’t,” he yelled.

She hesitated but knew perfectly well what Nick would say. “I’m not allowed to talk to you,” she stated and then winced because, of course, that’s exactly what she was doing. She remembered Mack giving her a warning about still being under the influence of her ex, and she wondered if this was yet another symptom of that. “What do you want?” she asked calmly.

“I want you to be reasonable.”

“And I don’t even know what *reasonable* is in this matter,” she declared. “So I trust my lawyer.”

“Yeah, well, you trusted the last one too,” he growled.

“Yeah, and look how far that got me.”

“She made my life miserable too. And what’s this I understand that you’ll inherit from her?”

“I don’t know anything about that,” she lied smoothly, wincing at her ability to do that. Not exactly the personal growth she was hoping for. “The will’s supposed to be in probate.”

“Yeah, I already called her lawyer and talked to him.”

“Why? Were you expecting something from Robin?” she asked, with a giggle.

At first, silence came from the other end. "No reason for her not to." But his tone was defensive, angry even.

"You weren't together long enough," Doreen noted. "If you hadn't been so pissed off at her, she might have had time to change her will. But she didn't, and the lawyers already got the official will, so you're out of luck."

"And, if you're getting money from her, you don't need money from me," he replied craftily.

"I don't know anything about Robin's will," she stated. "I don't know what I might be getting."

"That's a lie," Mathew snapped. "The will has already been read."

"Sure it's been read, but an awful lot of parts and pieces of her estate must be sold," she snapped right back, "and that's nothing that I know anything about. Remember? *I don't know anything about business,* according to you."

"Because you don't," he said, with that sneering tone again.

She shook her head. "If you've got something to say, spit it out. Otherwise I'm hanging up now."

"Wait," he cried out.

However, this time she didn't wait. She ended the call for good. She sat, staring at her phone, as if it were a viper, and knew that she would be in trouble because now she had to phone Nick and confess. Groaning at that, she quickly picked up her phone, and, when she got no response on the other end, she smiled, thinking she had a lucky escape. She quickly left him a short message to tell him what happened and hung up. When her phone rang only a few minutes later, she groaned because, of course, it was Nick. "What?"

"So, are you angry at *me*?" Nick asked.

"No," Doreen corrected, "but I do feel like a kid who

has done something wrong."

Nick laughed. "Well, you did. So why did you answer the phone in the first place?"

"Because I didn't look at who it was first. I was expecting your brother to call. So I picked up the phone and answered it."

"Ah, so back to my brother again."

She groaned. "Don't tell him that. It'll just go to his head," she muttered, "and I'm not talking to him."

"If you're not talking to him," Nick stated, half chuckling, "how is it that you were answering the phone to talk to him?"

She glared at her phone again. "Stop with the mind games," she mumbled.

At that, he burst out in a big guffaw. "Oh, I do like hearing all this. You two are meant to be together. You'll be good for him."

"I don't think *he* thinks so. Right now he's more than a little frustrated at me."

"Why?" he asked curiously. "What happened?" She told him about the walk in the cemetery and what they found.

"Good Lord. In one of those mausoleum boxes?"

"Yes," she confirmed. "I'm sure there's a proper name for them. I don't know what it is. But, yes, in one wall with plaques and urns behind them. One had been broken open, yet nobody seemed to take away what was inside it."

"So maybe it wasn't so much vandalism as an accident—think of a child and a baseball bat."

"I guess it's possible. It was the only one damaged." And then she thought about it for a second. "However, I don't know that for a fact—that this was the only one broken into. We didn't get through them all. *Hmm*, maybe I should go back and take another look."

"Or maybe you should stay out of it, so that my brother doesn't get angry at you," Nick suggested.

"He already is," she stated. "I didn't want to leave the cemetery, and he was not very happy about that either."

Nick chuckled. "Mack does have a job to do, and he is trying to make these cases stick in a court of law," he explained. "So the least outside interference, the better it would be for making a successful case in court."

"I know. I know. I know," she muttered. "But he made me come home, after we found something awesome like that, and then he wouldn't let me talk about it. He wouldn't even let me see anything more. He went ahead and called in for backup of all things, as if an active shooter were at the cemetery at that time. … And when there was some excitement, he sent me home. On top of that, he didn't even drive me home himself. He sent me home with Arnold. And you can bet Arnold was busy chattering the whole time about what they found."

"I'm sure Arnold won't get a good reception, not when Mack finds out that he did that either," Nick noted, still chuckling.

"Maybe not," she agreed, "but then Arnold shouldn't have done quite so much talking."

"I think that's part of Arnold's charm, isn't it?" he asked.

"Sure, but he's not very good at sharing straightforward information though," she muttered. "He does go around in circles."

Nick laughed again. "So what did your husband want?"

"He told me to be reasonable, and, now that I'm getting money from Robin, I shouldn't need his money."

"What did you say?"

"I told him that I didn't know anything about the money from Robin. Her estate was all in probate. Yes, I know that I've been left something, but I didn't share that with Mathew. Plus, a lot is still left to be done with Robin's property, like selling stuff. And it had nothing to do with Mathew."

"Good," Nick replied, "and that's quite true. A lot is still left to be done, and it has nothing to do with your husband. Regardless of whether you end up inheriting millions from Robin, it still doesn't change the fact that Mathew owes you millions too."

"What it does mean is that he's getting desperate, and desperate means dangerous," she muttered.

"Any animal's dangerous when cornered, but this guy? … I keep warning you that something ugly can come from this," Nick reminded her. "I keep asking you if you have any serious problems with him, but you keep telling me that you don't think so."

"Yet, at the same time, I'm terrified that he *does* have serious problems with me," she admitted.

"It would be nice if my brother were there a little more often to keep an eye on things," Nick muttered. "However, if he's got a hot new case …"

"He does. It's a very hot new case, and he won't let me anywhere close to it," she wailed.

Nick burst out laughing, then got serious. "Don't answer the phone if it's your husband. Look at who's calling you, for heaven's sake. That's what Caller ID is for after all. And don't answer if he ever calls you again."

"How close do you think he is to signing?"

"I thought we had an agreement, but we have a couple sticky points yet to resolve, and I want you to get paid right away. Now he knows that you're not sitting there starving, and he wants to hold off and pay when the divorce deal is done and dusted."

"But then that gives him more time, doesn't it?"

"Absolutely it does, more time to potentially move money, to declare bankruptcy. He can pull all kinds of shenanigans," Nick declared. "And, if he already hired one crooked lawyer, he's likely to hire a second one. Litigations could go on for years. Hence a court date."

"So then a money payout," she noted. "That makes sense to me. Maybe even the court case makes sense."

"That is starting to look like a better option for me too," Nick concurred, "but obviously it's not what Mathew wants."

"Yet he doesn't appear to be fussing too much about it, at least in court or with his attorney. Yet he's fussing at me often enough," she stated.

"I think he's worried about the impact that you'll have on his bottom line."

She thought about that and frowned. "I'm not so sure about that. I think it's more about control. For him, it's all about winning. So it's more about winning and … *not* losing. The case, the money, all of it."

"Do you think so?" Nick asked curiously.

"Yeah, one thing he hates, and that's losing. So, if it looks as if he'll lose, he might do something so that nobody wins. He is unpredictable that way."

"*Huh*. I wondered about that."

"He is dangerous," she murmured. "I just don't know how dangerous."

"And that again is something that we should take another look at apparently," Nick muttered. "I don't like hearing all that."

"Nor do I, so the sooner you can get this to a conclusion, the sooner it will be better for me."

"Got it. Maybe I'll turn up the heat."

"And what good will that do?" she cried out. "Mathew will just get angrier."

"Maybe, but, if he gets angry faster, maybe he'll get over it faster too." And, with that, Nick hung up.

She wasn't at all sure what Nick meant by that, but it didn't seem to be a good deal for anybody, especially not her. She pondered that for a long moment, and then her phone rang again. When she realized it was her ex, she winced. She didn't answer it, and it went to voice mail. She quickly listened to the message.

"How this will end up now," Mathew declared, his voice silky, *"you really don't want that ending, do you? No point in having money if you can't spend it."* She froze and phoned Nick back. When he answered, she asked, "Did you contact him?"

"I did. Why?"

"He left me a voice message."

"Send it to me."

"How am I supposed to do that?" she asked, looking down at her phone. Following his instructions, she managed to get a copy and then send it to Nick.

He phoned her back almost immediately. "I'm moving the court case up. This has got to stop."

"Yeah, ya think?" she quipped. "This is what I was afraid of."

"And that won't be the answer. He needs to come before a judge, and a judge needs to decide what'll happen. I need to tell Mack."

"That won't make Mack happy," she said.

"Why is that?"

"Because, one, I answered the phone when I wasn't supposed to," she explained, "and, two, he's already worried about this guy."

"So he should be, especially after that voice mail. Now he's threatened you. Stay close to home, and lock the doors." And, with that, he hung up.

She glared at her phone, not at all happy with the sudden turn of events. She stared outside because this was not what she had hoped would be her day.

When Mack called her twenty minutes later, she groaned. "Wow, that didn't take long for him to tattle."

"Who tattled?" Mack asked in confusion.

She winced. "Oh, you didn't talk to your brother?"

"No, but I will now," he declared softly. "So, do you want to tattle first?"

He imitated her tone and added a layer of lightness, but this would turn ugly when he found out. She took a deep breath. "I accidentally answered a phone call from my ex."

"Accidentally?" he repeated in that very slow and precise way of his.

"Yes," she stated. "I was expecting a phone call from you. I didn't even look. I snatched it up because I was irate that you took so long to get back to me, and it was him."

Dead silence was her answer. "You were angry that I took so long to get back to you?" he asked, his voice deepening.

"Well, you got me out of the cemetery pretty darn fast," she cried out, "and here I was hoping for some answers."

"What answers did you think you would get?" he asked, a note of humor in his tone. "We want answers too, but it's not as if I can just sit here and create them out of nothing."

She groaned at that. "I know. I know. I'm sorry."

"And what did your ex say?" She gave him an abbreviated version, right up to the point of his brother saying he needed to contact Mathew.

"He threatened you?"

"I can send you a copy of the message. And, yes," she confirmed, with a sigh, "I don't like it. I do understand I shouldn't have answered in the first place, but Mathew's getting angrier."

"He's crossed a line now too," Mack stated. "Sounds to me as if we need to pick him up and have a talk with him."

"And do what?" she asked. "Shake him down? He'll get more pissed off when he gets out. You don't have any way to keep him off my back, and this divorce mess is now becoming a big headache, and that's what I was afraid would happen in the first place."

"We will fix it," Mack replied, his voice firm.

"And you'll identify my body while it is laid out on a cold slab in the morgue," she snapped. "He's dangerous."

"Apparently, but we can't let him get away with this. You can count on that."

"Yeah? What will you do?"

"I've got a lot of ideas, but I will talk to the captain, and I will also talk to my brother, and we'll get back to you. Stay indoors, and lock everything up."

"I'm out on the deck," she protested. "It's a beautiful day, and I want to visit with Nan."

He hesitated and added, "He could be out there right now."

"Then find out where he is," she said, "because I don't want to sit here and be terrified that he'll come popping around the corner, if there's no need to be scared."

"You need to keep an eye out for him."

"Sure, but keeping an eye out is a very different story than spending every waking moment terrified."

"I'll get back to you." With that, Mack hung up.

She shook her head, frustrated and angry. He was right. All of this is because she'd answered the phone. And now she didn't know what to do, but they were right. She shouldn't have talked to Mathew, and that made her even more upset with herself.

Why was it things always ended up going south when she was trying hard to do the right thing?

She sat here nervously looking around, and, when Mack phoned again, he told her, "No sign of him having flown in this morning."

"No, I wouldn't expect there to be. That is, however, good news."

"And yet you're expecting him to follow up?"

"You're taking away the one thing he really loves, his money. This is all about control, which I already told Nick today. Mathew doesn't like to lose."

"Right," Mack muttered, "and yet apparently he was totally okay to get rid of you back then."

"Of course." She winced at the phrase. "I was a liability in his world. He had bigger and better things at the time."

"He can have bigger and better things again, but he won't get you. So … stay strong, and I'll come by in a bit."

"You got any more information to share?"

He groaned. "It would be a whole lot nicer if I could come by for a visit and not feel as if I'm being interrogated."

She hesitated and then said, "Fine, come on anyway."

He laughed. "I'm sure that was not easy for you to say."

"It wasn't." She grinned. "However, I'll think about how to get under your guard when you're here."

He groaned at that. "I'll be by in a bit. If you go to visit Nan, send me a text."

"Fine," she muttered and hung up.

She had barely set her phone down when Nan called. "You coming down for tea?" she asked.

Suspicious, Doreen replied, "Not even a *Hey, do you want to come down for tea*? Would have been nice to hear that or *How are you? How you doing? What's going on?*"

Nan laughed. "I figured that you would have information on what's going on down at the cemetery."

"I was there when it happened," she muttered, "but I sure don't have much information."

"That's it," she crowed. "Tea, come down for tea. I'll go see if I can find some treats." With that, her grandmother hung up on her.

Doreen groaned and then sighed because what was she supposed to do? Her grandmother lived for these cases, almost as much as Doreen did. They were two peas in a pod in some ways, except her grandmother had been badly hurt in one of Doreen's cases, and she didn't want Nan to get hurt again. And, of course, her grandmother would say the exact same thing about Doreen. And, for that matter, so would Mack.

Everybody wanted Doreen to stay out of these cases, but they'd gotten into her blood seemingly. Given that she hadn't gone actively looking for any of it …

With Mack's warning in mind, she quickly sent him a text, saying she was heading to Nan's. With that done, she hopped to her feet, grabbed the dog leash, and gave it a shake. "Anybody want to go for a walk?"

Chapter 3

ALMOST AT NAN'S, Doreen stopped and sniffed the air. Something was special about a late-summer day, which, if she were honest, was gloriously springing around her. It was definitely a one-of-a-kind day. Not quite so hot, beautiful, the creeks still ran freely. The sound of the water moving slowly down the rocks sounded delicate and musical.

When she walked onto Nan's little patio, Doreen heard Nan talking with somebody inside her small apartment. As Doreen called out, the patio door opened, and Nan stepped out, with a bright smile. "There you are," Doreen noted, looking through the patio doors to see various other people staring at her. "If you already have company"—she glanced at Nan—"I can leave and come back later."

Nan gave a wave of her hand. "They're all looking for information. So now that you're here, we can get some."

"But I don't have much," she warned her.

"No, of course not. I'll tell them to come back later." She quickly stepped inside and addressed the crowd. By the time she was done, the others had left.

"And you can't be a source for everyone either," she warned her grandmother, when Nan returned.

Her grandmother sighed. "That's easy to say, but everybody knows that you're here, and that means, everybody knows that information is at hand."

"Some information, yes," Doreen acknowledged. "Some information is good, but I don't have tons of information. It's all a bit confusing."

"We heard that somebody desecrated one of those vaults down at the cemetery."

"That's correct."

"How did you hear that?"

"I was with Mack. We hung around, after Annabelle's funeral, to put fresh roses on a couple graves from some of the cases that I've been involved in. Afterward we walked around, talking, commenting on how beautiful some of the gardens were. We found this mausoleum with marble markers, and I thought they were beautiful. We read the names and walked farther around, when we saw one of the plaques had been smashed. But the burial site itself didn't seem to be looted. Or not all of it anyway. Maybe something was taken, and the looter left the rest."

"But that would be …" Her grandmother stared at her. "You don't want to think about somebody looting your grave," she muttered.

"Yet it's an age-old crime," Doreen reminded Nan, who gave a mock shudder.

"Yes, but still, what a horrible thing to think about."

Doreen didn't really see how different it was than killing somebody or any worse than a lot of the things that they had seen already, but grave robbing appeared to bother Nan more, so Doreen didn't belabor the point.

"Anyway, as soon as Mack saw what was inside, he quickly phoned to get other cops down there, and then I got sent home." She frowned. "So I don't have any other information."

"Yes, but what was in it?"

She hesitated, not sure what Mack would say; then she shrugged. "I think it was a gun. He mentioned something about an Uzi."

"Wow," Nan stared at her, nonplussed. "Somebody loved their gun so much that they were buried with it?" For some reason that struck Nan as funny, and she went off in a peal of laughter.

"I thought maybe …"

"What else would it be?" Nan asked, shaking her head.

"I don't know. I seriously don't know. I don't even know what name was on the plaque."

"No, and that would have been interesting too," Nan replied.

Doreen continued. "All these thoughts ran through my head. Was that vault targeted on purpose? Did that person want to be buried with the gun? Who knew the gun was there and thought to get it themselves? Although that doesn't make sense, considering the gun was still there. And I don't have a name yet for the bashed-in vault. I'll keep trying to get Mack to tell me that much. Then I can research the dead person's name, maybe find something interesting."

Nan sighed. "You're right. That's definitely slim pickings on the information."

"I told you that," she warned Nan, before any other caustic comments came regarding her way of handling information.

Nan nodded. "You did mention that, and we keep hoping that more tidbits will come."

"What do you know about it?" she asked her grandmother.

"Richie talked to Darren, but he didn't have a whole lot to say either, just that he hadn't been down there yet. He didn't really know what was going on, but he was on his way."

"And then maybe you can get some information from him a little later," she murmured.

"Maybe, but then he'll get the riot act from Mack," Nan noted, sliding a sideways look at her.

"Yeah, same as me," Doreen agreed. "The police try to muzzle the gossip in order to keep some of the information secret."

"That's one thing," Nan noted, with a sigh, "but those of us want another mystery to solve. It's been at least a few days."

Doreen laughed, giving her grandmother an eye roll. "Yes, it has. And a few days between crimes is a good thing."

"For you, it definitely is a good thing," Nan stated. "You needed a break."

"And so do you," she reminded her.

Nan waved a hand, as if to completely ignore that statement. "I'm perfectly fine."

"You also have a busy life, and you're enjoying all the things that you're involved in," Doreen noted, "so this is something that you can ignore for a while."

"I would ignore it if I thought it would do any good," Nan retorted. "However, ignoring things around here isn't so easy. Always so much is going on." Then she clapped her hands together. "Speaking of which, the teakettle should have popped by now. Let me go make tea, and I'll see what I've got leftover from the Rosemoor kitchen."

"Did you get something?"

"I did, but they gave me a covered basket, so I don't know exactly what is in there."

At that, Doreen pondered why the kitchen would give her grandmother a basket of food. When Nan returned with the teapot, Doreen asked her, "What did you tell the kitchen that they gave you this basket?"

"I told them that I had company coming and that we would sit out on the patio and have some treats, if there were any that I could have," Nan explained. "They didn't have a problem with it at all."

Doreen wondered at that, but considering it'd been going on for quite a while, she wasn't sure that she should say anything either. When her grandmother took the tea towel off the basket, Doreen frowned. "Good Lord, how many people did you say were coming?"

"Six," Nan stated, with a nod of satisfaction, and then gloated at the hoard in front of her. "I figure a forty-sixty split. What do you think?"

Doreen looked up at her grandmother, back down at the basket, stuffed full of treats, and shook her head. "I'll be happy to even have one," she admitted.

"No, you'll get 60 percent, and take them home and enjoy them for the rest of the day," Nan stated. "I don't need more than a couple myself. But, if I don't have some, I'll feel guilty."

Doreen laughed. "I'm glad you can feel guilty over something because I'm sure the kitchen didn't know it would be just me visiting."

"You brought three with you," Nan pointed out. "So it's not as if I was lying." At that, she looked down at Mugs, whose tail was wagging heavily, and Goliath, who was getting closer and closer to the basketful of treats.

Doreen smacked him gently on the shoulder. He glared at her, while Thaddeus hopped up and snagged part of a baby croissant and hopped down. Goliath raced after him, and so did Mugs. Squawking, Thaddeus went around in circles, until Doreen quickly lifted him up higher than the other two.

"If you're going to steal and then flaunt it in front of them," she told Thaddeus, "you've got to expect to share." At that, the bird settled on her shoulder with his croissant, and, using her shoulder as a plate, he ripped up his treat into bits and pieces.

"Oh no you don't," Doreen wailed, as croissant crumbs fell onto her shirt and even into her hair. She quickly put him on the table. "Eat here," she stated sternly, as she got up and brushed off the crumbs. She looked over at Nan, who was grinning widely. "Sometimes I think they do this to keep you entertained," Doreen muttered.

"And I'm all for it," Nan agreed instantly. "Life's too short to not find something to laugh at every day. I just see you guys once, and it puts a smile on my face."

Regardless of the reason for the visit, it was still lovely to see Nan. Doreen was now thoroughly stuffed herself, after not eating much breakfast, and Nan was happy to have time with her and the animals. "As much as I hate to say it, it's time to go home."

Nan looked at her and nodded slowly. "I guess Mack wants to keep you pretty close, huh?"

"I don't know about keeping me close, yet he is a little worried about me." At Nan's stare. Doreen shrugged, then added, "My ex is causing trouble again."

A frown settled on Nan's face. "The sooner you get rid of him, the better," she declared in a severe tone.

"I agree with you." Doreen grimaced. "Believe me. I do. It's a matter of making that happen though. The Moreau brothers don't want me to walk away from the marriage without getting something, and I warned them that Mathew's dangerous, but I don't think anyone thought he'd threaten me."

"As you already know firsthand, he's all about control, and he's all about money, and you're threatening both of those."

"He's already lost control, which is the problem, and now Nick, my lawyer, is pushing Mack to pick up Mathew on charges of threatening me. Plus, Nick's trying to push for this divorce to be adjudicated by a judge."

"So Mathew will have a lot of trouble with all that, won't he?"

"He sure will. Big-time too," she stated. "I'm not looking forward to the fallout."

Nan nodded wisely. "No, and I won't be happy if anything happens to you because of that man," she declared in her severest of tones. "He was never good enough for you to begin with. I sure don't want to be giving ground to him, now that you're free and clear."

"I agree with you there too," Doreen added. "You also know that sometimes things don't go the way we plan."

"I know. I do know that."

As Doreen stood, she leaned over to give her grandmother a kiss. "You look after yourself."

Nan gave her granddaughter a troubled look. "*You* look after *yourself*," she murmured. "I don't want anything to happen to you."

"Ditto," she murmured back. She gave her a gentle hug again for good luck and then called the animals. "We'll head home and spend the afternoon doing something," she told Nan. "Maybe I can find another case to go after."

"How about the Bob Small files?" Nan suggested. "I keep thinking about Hinja lately."

"Right," Doreen murmured. "Hinja compiled all that info. Maybe, maybe it's time for that. It's certainly big enough that it'll keep my focus, particularly if Mack ends up forcing me to stay grounded at home." Nan frowned at her. Doreen shrugged. "He's worried that Mathew would come here and attack me."

"I think it's pretty far-fetched, but … I don't know," Nan admitted. "That man's dangerous."

"He is," she murmured. "I tried to warn Mack and Nick both, but probably not as much as I should."

"Did you tell them the truth about everything Mathew did to you?"

She stared at Nan. "Probably not. … Only so many things I want to bring up."

"And yet," Nan snapped, "they can't deal with things properly if they don't know everything."

"I've certainly told them a lot. So it's not as if I have tried to minimize what kind of person Mathew was," Doreen added. "I don't think anybody needs to go into all the details."

Nan winced. "No, of course not, especially you. As long as they're aware that Mathew is very dangerous, … that should do."

"Mack's aware." Doreen nodded. "I don't know about Nick. He's the one pushing to end this divorce faster—which I want too—thinking it'll protect me, but that just makes Mathew irate," she muttered. "Maybe I didn't make it as clear as I should have to him."

Nan looked at her, her voice and tone severe. "Maybe it's time that you do."

She stared at her, then shrugged. "I'll see." And, with that, she headed back up to the creek and home.

Chapter 4

WHEN MACK TOLD Doreen that he'd be by soon, apparently *soon* meant well over an hour. And that was an hour *after* she got home from Nan's. When his truck drove up her driveway, Mugs took off in excitement, as if he hadn't seen Mack in forever. And maybe in his mind he hadn't. She'd talked to Mack on the phone already several times, and that was a whole different story. When he came in through the front door, she sensed a buzz of excitement. "Oh," she noted, her hands on her hips. "I sure hope you can explain that look on your face."

"What look?" he asked, trying for innocence.

She shook her head at that. "Oh no you don't. You don't get off that easy." He glared at her, but she was not deterred. "Something has lit a fire under you. I'm not sure what's going on, but you're pretty excited about it." He stared at her, nonplussed. She nodded. "Yes, I do know you that well."

He laughed. "Maybe that's a good thing, maybe not. At times it would be nice if you weren't quite so perceptive."

"Well, I am, particularly when it comes to you." She crossed her arms over her chest. "So what's going on?" He shrugged. "Or did you find who's vault had that Uzi?"

"No, not yet," he replied evenly, but that steady note of indifference in his tone gave it away—he was trying hard to not let her know something about it. "I guess it's too late to get any forensic tests done on it, isn't it?"

He nodded. "Yeah, sure is."

But that answer came too fast, and she smiled. "Or not," she murmured. "Maybe you should tell me what you have so far."

"Or not," he said, with a grin.

She sighed. "So then why are you here?" He raised his eyebrows at her tone. She flushed. "If you're not here to share information, and you'll keep stuff from me, that'll make me cross."

He chuckled. "Yeah, we'll keep coming up against this same wall time and again because some things I can share, and some things I can't."

"I'm sure you could share this," she declared. At that, he burst out laughing, but such joy filled his tone that she stopped and looked at him. "It's that Uzi, isn't it?" His facial expression gave it away, and she smiled. "Yeah, it sure is. Now isn't that exciting," she said, clapping her hands. "So, is it involved in another case? Whose gun was it? Whose vault was it? What's going on? It's too early for ballistics, I'm sure." Then she stopped and shook her head. "Or maybe not. How often do you get an Uzi falling into your lap?"

"Not very often," he admitted.

"Then, of course, it could be connected to something big." She still eyed him, her mind rapidly going over all the cases she knew about. "Or was it something locally?"

He stepped forward and placed a finger on her lips. "Stop." She glared at him. "You're too good at this. You know I can't tell you anything."

"Bob Small," she said.

Mack froze and stared at her, his eyes going wide.

She grinned. "That's it. This is connected to Bob Small."

"I can't tell you anything," he murmured. Then, as he paced the living room, a blue streak of swearing burst forth out of frustration. Finally he stopped, his hand on his hips, still glaring at her.

She nodded. "No, you might not be able to *say* something. However, that doesn't change the fact that I can see it in your eyes."

"Well, dang it, don't look so close."

At that, she burst out laughing.

"Besides," Mack added, "we don't know that it's Bob Small. It's a case that might be connected to him."

She nodded. "A lot of cases could be connected to him."

"Exactly," he agreed smugly, "and that's part of the problem. We can't do as much as we want or as fast as we want because we have a lot of things to check on."

"Okay," she replied. "I can work with that, and checking is very important."

"It very much is," Mack agreed, "so give us a chance to do what we need to do."

"Give me the name on the vault."

Mack shook his head. "Doreen ..."

"Just tell me whose vault was broken into."

Mack seemed to consider it, with an eye roll for her. She quietly waited. "Joe Smith," he said.

Doreen snorted. "Nice try, Mack. Giving me a fake name."

Yet he only shrugged.

"I can't search Joe Smith," she complained. "Well, I can,

but I'll get a gazillion hits. Do you know how long it'll take to go through all that to get relevant information?"

Mack smirked.

"Fine. Be that way." Then she added, "And then there is Annalise, Hinja's niece, who was killed down on the coast."

"And again, remember," he stated. "We have no body in that case. We can't know for certain she didn't just run away."

"That fifteen-year-old girl did not just up and leave," Doreen stated. "No way that happened."

"No, but we've also seen cases where they were kidnapped, and the girls managed to escape later. Sometimes the things people do are pretty hard for any of us to understand, but eventually the truth comes out."

"You hope," she corrected. "I think, for a lot of these cases, people gave up hope a long time ago."

He winced at that. "No, you're right," he agreed. "We do the best we can, but we can't always get all the answers."

"I'm not trying to say that you should," she clarified, then she turned and walked into the kitchen. "I could use coffee. How about you?"

"Coffee would be good."

"You look awfully tired, Mack."

"It was a crazy morning."

"You didn't really think anything dangerous was going on right when we were there, did you?"

"No, not necessarily, but, when you get a specialized weapon like that, you wonder what it might be connected to."

"You've mentioned a lot of cases here in Kelowna lately, and yet I don't remember anything to do with an Uzi," she said, thinking out loud.

"No, and neither do we, and that's part of the problem. Until we got a hit on one of the databases …"

She asked, "As in the weapon used or as in ballistics that matched?"

"Originally, any weapon potentially used, but, when we ran ballistics on a special request, yes, it matched."

She looked at him in excitement. "Wow, that means it's a cold case."

His eyebrows shot up. "No, it means it's an active case. Remember? We were there and found the gun …"

She shook her head. "Obviously it's not an active case."

"It is now," he stated, his voice firm. "You know what that means." He glared at her. "Right?"

She studied him but could see him willing her to do the right thing. She nodded. "I know what it means," she admitted calmly, "but, if it connects to a cold case, that's a different story."

"No," he stated flatly. "This is a whole different circumstance."

"I'm not sure what that means," she muttered.

"I'm not sure I can tell you much more."

"Fine." She considered him for a long moment. "An awful lot of people are looking for information on this."

"There always is," he agreed, "and it's one of the reasons why you need to stay out of it."

"Nobody I know would tattle."

He sighed and shook his head.

"Okay, fine, so Nan'll be curious, but, if I tell her not to tell others, then she won't."

"Yeah, just like when I tell you not to, and you don't?" he asked curiously.

She frowned at him. "That's not called for."

He laughed. "It absolutely is. Remember? We don't know what's going on with this case. So I need you to stay quiet on it."

"Fine, I won't tell anybody now."

"*Now*?"

She nodded. "I told Nan that we found a gun in an urn, but that's all."

"That's already enough," he muttered, with a sigh.

"Well, if you've got it connected to another case, then that's a good thing. You should have this solved in no time."

"Maybe," he agreed. "It's also possible that we won't get it solved for a long while. An awful lot of threads need to come together."

"It wouldn't be Bob Small though."

"Why's that?" he asked her.

"Do we know what weapons he used?"

"No, we don't. Remember? No bodies."

"So how did anybody get onto him anyway?"

"He was in the area a little too often to make people happy."

"So circumstantial. You realize, with a trucker, that he could have been dumping the bodies anywhere."

"And that is one of the concerns," Mack admitted calmly. "As I mentioned before, a lot to sort out."

She stayed quiet and made the coffee, thinking this over. When the coffee was done, she took two cups and motioned at the back door. "You want to open the door for me?"

He stepped up, opened the door, and they went outside to sit on the patio. "You're being awfully accommodating," Mack noted hesitantly.

"Is that what this is?" she asked, with a note of humor. "I get it. The bottom line is to solve these cases and to have a case that you can take to court and win, but my understanding was Bob Small would be a very old man by now."

"That doesn't alleviate the fact that he's still guilty in many of these cases."

"Or at least you're assuming he is," she corrected.

"Exactly, and, considering the amount of time that has gone by, we can't make a mistake on this."

She sighed. "It really does boggle the mind to think that somebody could have committed all these murders without getting caught."

"At least we're assuming …" Mack stared at her, and then his gaze turned inward. "Most of the killings were thirty-plus years ago."

"And you did say some of the reasons people stop is they are incarcerated."

"Yes. … That's a common reason, but it could be a lot of things. Maybe he lived in a different country, and he didn't stop but continued there."

She stared at him. "And that could be quite possible in this case, when he's a trucker, right?"

He nodded. "It is possible. It's possible he's still out there doing his thing and has been all these years."

She shuddered at that. "To think that somebody could kill all these young women boggles the mind," she muttered. "Hinja was deadly certain that Bob Small was responsible for her niece's death."

"Yet there's no proof either, and it would be nice if we had some DNA from her that we could utilize."

"Well, he came and got a bunch of stuff from Hinja's bathroom, but I don't know if anything might have been missed. However, she has passed away now, so I can't be sure. I have Hinja's letters and the notebook in my Bob

Small files."

"But none of that would have his DNA."

"No, but that doesn't mean there isn't some of her personal things that might still have something," she suggested. "I can always contact the estate."

He frowned at her and then shrugged. "But we'll never know whose DNA it is."

"No," she agreed, "and even if we could place him at Hinja's place, that doesn't necessarily place him at the niece's place."

"Exactly," Mack murmured. "It gives him a connection to the case, but that would be it."

She pondered that, then slowly nodded. "Having to make it legal really does screw up the flow, doesn't it?"

He burst out laughing. "It absolutely does," he agreed affectionately. "Maybe find something else to work on."

She stared at him, with that knowing look. "Something not connected to Bob Small?"

He shrugged. "I don't know that we'll have a connection here that's workable, but ballistics has evolved with a case from more than a few years back. And even better, I believe they've lifted some fingerprints."

"Now that," she said, almost bouncing off her chair, "is very exciting because that bit of forensic evidence is something that's been long missing with Bob Small, hasn't it?"

"Again, we don't know that it is him. However, if it is him," Mack explained, "why would he have an Uzi? And, if he's got an Uzi, why would he leave it there?"

"It's an emergency stash," she offered. He raised one eyebrow. She shrugged. "If you're traveling, and you don't want to get caught with that gun in your vehicle, especially if you're crossing the border all the time, what you really want is a place to keep stuff. And although a burial vault is an odd place maybe to keep it …" She frowned at him and asked, "What was the name of the person buried there again?"

He gave her a quiet smile. "Joe Smith."

"Right, got it. You're thinking this gun is somehow connected to Bob Small."

"I don't know that it's connected, but we don't want to rule out other unsolved matters that could be related. Therefore, we look for some connection."

"Yeah, the assumption would be that the deceased *Joe Smith* was buried when our gun owner was there as part of the ceremony or maybe said gun owner paid off somebody to bury it with the next body that came along, or something in between those two events, whereby the gun owner managed to bury it and was there while they sealed it up."

He nodded. "If you wanted to put something special in there with a loved one, I'm sure it wouldn't be much of a process to get away with that. And, as long as our gun owner knew the name on the vault, he could come back and take that back anytime."

"But we are assuming the gun owner and the dead man aren't family, not blood related," Doreen replied. "So would anyone in the family knowingly let a gun be sealed in the family vault by some unrelated person and not say anything? And was the damage to the vault accidental, considering the weapon was still there, or"—she turned to him in excitement—"or did we interrupt the person attempting to retrieve the weapon? So the question really is," she added, "why did he do that? In particular, when did the vault get broken into, and why was the gun still there?"

He looked at her and smiled. "You would have made a great detective."

"Don't put that in the past tense," she warned. "I might surprise you yet."

He chuckled. "Anytime you want to apply for the training, I'll give you a recommendation, but it's not easy."

"No, and I don't think I want that kind of restriction on my viewpoint," she muttered. "You constantly hamstring me."

He shook his head at that. "You know that's not what we're trying to do, right?"

"No, you're not trying to do it, and that's what makes it even more frustrating. Even when you're *not* trying to do it, you're doing it anyway. So I feel as if I can't go forward or backward because of all your rules," she complained. "But I really would like to know more about whose grave that is."

"So would I, but the plaque's gone."

"Sure, but the cemetery management should have records."

"Yes, and remember the part about how I know how to do my job?"

She sighed. "You won't tell me, will you?"

"Wasn't planning on it," he quipped.

"I could be a help to you," she stated.

He shook his head. "Everything has to be by the book."

"Of course it has to be by the book, but I wasn't planning on going against the book."

"You never plan on it," he noted, "but somehow …"

She snorted. "I don't understand how that happens though," she replied indignantly. "I try so hard, and then, all of a sudden, things blow up."

"And you can't blame the animals for that."

"I wasn't planning on blaming the animals at all."

His lips twitching, he added, "I know exactly where to

lay the blame." And he stared at her deliberately.

She glared at him. "Not funny."

"Sometimes it's *really* not funny. I agree with you there too."

She groaned. "You'll be difficult, won't you?"

"Nope, I won't." Then his tummy rumbled.

She stared at him. "Have you eaten?"

"Not a whole lot. It's been pretty busy. Have you any food around?"

"In my place?" She laughed. "Do you think any food is around?"

"I can always hope," he muttered.

And then she remembered the stash that Nan had sent home. She hopped up and quickly returned with the basket.

He eyed her, sniffing the air on a slow grin. "You got leftovers while you were down at Nan's, didn't you?"

"I did, and yet I feel as if I shouldn't be going there because she keeps snagging food for me."

"Considering the number of cases that you've helped them on, I don't think they'll begrudge you some food."

"Yeah, until the next new person comes along and causes Nan problems because of the retirement home's generosity," she muttered, with a sigh. She lifted the tea towel, so he could see inside.

"Oh, wow." He looked over at her. "Have you had any?"

"I had two with Nan, and she sent the rest home with me." Four croissants and two little fruit scones remained. "I haven't had any of those yet." He held the basket out for her, and she took one, and he took another. And they sat here, munching through the pastries with their coffee.

When his phone rang, he sighed, checked the screen, and answered it. "Hey, Arnold. What's up? … Yeah, fine.

I'm at Doreen's." Frowning at something else being shared, Mack replied, "Okay, give me ten, and I'll be there." He quickly popped the rest of the treat in his mouth, looked at another one, and asked, "Do you mind?"

She shook her head. "Take another. Now go, and make sure you eat next time."

He laughed. "Or I'll pop by here and hope for the best. Lately you've done pretty well."

"I've done pretty well in what way?" she asked.

"Well, that whole *getting food from Nan's place.*"

"Yeah, makes me feel worse though." She watched, as he snagged another treat, and then she grabbed one herself. "Do you want to take one more with you?"

"No, this should hold me for a while." And, with that, he got up, tossed back the last of his coffee, and said, "I've got to go."

"Where are you going though?" she asked curiously.

"Something came up."

And that was a cagey-enough answer for her to raise one eyebrow and note, "That sounds interesting."

"Maybe, but it's too far for you to walk, and I'm not taking you with me."

"And you won't tell me where you're going?"

"No, I won't." He laughed. "Besides, you don't need to know any of this."

"Maybe I don't need to know," she admitted, "but it's fun to know it."

"Maybe, but not this time."

Trying to hide her disappointment, she bid him farewell.

Mack said goodbye to the animals, with a hug for Mugs, a scratch for Goliath, and a brush along Thaddeus's feathers. "Look after her, guys." And he was gone.

Chapter 5

THE NEXT MORNING Nan woke Doreen up bright and early.

"What's the matter?" Doreen asked, still rubbing the sleep from her eyes.

"Did you hear?"

"Nope, I didn't hear anything."

"They're opening up a grave at the cemetery."

"What do you mean, opening up?" Doreen sat up in bed to see Mugs beside her, his four paws pointing to the ceiling. Goliath was curled into a tight ball at her feet, yet Thaddeus soldier-marched along the bedroom windowsill.

"Heavy equipment is opening up the grave." Nan's voice rose in excitement.

Doreen wondered what that meant to her ongoing investigations. "I hadn't heard anything, and Mack has not been sharing."

"No, of course not," Nan stated dismissively. "They've got that whole area of the cemetery cordoned off too. A bunch of us are going down there later today."

Doreen bolted out of bed. "Really? Why?"

"Because we want to see," Nan declared, brimming with

cheerfulness.

"Right, you want to go to the cemetery to see a grave that you won't see because you should stay behind the cordoned-off area."

"They won't keep it cordoned off all the time," Nan stated crossly. "Besides, anything right now is needed to break up the boredom. I thought you were looking for something to do?"

"I wanted you to have a rest," she told Nan.

"Me? I've got more-than-enough rest coming when I'm dead," she muttered. "I would just as soon live a little bit right now."

Doreen winced at that because that was a heck of a reminder of her grandmother's age. "Fine." She yawned.

"Did I wake you, dear?"

"Yes, I didn't have a great night last night."

"Oh my, well, you better get up, rise and shine, because I told them you would come too." And, with that, she rang off.

"You said what?" Doreen cried out, but the phone was dead, and Nan was long gone. The last thing Doreen wanted to do was go with a group of seniors from Rosemoor and see a grave that was being reopened. She'd already been through similar things with other cases.

As soon as her brain fog was gone and her first cup of coffee poured, she texted Mack, asking him to call her.

When he called a little bit later, his voice was distracted. "What's going on?" he asked. She told him what Nan had told her. He groaned. "The best thing you can do is keep them at home."

"You don't understand," she cried out. "There's no keeping these people at home. They're bored and plan to make a day of it."

There was silence in the other end. "Good Lord, how did they even find out?"

"I don't know because they're the ones who told me, so you can't blame me. And are they correct? Is that what you're doing?"

"Yes, a grave will be opened today," he confirmed. "And, no, nobody will be allowed to get close enough to see anything. You'll all be kept behind a cordoned-off area. So why don't you try to keep them home?"

"Trying to keep them home and keeping them home," she stated in exasperation, "are two completely different issues, and neither are very workable."

"Right, so what are you planning on doing?"

"I don't know, but a part of me says, if I don't go with them, it won't go well. Yet, if I do go …"

"It won't go well either," he finished for her.

"Maybe I can keep them out of trouble," she said, "and I get that you don't seem to think that I can do that, but, when they get off on their own, they are quite a handful."

He groaned at that. "I won't be there, and I can't help you if you get into trouble."

"How much trouble can I get into?" she asked. "They'll be wandering around the cemetery, some of them probably visiting old friends."

He laughed at that, then sobered. "I guess for a lot of them that's how they view it too, isn't it?"

"Absolutely," Doreen agreed. "Lots of people look at it that way."

"Right," he muttered, "and that's a good thing, visiting loved ones at the cemetery. However, I would still prefer if you would stay home."

"Yeah, I would too, but I'm not sure I trust Nan and that group."

"I don't trust them at all," Mack declared.

"So I guess I will go along and try to keep them contained," she agreed. "Who's driving anyway? I'm not sure any are valid drivers, and that's another part of the problem. If it's Richie, that's bad news."

"Did he get his license again?" Mack cried out in horror.

"Maybe. Nan mentioned something about having a new lease on life and that they were free again."

"*Uh-oh,*" he muttered. "I will phone Darren." And he quickly disconnected.

She grabbed the last treats that Nan had given her the day before and sat with her coffee. When Doreen heard incessant honking from a vehicle out front, she got up and walked to see the Rosemoor minibus sitting outside Doreen's house. As Doreen stepped into her front yard, Nan stepped out of the bus long enough to call out, "Hurry up, child. Hurry up. We can't wait for you forever."

She stared, nonplussed.

But then Richie poked his head out from the driver's side and called out, "Come on. We've a free pass for freedom today."

Doreen realized there really was no choice.

Nan added, "Bring the animals too."

And, with that, Mugs raced out the door and headed toward Nan, jumping up into the bus already. Groaning at that, Doreen quickly grabbed her purse and snagged Thaddeus off his roost, while Goliath already was halfway to the bus himself, even though he hated the noise, but he wouldn't get left behind. Doreen locked up the house and headed to the bus.

Finally she was on board, with the others cheering and clapping because she'd joined them on their outing. She looked at Nan and whispered, "This is a bad idea."

Nan laughed. "Maybe, but it's fun."

Chapter 6

IT MIGHT HAVE been fun for some of the Rosemoor residents to see a coffin dug up and brought to the surface of the cemetery. However, soon they realized that they wouldn't get close enough to see anything, and they couldn't do anything because they were being kept so far away.

Doreen had corralled her animals, with both Mugs and Goliath on leashes, and Thaddeus on her shoulder, so that they wouldn't get hurt by the big machinery at work here. When several of the senior citizens turned to look at Doreen, upset about the barricades in place, Doreen raised her hands in mock surrender. "I told Nan that we wouldn't get close enough. And she said it didn't matter because you guys were here for the adventure." They all nodded and turned back to Nan.

"It still would be nice if we could see something though," complained Maggie, one of the Rosemoor residents, now visibly pouting.

At that, Nan nodded. "Let's go for a walk around. I don't know about the rest of you, but Chrissy's grave is here, as are a few other of our other friends. So why don't we go have a visit, and, when we come back, we'll see if they're any closer to being done here digging up a grave." And the bulk of the seniors headed off in three subgroups of three, while Doreen remained with Richie and Nan.

Doreen looked over at Nan. "Did you do that deliberately to get rid of them?"

"Of course I did, dear. Now you can go work your magic."

She stared at her grandmother. "You expect me to go get information from the workers about this case?" she asked in astonishment. "You know how Mack'll feel about that."

"I tried to ask Darren about it too," Richie mentioned. "He wasn't very generous with his information."

"No, I think they've been given a blackout order on this case." Doreen looked from one to the other. "Still, it sounds pretty exciting."

"That means you know more than we do," Nan stated, eyeing her granddaughter, and noting how still the animals were.

"No, I really don't," Doreen countered. "Maybe the fact that I know that they're working so hard to keep it quiet is what's making it very interesting."

"Maybe," Nan replied suspiciously.

But Doreen managed to keep her face straight. "I think there are times," she noted cautiously, "when there's not a whole lot we can do about keeping it clean for the police. Obviously I don't want to upset Mack too much."

"Well, there's too much, and there's not at all," Richie stated, looking at her. "Now, based on your wording, I believe you're okay to upset him a little bit."

"Not really." She sighed. "Particularly after I know that he asked me to be good about it all." As she watched the Bobcat at work, she heard a sudden noise. When she got closer, holding the leashes firmly on Mugs and Goliath, the Bobcat slowly raised the casket from the grave, but then came this crunching sound and a man's groan. She and her animals raced closer, with Nan and Richie coming up right behind her. "Are you okay?" she asked the man, who had fallen into the grave, the top of his head bleeding.

She motioned for him to come closer to the other side, and she moved a nearby ladder into the hole. "Here. Come on. Let's get you up there."

The other workmen raced over to help too. She got the injured man out and sat him down and checked his head. "I'm sorry. I guess the bottom of the casket dropped on you, didn't it?"

"Yes." He gasped in pain, as she gave his wound a once-over. "I wasn't expecting that. When the weight in the casket broke free, the coffin swung free and knocked me in."

"Understandable, I guess, after so many years of decay," she guessed, trying hard to see what was now inside the grave, with the casket busting apart. The animals were intent on the big hole too. Yet the cops had rushed in to hide whatever was in there now. She heard muted voices. "What hit you anyway?" she asked the injured man.

He looked up at her and in a low voice said, "Honest to God, it seemed weapons came out of that thing instead of a body. It shouldn't have been that heavy. Not only should the casket have held, but the body decay alone should have made its load lighter. Whatever hit me wasn't light."

She pondered that for a moment. "So it's more hidden guns, *huh?*"

"Yeah, I think so," he agreed.

One of his coworkers came over to him. "Are you okay, man?" And, with his buddy's help, the injured workman slowly stood, winced a bit, and added, "I'm okay. Got hit as the coffin swung around, then sent me flying in the grave."

His buddy nodded. "We'll get your head taken care of, get you down to the hospital, and get you checked over."

"Man, I hate the hospital," the victim grumbled.

"Yeah, but you took a blow though," Doreen noted, with obvious worry. "Let's not be foolish about that." She looked back at the guys to see Darren leaving them to join her. "Darren, have you called an ambulance?"

He nodded. "We're getting somebody over."

"Good." She lowered her voice and asked Darren, "Do you realize that your grandfather drove that whole group here, including me?" Darren stared at her in shock. "Yeah, I came because I figured that I was probably better off to come and keep them in line than having them come here and raise Cain on their own. But they're upset at me because I can't get any information."

Darren rolled his eyes at that. "Yeah, how do you think Gramps was for me this morning? There's just no making him happy." He looked around. "I see Gramps and your grandmother. Where are the rest of them?"

"They've gone to visit their friends." He looked at her puzzled, so she explained, "The graves of their friends who have passed."

"Ah." He still wasn't terribly happy with that idea.

"I guess you've got this under control here," she murmured.

Darren shook his head, as he looked back at the excavated grave. "Not exactly what we expected."

She nodded. "But considering that Mack and I found the one weapon already," she added in that low voice again, "it does make sense."

"How does it make sense?" he asked, staring at her.

She turned to look back at Richie and Nan. "I don't think it's connected with the Bob Small case file, but we need to hear from forensics first."

He stared at her. "Why isn't it connected?"

"Per my notes, Bob Small didn't need weapons," she murmured. "He was a one-man show. This right here very much has overtones of gang activities."

He smiled. "Mack said you were talking about going into the police force. You'll be a great asset."

She grinned at him. "Thank you."

"I mean it, and that's exactly what Mack was saying earlier about this. Wait till he hears about this one now."

"The good news is that this can all be locked up safely. I don't know how you found this …"

Darren lowered his voice. "It's the same name, as the urn in the mausoleum."

She stared at him. "So, in theory, somebody buried the same person twice?"

"Exactly, and that's what started this."

"I like it. It's devious thinking."

He burst out laughing. "Glad you think so." A shout came from behind them. He turned and said, "Here's Mack." He walked over to talk to Mack, while Doreen headed back to join Richie and Nan. They both looked at her inquisitively. She gave a small headshake, and both of them nodded. She knew Mack was coming up behind her, especially with all the yipping and wiggling coming from Mugs.

He came up, greeting all the animals who demanded to be acknowledged first. Then Mack settled a hand on Doreen's shoulder, sternly looked over at Richie and Nan, and said, "Anything you find interesting right now, we need you to keep very, *very* quiet about." The two of them grinned at him, thrilled to be involved, and nodded.

"Of course we will." Richie straightened up proudly. "You can count on us."

Mack, his voice even more serious than she'd ever thought possible, stated, "I need it to be that way. This could be very dangerous for anybody who hears the wrong information right now."

"Got it," Richie replied, puffing up even more with importance.

Mack squeezed Doreen's shoulder gently. "And what about you?" he asked.

She turned to give him an innocent smile. "I don't know anything."

He rolled his eyes at that. "It'll be easier and safer if you didn't, but Darren already told me."

She sighed. "Fine. I'll be good."

"You need to be, and your theory that you just mentioned," he noted, eyeing her wryly, "unfortunately I think you're right, and that makes this a very dangerous game."

"A whole bunch of bikers' gangs are in the north end of town, aren't there?" she asked.

He nodded. "But because they're part of a biker gang doesn't make them killers."

"Nope, but they could be gun owners," she suggested. "And it sure ups the ante, doesn't it?"

"We'll see," he replied. "A lot of weapons are here."

"And when did this get buried?" she murmured.

He tilted his head, as if a combo shrug and nod. "That's a really valuable point. By the looks of the shape the guns are in, maybe around … Twenty-plus years ago."

She looked down at the grave. "Will those weapons still be usable?"

He nodded. "Yeah, they were kept mostly dry and clean at first. However, the wood coffin itself wasn't of the best quality, and water got in. So I don't know how long the weapons would have stayed in good working condition," he said, thinking out loud, "but anybody who knows weapons could clean them up."

He gave the three nosy civilians a stern look, while giving the three animals a cozy goodbye, and added for the others' benefit, "Now go home and be quiet."

Chapter 7

WITH EVERYBODY ON the bus, heading back to Rosemoor, Nan had Richie drive straight there instead of dropping off Doreen. Of course they would want to talk, whether Doreen wanted to or not. Digging up a fake grave filled with weapons added a whole new element. She was no longer thinking this had anything to do with the Bob Small case, not now with this newest element, which was something completely different. She looked over at Nan as they parked and asked, "Tea?"

"Absolutely, dear." Nan then frowned at her watch. "It's our lunchtime."

"Oh, good. You guys go have your lunch. We'll talk later."

"Are you sure you're okay with that?" Nan asked anxiously. "I don't want to send you away hungry."

She laughed. "It's fine, absolutely fine." With her animals in tow, Doreen slowly walked up the creek, heading home, her mind full of all these very interesting turns of events.

Who would have thought that people would bury weapons, and yet what a smart idea. Would the guns rust? Or deteriorate like paper money. Only their money was plastic and would likely last forever in a grave. Particularly if some attempt was made to keep it safe. You had the cache, and you needed it available. Plus, burying paper money was iffy, could be completely ruined by Mother Nature. Therefore, exchange the currency for guns and bury them, as they could withstand the elements better. Yet that was something else she didn't quite understand. Was it done in spite or was it done to have weapons available at a certain time? All these things rattled around in her head. By the time she got home, she was no closer to an answer.

When Mack called her as she walked in the kitchen, she said, "I'm fine. The seniors are all back safely at Rosemoor. They're having their lunch, and I just walked into my house."

"Good." He laughed. "Now make sure you keep quiet about this."

"I will, but you do know that one of the other observers was a reporter, right?"

"No, I didn't know that." And he started to swear.

"I wouldn't worry about it. Nobody really was close enough to see anything."

"Except you."

"Yeah, except me, but I was more concerned about the poor guy's head."

His voice softened. "And we appreciate that."

"I'm not trying to make life difficult for you, but a cache of weapons that size?" And she knew that the worry was evident in her tone.

"I know. Believe me. We're heavily focused on this. I'm not too sure what the outcome will be."

"No, I get it. This one's dangerous."

"I'm glad to hear you acknowledge that," he noted, his voice serious. "Please stay careful and out of the way."

"Will do." And she disconnected. It was hard to even imagine how completely different her morning had gone from what she'd expected. She hadn't even had a chance to relax and to enjoy her morning out with Nan, who was totally focused on ensuring that they got down to the cemetery early to garner the best seats in the house. Doreen rolled her eyes at that.

They wouldn't have even known about the grave being opened, except for Darren spilling the beans.

And, since he had, that would be something he needed to watch because his grandfather Richie was pretty cagey too. And the last thing they needed was Richie getting information on cases and then getting involved as well. She winced at that horrible thought because trying to keep Nan, Richie, and everybody else at Rosemoor out of Mack's business would take its toll.

As Doreen sat here, she wanted more coffee. No way the one cup from the morning would be enough for today. Now with fresh coffee brewed, she pushed open the back door and stepped outside. Almost immediately her neighbor Richard popped his head over the wooden fence. "What was all that caterwauling this morning?" he asked, glaring at her.

She stared at him nonplussed. "What caterwauling?"

"That group who picked you up, they looked as if they were inmates who broke free of Bedlam."

She snickered at that. And even he got a ghost of a smile on his face. "You're close, very close. That was Nan and a few of her cronies, heading down to the cemetery."

"The cemetery," he repeated. "Why?"

"Workers were opening a grave," Doreen shared, "and I

guess the Rosemoor crowd thought it would be something exciting happening."

He frowned at her. "Opening graves is not good for anybody," Richard declared in horror, "and what could possibly be exciting about that?"

"Not sure," she replied cheerfully. "But you know how Nan is. She is a force into herself."

"I thought you were supposed to be a stabilizing influence for her," Richard noted crossly.

"Yeah, well, I don't know that anybody on this earth can have much influence on Nan," Doreen admitted. "That woman does what she wants."

"So do you," he stated in disgust, and, with that, his head disappeared onto his side of the fence, leaving her shaking her head. She really needed to get a ladder or a chair or something, so that she could pop her head over *his* side of the fence for a change and see what was going on over there. See how much he liked that.

Of course he wouldn't like it; that was almost a given. But it was tempting. Maybe one day, when she was ready to get back at him for some of his nasty digs all the time. Yet she also knew that it would be better if she stayed out of it and tried to find the goodness in her heart to walk away from his comments. The trouble was that she could be good most of the time, and, well, she wasn't always *that* good.

She laughed at herself, walked back inside, poured a cup of coffee, and brought it back out to the peace and quiet of her backyard. Or for as long as her neighbor stopped popping his head over the fence.

As she sat here, she realized the animals hadn't even had breakfast. Shaking her head, she got up and quickly fed them. With all their heads tucked into their food bowls, she sat back down outside, feeling terrible that she'd forgotten them.

"I'm sorry, Mugs. Things got a bit chaotic." On the other hand, if he hadn't come with her on the impromptu bus ride, Mugs probably would have been even more upset.

Doreen pondered the earlier incident. That cache of weapons was so big that their combined weight had something to do with the casket collapsing. Although the injured guy had mentioned something about the water damage to the coffin also, so that made sense in a way. It was a unique set of circumstances that she couldn't forget about. She had caught a glimpse of the weapons in among the mess at the bottom of the grave, but not enough to identify the individual items. Something black and metal-looking though. And lots of them.

It would likely be a gang scenario, as too many weapons were here for one person. Even for some criminal like Bob Small; he got away with murder for so long because he kept it small, because he kept it simple. He didn't get other people involved, and he didn't get into trouble otherwise. He stayed quiet, and when he got into somebody's world, he got out fast too, just like with Hinja.

As she considered the Bob Small case, she realized that she had forgotten to contact Hinja's estate or have Nan call them about any personal items that they were getting rid of that might have had contact by Bob Small. What they really needed was DNA for this guy. And to at least find family members or some link that could lead them down the right pathway. Not that any family wanted to be connected to this, but, with this new online genealogy software, it looked to be the best bet.

It would be tough to find out that a serial killer was in

your family.

She called Nan later and asked her for the contact person who had sent the information to her from Hinja's estate.

"Hang on a moment." Nan returned with a name, phone number, and an email address minutes later. "Not sure about the phone number, but I did get emails from them."

"If you could forward that info to me," Doreen said, "I'd appreciate it."

"Sure." Nan's voice was alive with curiosity. "You'll work on that case next?"

"I'm not sure what I will do yet." Doreen laughed. "That trip to the graveyard was a little daunting."

"Very sobering, wasn't it?" Nan replied, all the laughter in her voice stilling. "Even some people who had gone to visit friends in the graves were perturbed by the burial site dug up with all that weaponry in the cemetery."

"Not exactly an easy thing to open up a grave and to do it quietly, without causing any desecration of the land around it," Doreen noted.

"No, and not everybody understands that," Nan added. "We didn't tell anybody what we saw or heard, but lots of them had things to say and felt that their friends didn't appreciate having their sleep disturbed."

"You mean, their dead friends?"

"Yes," she stated crossly. "And I know a lot of people don't believe that, and a lot of people would laugh at them, but, until you have friends who have died and have crossed over, it's a different situation to realize that their eternal sleep is not exactly very eternal, not when people go in with heavy bulldozers to open things up."

"Maybe so," Doreen admitted, nodding in understanding, "but, when you consider how much was hidden in that fake grave, I think it's a good thing that the grave was unearthed."

"I do too," Nan replied, "but it does give one pause for thought, doesn't it?"

"I don't think you'll be in a position to worry about it though. We should be responsible and not get involved in any of it."

"Well, it won't be easy," Nan declared. "And I don't think you'll listen to that advice yourself." And, with that, Nan laughed.

"Maybe not," Doreen acknowledged, "but I will contact this person who contacted you from Hinja's estate. So I'll talk to you in a bit." And, with that, she hung up.

As soon as she dialed the number in question, a young woman answered—a niece, actually a great-niece.

"Ah," Mila said, "I had heard a lot about you from some of the newspapers and, of course, from your grandmother. The news out there is that you're quite the detective."

"Most of it had been sheer luck."

"No," Mila disagreed. "I've read about some of these cases in detail that you've been involved in. Not sure that luck has anything to do with any of it."

"I don't know about that." Doreen was uncomfortable with this part of the conversation. "I did get all that information from Hinja's estate, and it's all sitting here on my desk now."

"Good. Do you think you can do anything with it?"

"I'm not sure. It's been a long time."

"I know, but it was my cousin who went missing."

"I'm sorry," Doreen replied. "That's got to be hard."

Mila sighed. "But to know that Hinja believed that she

had something to do with her niece's death, even unconsciously, has also been very hard."

"Did Hinja tell you that?"

"Before she died, she told me a lot of stuff," Mila admitted. "At the time I wasn't sure if I could believe it or not. … Then I went through those letters, before sending them off to your grandmother, so I know that Hinja felt that dating Bob Small made him responsible for her missing niece. I can't imagine any horror worse."

"No, no, you're quite right there," Doreen agreed. "Again it's been so long, and Hinja didn't go to the police. As far as I know, she didn't keep anything that may have had Bob Small's DNA on it. I'm afraid nothing will be here that I can really work with."

"Well, I do have her box of keepsakes," Mila shared. "I wasn't sure what to do with them."

"What kind of keepsakes?"

"Mementos. She's got a note here, along with some gifts from him, and more things she had collected during her time with him."

"And why would she do that? Was that normal for Hinja?"

"No, but my great-aunt didn't have good luck with relationships, and so I think she got a little possessive and kind of weird when it came to Bob Small. It's what my mother would have said anyway."

"Okay." Doreen pondered that. "And I realize that, as soon as this guy was out of her life, she really struggled with that. And according to my grandmother, Hinja didn't have any other relationships afterward."

"No, I don't believe she did," Mila confirmed. "Anyway, if you want, I can send you all these keepsakes."

"Yes, please. I would very much like that."

"Do you really think this Bob Small guy's alive?" she asked.

"I'm not sure if he is. It's quite possible he's gone to the US or has found a new hunting ground because it was getting too difficult up here," Doreen explained. "I really don't know."

"It's funny because, at the service for Hinja, a stranger was at the graveside, and I didn't know who he was. He was an older man, gray-haired, and he could have been anywhere from sixty to one hundred," she noted, with a laugh. "But he looked quite sad. When I asked him if he knew my great-aunt, he nodded and replied, *Yes, a long time ago.* He looked at me funny for a long moment, and then he walked away."

"Would you recognize him again?"

"I don't know. Why?"

"Do you have curly hair?"

"Yes, I do."

"In that case," Doreen stated, her voice raspy, "could you please look after yourself?"

"Why?" she asked again.

"Because the one thing that is constant, if you have read those letters, is that her boyfriend, if he's responsible for all these girls going missing, this Bob Small had a thing about women with curly hair."

Mila gasped. "That man did mention something about my lovely curls. Oh my. … Do you think that was him?"

"Honestly I think it's a good possibility, yes," Doreen confirmed. "And that means, more than ever, you need to be incredibly diligent, so that nothing happens to you."

"I don't want anything to do with him," Mila cried out. "I really don't want anything to do with this."

"And that's a good idea," Doreen noted, "but it might already be too late."

Chapter 8

DOREEN WANTED TO tell Mack about this odd development, but he was still so busy working that she didn't know when she could connect with him. When Nick phoned, she was impatient with him because she wanted him to get off the phone in case Mack called.

"What is wrong with you today?" Nick asked.

She sighed. "I was expecting your brother."

He burst out laughing. "I'm glad to hear it, but," he noted in exasperation, "can we at least take care of what needs to be taken care of?"

"Sure, but you haven't told me what you need me to do."

He sighed. "Yes, I just did."

"Oh," she replied in a small voice. "I'm sorry."

"It's okay. I'll be glad when this is over too."

And that reminded her that Nick was doing all this for free, even though she was due to get a substantial amount of money, which would make her feel even worse. She would end up insisting she pay him for all this work. "I really do appreciate it," she apologized. "This case that I've been working on has taken a really weird turn."

"I think all your cases do that," Nick stated. "I don't know how you find so many strange and bizarre cases to begin with."

"Hey, you weren't at the cemetery today, where they used a Bobcat to dig up a grave. When they brought up the coffin, the bottom fell away. Then the coffin and its contents hit one of the workers in the head and knocked him into the open grave. The casket was full of guns."

After a moment of absolute shocked silence, he said, "What?"

"Yeah, so pardon me if I'm a little distracted."

"Good God, was my brother there?"

"Oh, he came afterward. I did check the guy's head," Doreen added, "and he's okay. But the rest of us were a little bit on the shocked side."

"Maybe I don't want to move back to Kelowna after all." And then Nick started to laugh.

"Yeah, you're not the first one to say that to me." Doreen snorted. "I came because Nan told me what a beautiful place it was, so peaceful and so lovely. Yet all I've seen here? … Well, look at all I've seen here."

"I do. I have seen it." Nick was laughing now. "I was raised there, and I didn't know any of this."

"No, and I think that's the thing. If you're not in law enforcement, most of this doesn't touch you."

"Unless it's you," he noted warmly.

"Ah, I don't know. Sometimes I think I'm more a problem than I am a solution."

"I wouldn't think that," Nick disagreed. "You've done a lot of good there."

"And yet it seems as if sometimes it's not good enough."

"Now what are you working on?" he asked.

She sighed. "Mostly that Bob Small file. I was talking to the great-niece of the woman who went out with this guy."

"Bob Small, Bob Small," Nick muttered.

"Yeah, supposedly a prolific serial killer, yet no proof, no bodies, no idea who he is, but a lot of missing victims with curly hair. And this woman who dated him thinks Bob Small took her niece. So the aunt spent the rest of her life guilt-ridden because she feels as if, had she not been dating him, her niece would have been safe."

Silence.

"And, yes, her niece had curly hair. Her body's never been found. And honestly I'm not sure that any of the bodies have been found, but the estimated numbers of victims changed anywhere from supposedly dozens to upward of thirty or fifty."

"Without bodies? Then how do the police know that Bob Small is even real and did all this?"

She sighed loudly. "I'm not exactly sure, but, from what I've learned, it came from another inmate who'd been incarcerated with Bob Small for a while, and his cellmate tried to use this insider knowledge as leverage to get himself a better deal in prison. However, because he didn't have any proof, it didn't work."

"Interesting. So Bob Small confessed to his prison buddy about being a serial killer?"

"Yeah, apparently," Doreen confirmed, "and so we know him as Bob Small. But then sometimes you've got to wonder if the actual inmate didn't make it all up, just so that he could get away with a better situation for himself, if you understand what I mean. Without proof I'm not sure he got much of a better settlement at all."

"Good," Nick said. "Sometimes these guys are just out

to lie and cheat and steal."

"Maybe, but if he had any real information on this one possible serial killer …"

"You haven't contacted him, have you?" Nick asked her.

She beamed into the phone. "I haven't thought of that, but I will now." And, with a burst of laughter, she ended the call.

Chapter 9

DOREEN WAS STILL laughing, when Nick called her right back.

"You won't really call him, will you?" Nick asked, worried.

"Oh, I'll get in touch with him," she stated, "but that's not all that easy to do. I wonder if he'd even talk to me—or tell the truth?"

"He'll want something from you."

"Sure, but people also change over time," she noted. "So you never know. I could maybe send him a Dear John letter."

"Don't get involved with this guy. You don't understand what they're like."

"No, I don't." She pondered that. "Can't say I really want to either. Although I have had to deal with inmates before."

"*Great,*" Nick muttered, half under his breath. "Besides, I called you originally to ask if you'd heard from Mathew."

"No, I haven't. Why?"

"Because I've got a judge who'll hear this case early because of the problems Mathew is dropping in our lap."

"Oh, interesting," she murmured. "Do you think that'll make more trouble for Mathew?"

"Yeah, I think it will," Nick stated. "It's also possible he'll end up with criminal charges and a whole lot more legal issues than he expected out of this deal."

"*Nice.*" Doreen winced. "More things for him to blame me for."

"Maybe, but he had a choice to settle this without the judge."

"And now that you've got somebody on our side there, will Mathew try to settle this out of court?"

"Maybe," Nick replied, "hopefully, if you are willing."

"I want to settle," she stated. "I really don't want to go to court."

"You know that you won't be on trial, right?"

She hesitated and then continued. "I'm pretty sure that every person who has gone to court thinks they're on trial, whether they are or not. The circumstances and the environment makes it very dodgy."

He laughed. "Good point. Anyway it's not today's issue, but, if you do hear from Mathew, don't talk to him."

"Got it." She smiled.

And this time, he was the one who hung up on her.

She sat for a long moment, staring at her phone, realizing how much her life had changed. When her phone rang again, and she saw Mathew's name come up, she winced. "I'm not answering your call," she said out loud. It went to voice mail, but he didn't leave a message. She texted Nick. **He just tried to call. I didn't answer, and he didn't leave a message.**

Nick phoned her right back. "Good, make yourself unavailable," he stated. "I mean it. We don't want to antagonize him any more than we have, but he also needs to know that you're serious."

And, with that, she disconnected. But, with Nick's earlier suggestion—although he hadn't really intended to make one—she sat down and went back to the internet, looking for the name and location of the convict who had suggested Bob Small was a serial killer. It took some time but finally, with his name, Gary Wildorf, and the phone number for the prison in Abbotsford, she asked if Wildorf was there. When she got a confirmation, she asked, "How can I send him an email?"

It took a moment to get that info, and finally she was in business. She reviewed the email she had drafted, knowing that Mack would get really perturbed over the whole thing, and then, with a sense of bravado, she hit Send.

And when she got an email response almost immediately, she had a case of shock.

Come and see me. I'll only talk to you in person.

She wrote an email back. *No, I don't do those kinds of drives. A phone call is all I'm willing to do.* She waited and waited, assuming that he wouldn't have anything to do with her if she didn't go in person. However, finally she got his reply.

Fine. I can do a phone call this afternoon.

The email had a telephone number at the end. She looked at the number and realized it was the same one for the correctional institution, confirming that he was, indeed, there. She waited until the appointed time, and, when she dialed, it went through an operator and several other people, until finally a man picked up a phone on the other end and asked, "Who the heck are you, and what do you want with me?"

"I'm looking into the Bob Small case," she began. "So I'm hoping you have some real information."

"If I did, why should I care?" he asked. "Nobody did anything for me."

"No, and doesn't look as if you're getting out anytime soon either," she noted calmly. "So I guess it depends whether things have changed or if you'll still be that way."

"Be what way?" he asked, with a reckless laugh.

"Somebody who knows that you could right a wrong but couldn't be bothered."

"It's not just one wrong. That guy's killed, and I mean *killed.* But nobody believed me, so why should you?"

"Well, I'm one of those odd people who has a tendency to get involved where they shouldn't," she explained, trying to make it sound as sincere as she could, "and that's the truth."

"So you're some do-gooder?"

"In a way, yes, that's exactly what I am. And I'm looking out for the families of all these missing women, families who are trying to figure out what happened to their loved ones."

"Isn't it too bad that they didn't think about that before these women were killed," he snapped.

"Do you really think they could have done something to have stopped it?" she asked curiously. "Did Bob Small ever talk about his girlfriend?"

"Yeah, there was one with that really weird name. I know that she affected him more than he wanted to be."

"When did you last share a cell with him?"

"Oh, ten, fifteen years ago," Gary said, "at least. But I

won't talk to you if I don't get something out of this deal."

"And what is it you're expecting to get?" she asked curiously. "I'm not law enforcement. I'm not anything."

"No, but you'll probably write a book and make a few million bucks," he added. "Why should I let you have all that money?"

"But I'm not an author. I don't write books, and I sure as heck don't have one million dollars, so why don't you think about all those families and the women who died at this guy's hand, knowing that he got away scot-free, while you're still stuck in there? You might do something to put him back in jail."

"Do you really think this guy's even around anymore?" Gary's tone was gruff.

"How old was he back then?"

"Old, but he was still a cocky jerk."

"This is your chance to help put away this cocky jerk," she replied. "So what'll it be?"

"I'll think about it." And he hung up.

Chapter 10

THE NEXT MORNING Doreen woke up, made her coffee, fed the animals, but was still out of sorts after the odd phone call with Gary from the day before, so she went out onto the deck. Almost instantly she froze. Something was different, but what?

Mugs headed out behind her, sniffing the air experimentally. But he didn't *woof*; he didn't do anything to show that he was upset. He wandered around the space. She frowned at that and watched. As she sat here quietly on her deck, she saw a deer down at the creek, slowly walking his way toward her rose bushes. She stared in astonishment. It was the first one she'd seen at her house and didn't even realize that they would come up on her property. She was ultimately delighted and then worried about her roses, but considered the roses a small price to pay, as she watched the flowers disappear down the animal's throat.

As she watched, a second and a third deer slowly meandered toward her. She lifted her phone and took several photos, sending them to Mack. And then, as an afterthought, sent a few to Nan.

Nan phoned a few minutes later. "Isn't it lovely when

the deer come?" Nan was truly delighted.

"You never told me they would come up here," Doreen replied in a hoarse voice, unable to take her eyes off them.

"They do, and now you know that yourself."

"It's a whole different story to see them. And all the flowers they eat," she added, with a slightly disgruntled tone.

Nan laughed. "My dear, you grow so many flowers that I'm sure you have enough to share."

At that, Doreen smiled. "I guess that's a good way to look at it, isn't it?"

"Absolutely. Everybody needs to eat, including the deer." And because there had been plenty of times when Doreen herself hadn't had food, she wouldn't begrudge the deer a few flower blossoms. She sat here, rapt, watching as they meandered down the lower part of the garden, crossed to the other side, and then meandered farther up again. She wasn't sure whether they even knew she was here or if they cared. For that matter, they seemed to ignore Mugs, who didn't bark.

Long after she hung up the phone call from Nan, Doreen sat, in joy and gratitude, for the changes in her life and in her circumstances, so that she could sit here by the creek at her own place and watch the deer meander through her world. The joy lasted until the phone rang yet again. She glanced down at it, and all her joy fled.

Mathew again.

She glared at the phone, back at the deer, and realized that they had disappeared because of the ringing phone.

"Yeah, now that is just like you," she muttered to the phone. "Ruining everything." But what would she do? Sit here and ignore him?

She knew that was what everybody wanted her to do,

but it was hard. The phone rang and rang and rang. Finally it stopped and went to voice mail. She waited a moment to see if he would leave a message and then checked to see if he did. His words were harsh.

"I won't go to court, so don't think you'll play that game with me."

She winced and sent Nick a text message, saying that Mathew called again but left a message, stating that he wouldn't go to court.

At that, Nick called her back. "Hey, how are you doing?" Nick asked her.

"I was having a gorgeous morning," she began. "The deer were in my backyard, and I was sitting here, absolutely loving every moment of it—until he called."

"Don't let him ruin it for you," Nick told her. "That man has a lot to learn yet."

"Yeah, I don't think he's planning on learning any of it, since he says he won't go to court."

"That's good," Nick stated. "Believe me. I'll be phoning his lawyer right now, letting him know that he broke the no-contact agreement. Make sure you keep that message."

"Sure," she muttered. "I really would do a lot to get this divorce over and that man out of my life."

"I know you would," Nick stated gently. "We're almost there."

"I don't think I believe you," she muttered.

"No, that's because you're too entrenched into believing him."

"Yeah, well, he's scary," she murmured.

"And I'm not?" Nick asked in mock horror.

She burst out laughing. "No, you're not scary, and neither is Mack."

"Mack and I work on being scary a lot," he declared, with sham indignation. "It's part of our job."

"Nope, doesn't work, at least not with me. But then I've been terrorized by the best," Doreen stated, with a note of bitterness that surprised her.

"I get that. I really do," Nick told her. "Let me talk to his lawyer and see what's up." And, with that, he ended the call.

She sat here, trying to regain some of that early morning joy that had been so dominant just moments ago, but it was hard to recapture that sense of innocence and joy, not when Mathew was constantly ruining things.

Then she remembered something somebody had said about *giving away your power to such things*. She frowned at that, trying to remember what the message had been, but it wasn't an easy thing to do because to not listen to Mathew and to not just do as he says still felt so foreign to her. When you have that fear, you give away the power of who you are to the person intent on making you pay.

And that wasn't the exact quotation, but it was something close to that. She did realize just how much of her own power, her own decision-making, her own ability to be herself, that she had given to Mathew. It was easier to say he'd taken it, but, in truth, she'd let him take it over the years, as her fear had gotten worse and worse.

It had been easier for her to give in than it had been to fight. Now a lot of women wouldn't have a hard time with that, and they would understand. However, Doreen had to change this part of her. Doreen had also seen how all those self-improvement goals would say to stop and to define her own sense of balance, her own sense of power again. Doreen wondered what that would take.

She was totally fine with everything else in her new world. Even the fact that she had little-to-no money, plus dealing with all these crazy murders, even some dangerous people. Yet she was fine to talk to them, fine with everybody except her ex. And that fear of him always encroached, always ruined her day, because he'd done such a great job training her to be his victim.

And, with that, she started to get angry. Angry that she had succumbed to her bullying husband all those years. Angry that he had managed to keep her under his thumbs for so long. Angry that he had been such a controlling jerk for as long as he had been. She didn't know what the anger would do, but it was cleansing.

That angry fire burned deep within, as if burning away all his influence. And, when the phone rang again, it was once again Mathew. She snatched her phone and snapped, "I told you to stop calling."

He laughed. "Yeah, but you didn't mean it. And, besides, I have a message for you."

"Oh, I have a message for you too," she declared, her tone blunt and hard. "I'll see you in court." And, with that, she hung up the phone.

She grinned widely, her face completely split in joy, as she realized that she'd talked to him like a powerful human being, instead of being afraid of everything Mathew said. She knew that Nick wouldn't be happy, but she herself? She was *ecstatic*.

Although she felt a bit of that fear creeping back inside again—because now she should confess what she'd done. She winced, picked up the phone, and, as soon as Nick answered, she admitted, "I blew it."

There was a moment of silence on the other end. Nick

asked cautiously, "What did you blow?"

She explained what had happened.

"And you told him what again?" Nick asked.

"I told him that I'll see him in court."

And Nick started to chuckle. "I can see why you would want to say that, even though I did tell you to stay away from him," he noted, "but I imagine that probably felt very good."

She burst out laughing. "Oh my," she cried out, "it feels awesome. You have no idea how much so. It was *awe-sooome*," Doreen swore she heard Nick's smile over the phone.

"In that case," Nick stated, "I'll let you off the hook for not following instructions."

She chuckled. "I did try. I really did, and then I got angry, as I realized how much of my life had been affected by him and how much fear and how much control he'd had over me all these years, and I just became furious," she explained simply.

"Now that that anger has come and gone," Nick said, "do you think you can step out of all that mess with Mathew and let me handle this?"

"Maybe," she replied, "unless he calls me again, and then I'm not so sure."

He groaned at that. "I talked to his lawyer, who had no idea he contacted you."

"Well, he contacted me again. Can't we charge him with harassment or something?"

"Yeah, and that's next," Nick told her cheerfully. "The more of this he does, the larger your paycheck will be."

"How does that work?" she asked in confusion.

"Because I was prepared to be somewhat nicer to settle

all this, but, now that he's hassling you, no way," Nick declared. "So hold tight. I'll be calling his lawyer right back." And, with that, Nick hung up the phone again.

She sat here, half a smile on her face, as she realized that maybe for the first time she'd done something right when it came to Mathew. After several more minutes of sitting here, waiting and wondering, Nick finally called back.

"His lawyer will speak to him," Nick relayed. "I've told him that we're adding harassment charges and that we'll get a court order to keep him away from you."

"Interesting," she murmured. "That'll make Mathew angrier."

"Yeah, and his lawyer knows it too. So we need to bring this to a conclusion, before something really stupid happens."

"Yeah, something stupid—like he hurts me."

"Yeah, exactly," Nick confirmed, his voice carefully low. "So the question is, do you think you can stay away from him for the next little while?"

"*Hmm.*" She pondered that. "Any chance he can stop calling me?"

"Any chance you can stop answering?" he countered.

"Yes, I guess so," she agreed, with a heavy sigh. "Particularly if that'll bring this to an end."

"It will, and he won't want anything to do with you once he pays, but, in the meantime, things could get potentially uglier."

"I don't understand why, if he knows his lot, he won't just suck it up and deal with it."

At that, Nick burst out laughing. "Because a lot of money is involved, and the law is not on Mathew's side in this case."

"But if he has as much money as you say he has," she muttered, "surely he could take a cut and carry on."

"He could," Nick noted, "but I'm not sure it is in him to concede."

She winced at that. "That," she confirmed, "he won't do."

"So then we'll have a bigger problem," Nick declared. "But, if I can bring him to court anytime soon, we will. Otherwise we'll have the cops pick him up, give him a warning, and then we'll see him in court."

"*Great*," she muttered, not convinced this was a good idea. And that concept gave her a lot to think about over the next little while. She spent the morning puttering at home, looking after her ruined garden for an hour. She then visited Mack's mother. And still she heard nothing from her ex.

Chapter 11

BACK HOME AGAIN Doreen started to relax. Mack called her in the early afternoon.

"I heard from Mom that you were over there."

"Yeah, I was. Your mom's doing lovely."

"She didn't seem to think you were. She told me that you were distracted and obviously worried about something."

She hesitated. "So I might be a little worried about something, but your brother's got it in hand."

"Mathew again?"

"Yes," she murmured. "I told him that I'll see him in court today," she muttered, "and I was supposed to ignore his phone calls." Mack sighed. "Before you get angry at me," she added, "I think I needed to do that."

He listened, while she explained. "Well, in that case, it probably was something you needed to do. But it would be awfully nice if we could get past this."

"Yeah, you and me both," she muttered. "And I think your brother's crazy to think that Mathew will give up anytime soon."

"I don't think Nick is planning on Mathew giving up

anytime soon. I think Nick is hoping that Mathew will do enough wrong without hurting anybody seriously to basically hang himself."

"I don't know about Nick having much luck doing that," she replied, "because Mathew's got some pretty smart lawyers."

"He's also crossed the line legally, and he knows that the judge would have a heyday with that. So, if he can keep this out of the courts, he would get away a lot easier. But, once the judge finds out what Mathew did, with your previous divorce lawyer and then with Mathew harassing you, that's a whole different story."

"And that's what worries me because, the closer we get to court date, the closer we get to him being very unsettled."

"I do have an alert in place, in case he flies here," Mack shared. "Believe me. We're on that."

"Good," she replied, with a certain amount of relief.

Mack asked, "What else have you been up to today?"

"I'm still waiting to hear back from the convict. Other than that it's been a pretty good day."

"Convict?" Mack repeated, his voice flat, quiet. "What convict would that be?"

And she winced. "Oh, I guess I didn't tell you about that either."

"No," he stated, his voice low and very restrained, "You didn't. Maybe you could fill me in now."

She sighed. "I probably should—in case anything else blows up."

"Like what?" he asked, his voice rising.

"Nothing scary or damaging in any way," she hurried to reassure him. "However, every possible victim we know of in this Bob Small case was all because of this convict who shared a cell with Bob and later shared his statement. But nobody ever found this Bob Small. Nobody ever had any proof that there was this Bob Small. So I contacted the convict."

"You did what?"

"Yeah, it was Nick's idea." After an ominous silence on the other end, she hurried to say, "I don't think Nick meant for me to do anything like that. Nick had asked in passing if I had contacted Bob Small's cellmate, and that made me realize that I should."

"Oh, for crying out loud," Mack muttered. "Why, when you already have enough cases to work on, do you need to bring more convicts, more criminals into your world?"

"I wasn't thinking of it that way," she explained. "I was thinking of it more along the line of seeing if this guy wanted to change his story after all these years."

"And? What did he say?"

"He says he wants something out of this deal."

"Of course he does," Mack muttered in disgust. "That's a common ploy among criminals."

"Well, that's nice. Yet I don't really have anything to give him, and he was pretty disgusted to realize that I wasn't law enforcement and that I was—what was it he called me? Something about a nasty do-gooder."

At that, Mack chuckled. "If that's the worst he called you, you're doing okay."

"Right? I figured I was doing okay too. Anyway, I asked him if he wanted to share his info with me, and he said he'll think about it."

"And what was it specifically you asked him for?"

"More information on this Bob Small guy, so we can track him down. The convict roomed with Bob Small about ten, fifteen years ago, at least that long ago. Time goes by too fast. I don't think the convict really figured out when, but he said that Bob Small was old then."

"If he calls you back," Mack said, "let me know."

"I will," she agreed. "I guess there's nothing you can do to get any information out of him, is there?"

"No," he noted cautiously. "Obviously, if he had information that the police wanted, then it's possible a deal might be struck, but it's not within my power to make that deal. The prison system, even our files will have fingerprints, photos and possible aliases but I need more than a few newsletter clippings and a convict's words to get permission to open this."

"Right," she murmured. "Okay, I don't know whether he has anything to say or not."

"Because of what you're trying to do and hoping to gain from talking to him," Mack explained, "I do need you to keep me in the loop at all times."

Such a note of worry filled his tone that she immediately replied, "Of course."

He hesitated and then said, "I was expecting a big argument."

"Nope," she replied. "I don't have a death wish. I don't really understand what these guys are all about. I just know that he has information. So it was worth a conversation."

"Right," Mack noted.

There was almost visible relief in his voice. She laughed. "Besides, if we get anything from him, I might need your help to come up with something to tickle his fancy."

He snorted at that. "These guys want better living accommodations, different jail cells, all kinds of nonsense, but, most of the time, they don't get it."

"He's been in for a long time," she reminded Mack.

"Yeah, and that makes him cagier than anything. Some guys do really well in jail, and they come out in much better shape," Mack shared, "and then some guys are lifers. They come out, do some crime, just so they can go right back again."

"By choice?" she asked in astonishment.

"Yes, by choice," Mack confirmed, "because they no longer know how to function in the society that's out here now. It's so very different than what society looked like when they went into jail."

"I guess that makes sense too," she muttered in astonishment. "I hadn't considered that."

"You should because some of these guys are pretty dangerous," Mack told her, "and some of them don't have much left for a moral code or creed."

"Sure, but not all of them I hope," she said. "I need this guy to care."

"I wouldn't count on it," he replied gently.

"I know. I know. He tried to fob me off with that too, but he's also PO'd that this Bob Small guy's getting away with all these murders, and he's still stuck in jail."

"Yes, that would be one of the buttons you can push," Mack suggested, "but again you should be very careful."

"One more thing," Doreen added.

Mack groaned.

"I spoke to Hinja's great-niece, and she saw an old guy she did not recognize at Hinja's funeral. He told her that he liked her curly hair. I'm afraid she spoke with Bob Small." Just then she overheard somebody calling Mack urgently in the background on his end of the phone call. "You should go," she said. "Have a good day." And, with that, she hung up on him.

She sat here for a long time and realized that she may have gotten herself into a bit of a pickle. But, well, when didn't she? It seemed as if pickles were part of her everyday occurrence, and that dumbfounded her because who knew she would have these problems all the time?

When her phone rang again, she didn't recognize the number.

She hesitated, but when she finally did answer it, she recognized Scott from Christie's on the other end.

Chapter 12

"THERE YOU ARE," Scott said. "I wasn't sure if I would get you."

"Hey." She smiled in relief that the antique dealer was calling her. "I've been worried about what's going on."

"I understand," Scott acknowledged. "It's such a time-intensive process that we go through, and honestly some of these pieces did need a good bit of work to clean them up," he explained apologetically.

"I can see how some of them needed additional care. So how is it going?" she asked hesitantly.

"It's going well. We have an auction this coming weekend for a few of the lesser-priced items," he shared. "The books went out in a special newsletter. Although have you spoken with the antique book dealer?"

"I haven't spoken to anybody. Everything left the house, and, after that, I've been sitting here, wondering."

He burst out laughing. "Wondering if we were thieves who came, stole all your property, and left?" he asked in a teasing voice.

"Well, maybe," she admitted. "It has been a pretty rough go-round not knowing what's going on."

"You did know that the pieces must first be repaired," he asked, "right?"

"Yes, I knew that," she agreed, "and we weren't exactly sure what shape they would be in for any auction until some of the specialists had seen them. Even with all those things going on, yet, as the months went by, I wasn't so sure."

"No, I hear you," Scott replied. "A few of the smaller items and some of those antique books are scheduled for sale first, even some little kitchen items this weekend. Obviously it'll still be a few months before anything that's sold comes your way, but those sales give us an idea of what money is due to you," he stated, talking in an assured tone. "For the big-ticket items we'll do a special auction in another, jeez …" He had to stop to think. "We pushed it back so that repairs were done, but I think it'll be somewhere in November. I hate to mention an October date, until I can really promise you that."

She thought about that and nodded. "Since it's late September, that's not that far off."

"I'm glad you think so. I was afraid you'd be screaming at that."

"It's not that I'm screaming," she clarified, "but you know my financial situation."

He replied, "Absolutely. I know you need the money, and we're trying to get you the most for your antiques."

"I'm okay for a little bit," she added. "I did end up getting a reward for one of the jobs that I did recently. That was enough to keep me for a few months."

"Oh, that's wonderful," Scott exclaimed. "I never really had any ability to do the stuff that you're doing. I think it's wonderful that you've found a way to make some money to get you through."

"Well, it'll be nicer when I don't have to worry about getting through those periods," she noted, with a sigh. "Some months it's pretty rough."

"And we thought we would have the bulk of these already heading at auction," Scott admitted, "but we decided to split this up and put the higher-priced items in a separate auction. We thought it would be better not to get it confused with any of the smaller stuff. And already a couple private collectors want a few of the books. I was wondering if it'll be okay to call you with offers."

"Who's handling that?"

"John. He does private collections in auctions. Give him some rare old books, and you'll be lucky if you can talk to him again."

"I do remember thinking maybe he wanted a few pieces himself."

"I think that's what his question will be, whether you're open to him buying a few for himself."

"But how will I know if his offering price is a fair deal?" she asked in worry.

"And that's a very good question. I can tell you that he did get all the pieces evaluated, and he does have paperwork for you to take a look at," Scott shared. "Now the *value* is one thing, while the *selling price* is a different thing. And that's where you'll have a bit of a challenge."

"Right," she muttered. "So he'll want some and some go to this first auction?"

"Yes," Scott confirmed. "John wants two books, I believe. So the rest go to auctions. We have a special literature auction, including music, even art, all that stuff. You have a few pieces of artwork in there too, don't you?"

"Yes, my grandmother apparently had eclectic tastes."

"She had excellent taste," Scott stated. "I don't know about eclectic. I also don't know if she cared for these pieces themselves or whether she had a good eye for what would make money, but she will certainly make you a lot of money."

"And that, of course, would make her happy," Doreen said, with a smile. "I'm not against John having a few pieces. I just … No matter what I say, it makes me sound greedy."

At that, Scott took off laughing. "No, absolutely not. These are investments. We need to get the most for you out of them," he stated in a consoling voice. "You should keep in mind that some are more valuable than others, and John doesn't want to buy the super expensive stuff. He is interested in two of them," and he named two books.

"I'm sorry. The titles don't mean a whole lot to me."

"Understood. The paperwork I'm sending you puts the estimated value at seventy-five thousand and sixty-two thousand."

She stopped and stared down at her phone. "Per book?"

"Yes, yes." Scott chuckled. "I gather you weren't expecting them to be that much."

"Nope, I sure wasn't, and, on top of that, you mentioned how these are the not-as-expensive ones, right?" she asked quickly.

"That's correct. Some of the others he found to be worth a lot more."

She sat back and gasped. "Wow. My grandmother is something else."

"Not only is she something else, I hope she is still in good health and can watch you reap the rewards of all this," Scott shared.

"Well, if it doesn't take too much longer," she added,

with a note of humor, "Nan might."

He chuckled again. "I'll have John call you, and you can decide what you want to do about those two prices."

"Sure, but are you telling me that's a negotiable price?"

"Oh, absolutely, and, if you don't think that it's worth whatever John will offer you," Scott explained, "it can go to auction. Then, if you still don't sell them, you can offer them to him."

"Oh, that might be an easier way to do it."

"It might, but then, for him, it's a chance that he won't get them because some of these books, according to him, should sell pretty fast."

"Right. More to think about."

"There's always more to think about," Scott noted warmly. "But I do want to auction some of the small stuff this weekend and then the bigger items later in November, per the catalog I sent you."

And, with that, he rang off, leaving her staring at the phone. Then she hopped to her feet and started running around the house, screaming at the top of her lungs in joy. It sounded as if, for once, she would be on the receiving end of good things. She was still dancing around, crying out to the animals, when her phone rang again. She sighed, coming back to earth, yet still bubbling and buoyant. Nan was calling.

Doreen quickly explained the phone call from Scott, and Nan was laughing and cheering with her. "This is absolutely marvelous news."

"I still don't know what to do about the books that John wants."

Nan hesitated before speaking. "Well, to a certain extent, I would say sell them to him, as long as he has a good price."

"But what's a good price?" Doreen asked. "He won't offer less than what it's evaluated at, will he?"

"No, and a lot of people will offer a lot more than what it's evaluated at," Nan noted in that most prim teacher-like manner in her voice. "You can't afford to give any of this away."

"No. … And I don't even know what I would say because, for the moment, I'm too excited."

Nan chuckled. "No, this is huge. You've done very well for yourself."

"Not yet I haven't—and it's not me. It's you."

"And I'll take all credit coming my way," Nan stated in a proud tone.

Doreen chuckled. "Did you have a reason for calling?"

"I did. I wanted to see if you've gotten any more news."

"No, I haven't," she said regretfully. "Mack's being pretty tight-lipped about it."

"Yeah, apparently Darren has been too," Nan added, with a sigh. "That makes us that much more eager to get to the bottom of it."

"I'm focusing more on Hinja's problem," Doreen shared.

"Oh dear, that's such a sad one."

"It is, and I have finally gone through all the letters and all the notes, and I did contact Hinja's great-niece, the woman who had sent them to you, and she is sending me the last bits and pieces. So I'll see if you want anything to remember her by and if anything at all has to do with this Bob Small character."

"If he's the right man," Nan noted.

"That's the thing. Once again we're dealing with the *what ifs*. It might be him, and it might not be him."

"And that's always the worst," Nan agreed. "We can make such innuendos and assumptions all we want, but, at the end of the day, you must ensure you've even got the right guy. And, so far, it sounds as if Hinja was worried about not having any proof."

"You're correct there," Doreen agreed. "I think it tormented her right to the end."

"Oh, it did. It definitely did. It was hard on all of us when Hinja went so quiet because we could do nothing to assuage her feelings of guilt."

"I can't imagine, ... but, bottom line is, it's been a good day so far here." Doreen chuckled.

"That's good. I wanted to check in to see if you had any new information."

"No, I don't. I'm surprised you're not hauling me down there for tea."

"Oh dear, no, not today. We're back to lawn bowling again. Ever since that trip to the cemetery, I realized that we're behind in our winnings, so we should pick up the pace."

"Ah, so you set up another tournament?"

"They're working on it now," Nan replied. "We need enough players to make the trips worthwhile, and, of course, we'll hope that they live long enough to make their plays happen." She chuckled at her own dark humor.

Doreen smiled at that because death humor appeared to be alive at all times when it came to these retirement homes. "Have a great day then, Nan," and Doreen hung up.

She sat here, still so excited at the news that she would have some big money—for her—coming in soon so that she could eat and pay off some bills.

She wondered whether she needed to offer Nan some

money for all she had helped Doreen with, or would that upset Nan more? Doreen didn't want to upset her grandmother, but, at the same time, what was the right thing to do? That was always the trick. Supposedly the right thing to do was obvious, but, when you took the particular personalities into play, it wasn't always that simple.

Still, Doreen wanted to make sure Nan knew how much Doreen appreciated what she'd done for her and didn't want to make the mistake of taking advantage. She pondered that but no point in even thinking about it right now because it was still too far away. No money at this point anyway. And, according to Scott, it still would be a couple months, if not three months, before any money came her way.

She would offer to pay Nick something for all the time he spent on getting her a divorce too.

Finally she got up and made herself a sandwich, and she was still dancing when the doorbell rang. She froze, as Mugs went to the front door, barking like crazy.

She hesitated, then walked over to her front door. From Mugs's attitude, Doreen wasn't sure that she should open it. But she did and stared out at Mathew. She glared at him. "What are you doing here?" she muttered.

"I came to talk to you," he said, with a note of desperation in his voice. She frowned at him. He asked, "Can I come in?"

She immediately shook her head. "Nope, you sure can't. I already know that I'm in trouble for even opening the door to you."

"Well, you've already opened it," he replied in exasperation. "So stop letting the lawyers control everything and open the door and talk to me."

"Talk to you?" she repeated. "Every time I talk to you,

you end up threatening me."

He flushed at that. "I'm sorry. You seem to be pricking my temper these days."

"Not me," she declared, keeping the door firmly opened just a bit. "You know perfectly well you need to talk to the lawyers."

"Sure," he said, "but all they want to do is talk court."

"What did you expect? If you can't come to an agreement, then it's a court case."

"We can come to an agreement, but you should be reasonable."

She glared at him. "Is that what you came here to tell me?" she asked stiffly. "Because you know where you can go if it is."

It was his turn to glare at her. "When did you get so ornery?" he snapped.

"Maybe somewhere around the time that Robin betrayed me and that you stabbed me in the back," she muttered, brandishing daggers with her gaze, "and this divorce has nothing to do with anything except fairness."

"This is not fair," he roared. "I'm the one who built all this up. You shouldn't get any of it."

She stared at him, stony-faced, wondering how she was supposed to get out of this. He shoved the door hard, and it bounced in her hand. It was all she could do to keep it from pushing open again.

Mugs started barking in fury.

Mathew glared down at the dog and said, "Shut the dog up, will you?"

"No, I won't," she snapped. "You're the one trying to force your way in, and that goes against everything the lawyers are trying to get you to stop."

"I don't care. I can't go to court."

"Why not?" she asked. "You're always talking about having lawyers on hand and that you'll sue everybody."

He nodded. "Yeah, and somehow my name's become mud with lawyers."

"Go get yourself more crooked lawyers to handle this for you."

"I've got a bunch of them," he muttered, "but your lawyer's been a jerk."

She smiled at that. "Glad to hear that. All you should do is come to an agreement with my attorney."

"I can't come to an agreement if you won't talk to me," he snapped. "Why do you think I'm here?"

"I have no idea why you're here. Can't say I'm thrilled to see you."

"Well, that's too bad," he muttered, "because I'm here, and I'm not leaving until we get this settled."

"Get what settled?"

"I want you to accept the money that's been offered and leave me alone."

"Me? Leave you alone?" she repeated in astonishment. "Did you seriously say that?"

"I absolutely did," he snarled. "You don't get all my money."

"I don't want all your money," she clarified, "but you're really starting to piss me off. It would be better if you go away and leave me alone." And, with that, she tried to slam the door shut again.

There was Mathew, foot in the way, and he looked at her and gave her that smile that made her blood run cold. "Yeah, will you make me?"

Then someone behind Mathew said, "No, but I will."

Chapter 13

As Mathew turned, a bit astonished, there was Mack, an avenging angel, standing firm, his hands on his hips, glaring at Mathew. He looked back at Doreen and snapped, "And you have some explaining to do."

She winced. "I opened the door. I won't get off the hook on that one, will I?"

"No, you won't," Mack declared, turning his attention back to Mathew. "And I have a cell waiting for you." Mack turned and pointed to Arnold and Chester, big grins on their faces and handcuffs in their hands.

Before Mathew had a chance to argue, he was handcuffed and led away to a cruiser.

Doreen stared at Mack in astonishment, then called out to Mathew, as he was being led to the car, "That new jewelry looks good on you."

Mathew turned, and the sight of her with Mack seemed to be Mathew's undoing. He started swearing and cussing and threatening her. At that, Mack noted in a clipped voice, "That gives us a whole lot more ammunition," he told Mathew, "so keep it up."

Almost as if Mack finally got through to Mathew that

this was serious, Mathew shut up and allowed himself to be put into the back of the cruiser. With that, Chester got into the front seat with Arnold, and they drove off.

She turned to look at Mack. "I know I did wrong. I checked one of the side windows, but I couldn't see who was on the porch. And you told me that you were watching to see if he flew in and would let me know."

He groaned. "How is it you always turn this around to me?"

She smiled at him. "It depends on whether or not you'll yell at me."

He glared at her. "You know what you deserve."

She opened her arms. "Not to be yelled at. It was already bad enough having him here."

Instantly Mack's anger fell away, and he opened his arms.

She stepped into them, smiling, as Mack wrapped his arms tightly around her. She muttered, "I really don't like that man."

Mack snorted. "Fine time to figure that out," he replied, with a headshake.

"You'll tell your brother?"

"Oh, I'm so going to tell him. Now we'll charge him with threatening you again, trying to force his way inside, and anything else I can think of," Mack declared, with a glare in her direction. "What did he want?"

"He said that he wasn't leaving until we settled the divorce and that I was supposed to accept what he had offered and to stop being greedy and that I didn't deserve all his money."

"Of course, and what did you say?"

"I told him that he was supposed to talk to the lawyers."

"That would have maybe been okay, except he was already past it, I presume."

"Yeah, he started getting really angry at that point. I don't think he likes Nick very much."

Mack chuckled. "No. When my brother's on your side, it's a good place to have him. However, when he's against you, I'm pretty sure he's scary."

"Well, I'm done with enough scary in this lifetime," she muttered. "Can't say I want more scariness." He gave her a gentle squeeze, then nudged her back indoors. "We're creating a scene."

She looked around to see Richard, standing there, glaring at her. She glared back at him.

"You see? You're causing trouble again." Richard shook a fist at her.

She picked up her own fist and shook it at him. "You could have called the cops and given me a hand."

He looked at her in surprise. "You mean, you needed help?"

She nodded. "Yeah, I did."

"Oh." With that, he went inside.

She looked back at Mack. "You know that it's not easy living here, right?"

He sighed, pulled her inside, and closed the door. He then greeted the animals that were all over him. "What did Mugs do?"

"He wouldn't stop barking at Mathew," she replied, "which upset Mathew too."

"Yeah, I suppose Mugs knows what Mathew is like?"

"Somewhat, yes. Mugs always was perfectly groomed and looked after because of Mathew's strict rules, so I don't know if Mathew knows how badly dogs can act. Mugs was definitely on my side."

"In that case, good boy," he said to Mugs, who was quite happy to get any accolades coming his way, so took advantage and rubbed all over Mack.

She shook her head. "Even when I think I'm doing right, I'm not doing right," she muttered.

He sighed. "Don't start that. You're doing just fine."

"Yeah, doesn't feel that way," she said. "Even with your help and Nick's, I still can't get the divorce done."

"Oh, we'll get it through now," Mack stated, "and we'll have quite a few extra charges that Mathew must consider too."

"Will you really charge him?" she asked.

"Yeah, or use it as pressure to get him to do whatever he needs to do to get this done and gone and to ensure he never crosses your pathway again."

"And then what happens if he doesn't?"

He gave her a wolfish smile. "Then we get to throw the book at him," he said cheerfully.

"Can't you do that now?" she complained. "And skip all the rest of it?"

He burst out laughing. "Remember that part about still needing to follow the law?"

"I think the law needs to change," she announced.

He nodded. "A lot of parts in the law do need to be changed," he agreed. "What then? Will you become a lawyer now?"

She looked at him and shuddered. "I don't think I could do that job."

"No, I don't think you could. Besides, that's what Nick does best, and I don't think he wants any competition."

She snorted at that. "Yeah, I think he's scared of me as it

is."

"I wouldn't be at all surprised," Mack muttered. "Lots of people are."

"I'm not scary," she protested. "Why would you even say that?"

He rolled his eyes, as she led them into the kitchen, and asked her, "How about coffee?"

She looked at him in delight. "Can you stay?"

"I can stay a little bit," he replied, "while they arraign Mathew down at the station."

"Good. Can they throw away the key too, or at least give it to Chester to lose it for a while?" she muttered.

He chuckled. "They will treat him as well as they can, but they won't go overboard. They all know who he is, and they know what he's doing."

"Good," she muttered. "I never did anything to him, you know? It feels very strange to even be in this position now."

"Of course it does."

"When I think I'm getting better, he pops up into my life, and I open the door for him."

"Did you know who it was?"

"No, I didn't, honestly. I would like to think I wouldn't open the door if I'd known. I don't know whether that would have made a difference or Mathew would have kicked it down."

"Well, that would have been an interesting set of charges, if he had done that," Mack noted. "As it is, his lawyer will get him off pretty fast."

"He mentioned how he was having trouble getting lawyers now, something to do with his name being muddy."

"Yeah, that's not exactly an easy thing to come back

from, once you get disbarred because of your client."

"I don't think Robin particularly cared."

"Maybe, if she were still alive, she would," Mack noted, "or if she had any idea that her life would be forfeit in this instant."

Doreen nodded slowly. "I guess you don't really think about the cost because you never think it'll be *your* cost, do you?"

"No, everybody always thinks that they'll be the ones who walk away scot-free," Mack confirmed. "Got to tell you that it doesn't work out that way."

She patted his cheek gently. "Thanks for coming to the rescue again."

He nodded soberly, looking down at her. "It would be nice if I didn't have to keep rescuing you."

"Yeah, wouldn't it?" she quipped. "Did you find out that he had arrived?"

He nodded. "But I was out on a call," he explained, trying to keep his tone even. "When I got the alert, Mathew was already on the way over here. When I arrived, I saw him standing at your front door, ready to beat you to death."

"If you hadn't come then, I think he would have used his fists to get me to sign."

"Let me call Nick. You put on coffee, and we'll sit down and relax."

"Sounds good to me," she agreed, as she put on the coffee, listening to Mack as he explained to his brother what had happened. Some hard tones could be heard back and forth, as options were discussed. Finally, with the coffee poured, she opened up the back door and stepped outside, wondering what had happened to that absolutely glorious feeling that she'd started the day with. She looked in vain for the deer, hoping that maybe their presence would bring her back to some balance. Still, why would they stick around with this turbulence in the area?

They were smarter than that; too bad she wasn't. Almost immediately she was reminded that she hadn't been submissive. Instead she had gotten angry, and she had, at the moment, won this round. Thanks to Mack's fortuitous arrival. Now if they can keep Mathew out of her life, that would be perfect. And, with that, she waited until Mack was done with his phone call and then asked him, "So who did the guns belong to?"

He stared at her blankly.

She smiled. "The Uzi from the cemetery vault and the weapons' cache from that fake grave?"

"Still trying to figure that out," Mack replied.

"Do you think it's related to the Bob Small stuff?"

"I don't think so," he told her. "It's way too much weaponry for him."

"That's what I wondered. So what if it's a prepper?"

"A prepper?" he asked, amused.

She shrugged. "Somebody waiting for the end of the world."

"But why would you have the guns buried at the cemetery?"

She frowned. "Okay, so that doesn't make a whole lot of sense either, so now we're back to the gang theory?"

He nodded. "Yeah, that's the working theory."

"Have you talked to any of the gangs?"

"I have. Nobody knows anything." She rolled her eyes at that, and he smiled. "Right, isn't that always the way?"

"On the one hand though," she added, "I bet they're angry they didn't know about that haul."

"I think even the gangs are still trying to figure out exactly how and what went on there."

"What about cameras?" she asked. "When that vandalism was done?"

"We're still sorting that out. Cameras are at the cemetery but none at that area."

"Of course it's on the other side, right?"

He smiled and nodded. "Cameras can't cover every angle."

"No, but it would be nice if they at least cover the right ones," she muttered.

He burst out laughing at that. "I won't argue with you on that, but let's consider the fact that a lot of people go back and forth through there, just to visit the gravesites."

"But then, with cameras at the cemetery, how would somebody have known the best time to bury the guns?" she asked.

"Had to be working with the cemetery people, in my opinion."

"Still, why bury guns for twenty years?"

"And that's the trick. If one person buried the Uzi and all this other stash of guns, why did he leave it there for so long? However, if one person put the Uzi in the mausoleum vault and another guy buried the bigger stash, still the question remains. How did someone know the bigger stash was there or was it just a prank?"

"Do you think that's all it was, a prank? Because, if it were some kids, and they saw what was in the casket, they would have grabbed it right then and ran."

"And that's one of the questions to figure out—and, yes, we're on it."

"Of course you are. It'll be nice if we could, just you

know …"

He laughed and added, "Get answers sooner?"

"Yeah. … Are you by any chance spending a lot of time down there?"

"No, I haven't in a while," Mack said.

"Just wondered."

"It might not be a bad thing to do." And he waggled his eyebrows at her.

She gasped. "Hang on a minute. Are you telling me to go to the cemetery and to walk around, just to see what and who might be around there?"

"I can't tell you to do anything. Officially I need to tell you to stay out of this mess," Mack noted. "I suspect nobody would return, particularly now that the guns have been found and are in our custody."

She pondered that and nodded. "Unless they're keeping track of the police presence."

"And that's one of the reasons why it's probably okay for you to go down there now," Mack added. "The police presence is pretty well over."

She looked at him in delight. "Then I'll take the animals this afternoon, and maybe Thaddeus here can go visit Big Guy."

Mack nodded. "Not a bad idea, particularly if he wants to get out."

As it was, Thaddeus had woken up on his roost, popped his head up, and started crying, "Big Guy, Big Guy, Big Guy."

She winced because, now that he was on a roll, there was no stopping him.

"Big Guy, Big Guy, Big Guy."

"Oh my." Mack stared at the bird. "How long can he

keep that up for?"

"Too long," she muttered. "I shouldn't have mentioned it out loud."

"Nope, you sure shouldn't have," Mack agreed, "but the good news is, it will chase me back to work faster." And, with that, he hopped to his feet, drained the last of his coffee cup, and suggested, "Maybe you should take him over there now. … Don't take this the wrong way, but could you try staying out of trouble for once?"

When she hopped to her feet indignantly, he grinned at her. "That's better. You were looking a bit down."

She sighed. "So that's what this is, an effort to make me feel better?"

"Is it working?" he asked.

She laughed. "Maybe, just maybe."

"Good. In that case, go and enjoy. And remember. Leave the cops alone, if you see anybody there."

"Will do."

As soon as Mack left, Doreen turned to Thaddeus and asked him, "Shall we go see Big Guy?" He crowed again, raced up her hand, tucked his head against her, and whispered, "Big Guy, Big Guy, Big Guy."

She picked up her cell and phoned Jerry, Big Guy's owner, and sure enough he was at home. When she mentioned that Thaddeus was on a rampage to come visit Big Guy, Jerry laughed in delight and replied, "Sure, come on over. We can let them visit, and, if you're up for it, we can sit and have a cup of coffee."

"Perfect. There's never enough coffee in this world as it is." She laughed, as she set off for his place.

Chapter 14

BRINGING ALONG MUGS and Goliath, Doreen took Thaddeus to visit Big Guy. The bird's real name was King, but King's nickname, Big Guy, stuck with Thaddeus. She wasn't sure whether she should leave Mugs and Goliath in the car or risk bringing them inside.

As she drove past the cemetery to Jerry's house, she smiled. Her *Lifeless in the Lilies* case hadn't been the easiest one to solve, but it had come with the biggest benefits overall. She had found another animal-lover, Jerry—whose animals were hired for kids' parties and also shared with hospitals and whatnot for free. Plus Jerry had a bird friend for Thaddeus.

She soon parked in Jerry's driveway and decided to bring all the animals with her. As she walked up to Jerry's front door, it opened, and, sure enough, the other huge parrot was on Jerry's shoulder.

"Big Guy, Big Guy, Big Guy," Thaddeus immediately cried out. Laughing, Doreen let Thaddeus go up Jerry's other arm. "Is it okay if Mugs and Goliath join us?" she asked Jerry.

"Of course. The more, the merrier." Jerry led her into

the house, with both birds on his shoulders, and said, "We don't think about playdates for the animals often enough."

She smiled up at him. "I was coming down to the cemetery anyway, and this guy always seems to know."

"Any particular reason to go to the cemetery?" he asked, looking at her carefully.

"I certainly have enough people there, I should go visit," she shared, "but I'm sure you've heard about all the commotion with the weapons found in a coffin in a fake grave."

"Yes. That is fascinating."

"I was there with a cop, when we found one of the mausoleum vaults had been smashed. That's when we found the first gun." After telling Goliath and Mugs to be on their best behavior, she explained further to Jerry. "The same name on the damaged vault had also been on a burial plot in the cemetery. I'm not sure what strings the police pulled, but they decided to open the buried coffin, when they realized that they have no records of burying any deceased person in there with that name."

"Wow, and now apparently a cache of weapons was buried instead?"

She nodded. "And yet they still don't know who buried them."

"It is amazing though," Jerry noted. "You don't even consider that going on here. How could somebody stash a large supply of weapons, all without anybody knowing?"

"It's crazy. Why bury all those guns, and why there in the cemetery?"

He pondered that as he made the way into his kitchen. "Accessibility maybe?"

"Yeah, but that's a lot of work to dig that back up again," Doreen noted. "It was buried deep too. It took the big machinery to retrieve."

"Sure, the coffins are all buried at least six feet under to stop any animals from digging up the bodies. But still, grave robbers used to dig those graves by hand, so to dig them up at this point in time—to uncover the weapons—I wouldn't think that would have been all that hard." He pondered.

"Maybe not in theory," she replied. "Still seems to be such an odd thing to do. And you'd need a long window of time to accomplish that, to bury all those weapons, not making noise, watching for eyewitnesses."

He smiled at her. "Odd for us, yes, but for whoever had all those weapons stashed there? Wow."

"That's the other thing," she added. "The value of the cache is high, so I imagine it was being stored for a particular reason. I was thinking gangs and turf wars."

Jerry nodded. "Sure, but I would think a lot of other things were likely more viable."

"Such as?" she asked.

Jerry put on coffee, moving carefully because he had both parrots on his shoulders. The two birds were having quite the talking fest around him. He laughed and finally put them both on the table, where they sat together, preening and pecking away.

"They really do get along well, don't they?" she asked in amazement.

"They really do," Jerry agreed, "and yours is such a talker."

"He's *such* a talker," she confirmed, with an eye roll. "Have you ever seen anybody at the cemetery who might be involved in this? It had to have been done somehow."

Jerry frowned, as he considered that. "I imagine the police can tell how long that stash has been buried. If that's been buried for at least twenty years, then you're going back quite a while. If it's only been buried some six, eight years, that's still a while, but current records will be relatively easier to find," he suggested, "but older is a whole different story."

She looked over at him. "Have you ever heard any rumors about this?"

He shrugged. "There's been rumors about a cache of weapons for a while now," he noted, "but not exactly what people are willing to talk about."

She nodded, knowing the area. "I guess I'm still not cleared and deemed a local to be talked to either, am I?" she asked, with a note of humor.

He gave her a wry smile. "You've come a long way, with what you did for that little boy here in our neighborhood. Those events will stay strong in these people's heart, yet you're still technically a stranger to them."

She nodded slowly. "Plus I still work with the cops."

"Exactly." Jerry nodded. "So don't take it to heart, if they're still looking out for themselves."

"And I get that too." Doreen sighed. "It's too bad."

"I can ask around," Jerry offered. "There'll be a lot of excitement about these latest rumors. I'm not at all surprised that you're looking into it."

"I was there at the time that we found the vandalized mausoleum vault," she shared, "and it appears somebody was interrupted while doing the job because they didn't clear it out."

He stared at her. "Seriously?"

She nodded. "Yes, so we got the one gun that was in there."

He shook his head. "What if a child had seen that?"

"I know," she cried out softly. "Can you imagine? It

boggles the mind."

"But the buried stash must be a very old cache."

"I think you're right. And the collection of weapons was so heavy that it did some damage to the actual coffin. Not sure whether that coffin was made of treated wood or was just a plywood box, as they used to use."

"And for the longest time," Jerry noted, "that did the job just fine."

"Sure, then organized commerce came in," she added, with a wave of her hand, "and everybody had to get bigger and better quality, while more focused on the upsell."

"And that's a problem?"

"It is, if a pine box would do the job, then maybe a pine box is all that anybody needs for the job, but I guess people want to send their loved ones off in fine style."

"And yet some people can't afford it."

"And that just adds to the guilt, especially if you were unable to help them while alive, or you couldn't be there for them. So you want to do something right at the end of the day, but *wanting* doesn't mean *being able.*"

"Yet the dead don't care."

She chuckled. "They don't care. They don't know. However, you brought up some good points. So, when I leave you, I'll head to the cemetery and have a walk around, and maybe I'll see something," She shrugged and laughed. "Or maybe not."

"You never know," Jerry stated in a serious tone. "Apparently you see things others don't."

She flushed uncomfortably with the compliment. "Maybe, yet it does feel very much as if this were an old case. So whether that person who buried all these guns is still alive or not is a different story."

"If the person who buried this cache is no longer alive, then how would anybody know?"

She nodded. "A lot of times people leave hints to the next of kin, particularly if they are somebody who would understand and maybe honor the information."

He shook his head. "That boggles the mind."

"Well, think about it. If you stash one million dollars somewhere, and you couldn't go get it, and you have an only son, wouldn't you want to leave him that legacy?"

Jerry stared at her and then slowly nodded. "I guess I would, but the chances are good, when talking about way-too-many guns and not one million dollars, that'll just get him killed."

"Exactly," she agreed, "but the dying may hope that the son can find a way to get it, even though the original owner, the supposed father, might not have."

"Still boggles the mind," Jerry repeated.

She chuckled. "It absolutely does, and I don't know what the story is in this case, but it'll be nice to find out."

"It's got the whole town buzzing," he confirmed. "That's a lot of weapons."

"And thankfully," she shared, with a bright smile, "it all went into the lockup."

"Still, I guess the police should test them all for forensics."

"I imagine they are testing them all to ensure nothing connects to other crimes."

He winced at that. "And anybody who's stockpiling guns may have had an innocent reason, such as the doomsday preppers, or maybe they were intent on selling them or who knows what." Jerry shrugged and laughed. "I have no idea what other reasons there could be."

She smiled. "But why bury them all if a prepper or if they planned to sell them? Maybe burying the guns was to take them off the streets, but, in that case, why not destroy them? I think the cops often have amnesty buybacks, where you can take in weapons, and the cops won't ask any questions, just as a safe way to dispose of them."

"But if somebody had a criminal record, they won't do that."

"No, they sure wouldn't." Doreen pondered that. "Makes you wonder then, *huh?* I'd say that it was …" She stopped, shook her head. "No, that doesn't make sense either."

"Being in the cemetery, the guns were close enough that, if somebody local *had* to get them, they could. However, they were far enough from home and equally hard enough to get at that it wouldn't have been an easy job. Yet so many guns were involved to entice someone to go get them eventually. Did you see the stash?"

"I was there as the coffin gave way. When it swung, it smacked one of the workers up the side of his head, and he slipped into the grave. Then, of course, everything inside the coffin came down at the same time."

"Wow," Jerry exclaimed. "How is it you always manage to be on the spot?"

She rolled her eyes at that. "You won't believe how I ended up down there." She quickly told him about her grandmother. They finished their cups of coffee, discussing the case, but they didn't come up with any other answers.

He pointed at her. "If you solve this one, your notoriety would be out of this world."

She winced at that. "Not trying for notoriety."

He chuckled. "Maybe not. I will ask around here for

you. Give me a call back in a few days, and I'll share what I come up with."

"I can do that." She got up to go, looked at Thaddeus, and said, "Thaddeus, it's time to say goodbye to Big Guy."

He started squawking, "Big Guy, Big Guy, Big Guy," rubbing his head up against the other parrot. The other parrot—not to be outdone—was doing the same thing, but not talking.

She smiled. "It does us good to see them together, doesn't it?"

"It does." Jerry smiled. "And this guy's been a lot perkier since he met yours."

"Oh, that's good to hear. And you're still taking your guy around to schools and hospitals and such?"

"I am. It's been busy."

"That should be a good thing, isn't it?" She turned to look at him curiously.

He shrugged. "Yeah, but the support isn't what it's supposed to be. It's daunting."

She winced at that. "I think support for a lot of things is down this year," she muttered.

He nodded. "What about you? Do you have a job?"

"No, no job," she replied. "I do a bit of gardening, but I seem more embroiled in this cold-case stuff than anything, yet it doesn't pay."

He laughed. "No, I can see that. The stuff that we love to do doesn't seem to pay much, does it?"

"How does that work?" she asked, with a shake of her head. "You would think, if we're doing good stuff, we should automatically get money. Some people say that's how it works, but I'm not so sure."

He chuckled. "It would be nice. Just hasn't worked for

me yet, though."

And, with that, laughing, she and her animals headed out to her vehicle.

Chapter 15

DOREEN DROVE UP to the cemetery and parked. As she got out, her animals crowded close. She looked down at them and said, "I promise. We're only here for a visit. It's okay." However, Mugs was acting strange. Of course the last time she'd been here alone, she had been attacked. And that had set Thaddeus off on a hunt that had quite a different ending to what she had imagined.

Keeping the animals close, she walked over to where the grave had been opened up. It was empty, and nobody was around. The crime scene tape was all still up, which she thought was foolish.

On the other hand, if the gun owner or some mischievous kids came at nighttime for a lark, then maybe that was a good precaution. She never really thought about doing things like that when she was growing up. It wasn't part of her childhood to run around and to scare each other in cemeteries.

She stood here for a long moment, studying the excavated grave, looking around at the area. It was located in the back section. And older area. Roads were nearby. As far as accessibility, it was one of the easier-to-access graves, and, as far as visibility, it was one of the least visible ones. All in all, it wasn't a bad place to bury guns, without witnesses strolling by.

She frowned at that and wondered how anybody could possibly have had the opportunity to hide all those guns in one evening. Maybe it was an inside job. Maybe somebody who worked at the cemetery had been involved and had even suggested this hiding place.

As she contemplated that, she heard odd sounds around her. She turned to look but didn't see anything. Mugs got restless, Pilling on the leash, wanting to head back toward the car.

She decided that she should probably be smart and stay with him. She also had no guarantee that her husband was still locked up. She was pretty sure that Mathew's lawyer would have gotten him out of jail by now. And, with that thought setting her nerves on edge, she retraced her steps back to her car.

When she looked around, she thought she saw somebody standing in the trees, watching her. She wasn't sure who it was, and she didn't recognize him, but, being a friendly sort and not wanting anybody to think that she was being sneaky, she lifted a hand and waved. She waited inside her car for a long moment, watching as that person slipped back farther into the shadows. Not at all sure about that, she phoned Mack.

"Hey, how are you doing?" he asked her.

"I'm doing fine," she said, feeling a little nervous. "Is my husband still in jail?"

"Your ex-husband, you mean?" he asked, with emphasis on the *ex*, making her wince. "He was released an hour ago."

"Ah."

"Why?" he asked, his voice sharp. "Have you seen him?"

"No, I haven't. I'm at the cemetery, and it seemed like somebody's skulking around in the back area."

After a moment's hesitation, Mack replied, "And you're thinking it's him."

"No, I was trying to narrow that down and would feel better if it wasn't him."

"Well, I would hope not. I'm checking to see if he got on a flight out."

"But if he only was released an hour ago …"

"It's not him," Mack said, with relief. "He went into the boarding area at the airport."

"Oh, so he will be on that flight?"

"Supposed to be, yeah, but he can slip back out again, skipping his flight."

"*Great.* I would like a confirmation that he took that flight."

"Yeah, I would too," Mack added, "and it takes off in twenty minutes."

"And would that then be updated?"

"Ideally, yes, but …"

"Right, so maybe not." Doreen sighed. "*Great.* I think I'll head home."

"Good idea, but make sure you are not followed. … I'm craving some salmon. How about you?"

She stared at her phone. "I'm craving food," she replied in a wry tone. "If you've got salmon, and you want to share, I am absolutely up for sharing."

He chuckled. "It's been a heck of a day."

"Yeah, it has," she agreed, "and I could really use a good meal."

"Done. I'll be there around five-ish."

"Sure, can I get something ready to go with it?"

"Yeah, absolutely. You can prep some rice and veggies." And, with that, he hung up.

She frowned at that because, for one, she didn't know if she had any veggies, and he made it sound as if she already knew what to do to get rice ready. She didn't think she had ever tried that before. Still, nothing like the present to get started.

As she drove up her driveway, Richard was working in his front yard. As soon as he saw her, he stopped and glared. She shrugged. "Hey, nice to see you too."

She and her animals walked into her house, and Doreen locked the door behind her. She wasn't sure what Richard's problem was, and was he really as crotchety as he tried to make himself out to be or was he actually a nice guy?

All of it was open for debate in her world. She headed to the kitchen to see if she had any veggies or if she needed to go shopping. She found carrots and wondered if she could make a carrot salad, but that wouldn't be substantial enough for Mack. She searched her pantry and found rice, but what would she do for more veggies? Searching her fridge once more, she found zucchini in the back part of the fridge. She noted it was a little sad but maybe still okay. She took a picture of it and sent it to Mack.

He came back with a thumbs-up.

"Okay, good," she said out loud. That was settled then. She at least had something to feed him. She felt bad every time he came over when she had no food. Although lately she'd been lucky enough to have treats from Nan, and that went a long way to making her feel better. She sat down with the internet and sorted out how to set up a pot of rice. With that prepped but not on because he wouldn't be arriving for a while, she then went back to her Bob Small stuff.

As soon as she checked her cell phone for any messages, she wondered if Gary Wildorf—the inmate she'd contacted—had any ideas about the guns stashed here. But why would he? It's not as if he was from here. Yet, if Bob Small was from here, would that gun stash have anything to do with this supposedly serial killer? But that didn't fit right. Why would a serial killer bury a cache of weapons?

In her mind, the profile of somebody who would do that was very different than who she thought Bob Small would be. Of course she'd been wrong before, many times in fact.

Still, there was an urge to call Gary again. She frowned at that. If she initiated the conversation, it would make her look eager—something that she couldn't hide for long, particularly when she really needed to hear back from Gary. Yet, at the same time, she didn't want him thinking that he could get the upper hand.

As she sat here, she pondered who else she could ask. With everybody agog about the most recent news, and with that unidentified person standing in the trees at the cemetery, she should talk to Mack. But she wanted to have a list of questions she could talk to him about over dinner.

The one question she really wanted answered was if Mack had questioned any past employees of the cemetery. It could be a current one too, who had been involved in this buried guns mess twenty years ago or so, but an ex-employee made the most sense to her overall. It made more sense for somebody who had access to the records or to the lots and could maybe set up this special gun burial privately.

And then, depending on how long ago this mass gun burial took place, maybe nobody really cared much in the way of records. Maybe things were a little haphazard, and some money even crossed hands. Or maybe it was a private affair, and they wanted to do the burying themselves. She shrugged. So many possibilities that didn't make much sense.

As she started to wonder if Mack would get here on time, her phone rang. She looked down at the number. She answered the call from the penitentiary cautiously. "Hello?"

"I want something for it," Gary snapped.

"Yeah, and I told you that I don't have anything to give you," Doreen repeated.

"No, but I did some research on you." Gary snickered. "You and that cop are pretty tight."

"Interesting," she noted. "I'm surprised that even made it to the news, and we're friends, but we're hardly more than that." She heard a sound behind her and turned to glare at Mack, who had entered the kitchen and was even now studying her, with an odd look on his face. She pointed to the phone and continued to speak to Gary. "Besides, an inmate like you really doesn't have a whole lot of options when it comes to negotiating."

"I bet I have some options," Gary snapped.

She quickly put the call on Speakerphone.

"Because I won't give you any information without it."

"I don't know if you really have any information to give me," she replied. "Guys like you make up stories, just to make you look good."

"I didn't make up nothing," he growled, "and witches like you make life difficult for people like me."

"Yeah, how do you figure?" she asked in astonishment.

"Because that's how I got into trouble in the first place," Gary admitted, "all for the love of a good woman."

"Well, if she was a good woman, presumably she didn't get you into any trouble."

Silence came from the other end. "Aren't you smart," he growled.

"No, not a whole lot," Doreen noted in a cheerful smile. "Besides, if you don't give me something to make it worth my while, then it won't get off the ground."

"I'll give you something, but then you should do something with it before you get back to me. Otherwise I won't give you any more."

"Yeah, what is it you'll give me?" she asked, with a laugh. "I need something concrete, something lasting, that I can do something with."

"Oh, I've got lots." Gary was silent for a moment. "But, if you think you'll get very much out of me without me getting something in return, you're wrong. So I'll give you a name, … and that name would lead you to other names, if you can get them to talk to you."

"If they're still alive," she added, correcting him.

"Ha, she's still alive all right, but I don't know if she'll talk to you or not."

"Depends on who you're talking about because, if it's Bob Small's ex-girlfriend, she's dead."

"Both of them?" he asked in shock.

"Well, Hinja is." Doreen raised her eyebrows, as she looked at Mack. He sat beside her, listening in on the conversation.

"That was one of them, yeah." Gary waited a long moment, then finally added, "You need to talk to Ella. She knows more than she's let on."

"Ella who?"

"How am I supposed to know?" he blustered.

"You know how many Ellas are out there in this world? Doreen asked in astonishment. You think I will go through a phone book to try and find every Ella?"

"It shouldn't be that hard," Gary stated. "She used to live in Kelowna. Ella … Hickman, I think. You talk to her, and then you come back and talk to me—but make sure you've got something on the table for me." And, with that, he hung up.

She quickly wrote down the name, turned to Mack. "What do you think?"

"You got something." He nodded. "I didn't think he'd even give you that much."

"Well, I sure as heck wouldn't approach you for something for him if he didn't give me something doable," she replied. "But I will now make some phone calls to see if I can get a hold of this Ella Hickman."

"Yeah, you do that," he muttered in consternation, as he stared down at the name she had written in her notepad.

"Do you know her?"

He looked up at Doreen. "I don't know her. I know *of* her. There is a difference,"

"Oh, what does that mean?"

"She was a politician. She's now retired, but I can tell you that she's not likely to talk to you at all."

"Ah, don't tell me that she ended up being somebody with some power in this town."

"She did. However, I'm not sure that she still does though."

"Because she's retired?"

"Maybe," he said, "I don't want to say too much because I don't want to affect your impression of her. … She's a powerhouse in many ways." Then he laughed. "And, in many ways, the two of you are well suited. I would love to be there when you talk to her."

"Good, I'll see if I can set that up."

He shook his head. "No, I think in this case you'll do much better on your own."

She stared at him. "I think you need to fill me in some more."

He sighed. "She's a huge advocate for all things female and a huge hater on all things male."

She frowned at him. "Well, a lot of people have the sexist thing going on. I don't think that's necessarily the same thing as a hate on."

"Maybe not," he admitted, "and maybe that's my own perception. You're right on that count, but it'll be interesting for you to talk to her and then tell me what you think."

She nodded slowly. "I'll definitely do that now. Did you get anywhere on those guns?" He shook his head. "Did you look into the cemetery's previous employees?"

"We're waiting for information to date that coffin," Mack confirmed.

"Yeah, that would be necessary." She nodded. "I was trying to figure out who else could have made that happen, but twenty or so years ago versus ten years ago makes a big difference."

"Exactly," he agreed. "And twenty years ago puts this back a long time. Either way nobody would claim them, and we got them off the streets. So, outside of it being a curiosity and a worry that somebody else may know where there's more, I'm not sure we can do anything about this gun stash other than secure it."

She frowned at that.

"Stop frowning," he said, gently stroking a finger alongside her temple. "We are on it."

"Yeah, but what crimes may have been committed with

those guns?"

"A big one in the hoarding of the weapons," he noted. "Short of ballistics coming back and saying that they were used in any crime, that's a different story."

"And that'll take a while."

He laughed. "That was a lot of weapons. It will take more than a while. And, even when we've run ballistics, we should try to match them. And, depending on how long ago, we may not have that great a record."

She sighed. "It's never easy, is it?"

He burst out laughing. "No, but it's worth doing, so you can count on that while we're doing it."

"Glad to hear that." She got up. "I set up the rice, and I made a carrot salad."

He stopped, looked at her. "You did what?"

She frowned. "Is that okay?"

He looked at her in delight. "It's better than okay," he said, with a huge grin. "Didn't mean to sound quite so shocked."

She rolled her eyes at that. "Yeah, you did, and I guess with good reason."

He burst out laughing. "Hey, every day you're getting better and better."

She smiled. "I don't think so, but nice of you to say." And, with that, they went to work on dinner.

Chapter 16

THE NEXT MORNING Doreen woke up bright and early and knew exactly who to call. She wasn't even out of bed when she reached for the phone. When Nan answered, Doreen asked, "How did lawn bowling go yesterday?"

"We won," she stated cheerfully. "You're up early."

"I don't know what time it is," Doreen admitted, "but I woke up and thought that maybe you would be a good source of information."

"*Woo*, I like that," Nan replied. "What are we solving this time?"

"I wondered if you know who's been running the cemetery, who works at the cemetery, and who may have been working at the cemetery over all these years."

First came silence on the other end, then Nan said. "I should, shouldn't I?"

"I don't know if you should or not. I just assumed that, out of everybody in town, you would at least have some idea."

"It's not exactly a career path I've known very many people to be on," Nan noted, her voice still thoughtful.

"In other words, you don't?" Doreen asked.

"No, I'm not sure that I do, but I'm sure somebody here will."

"That's what I figured. So I'll get up and have a shower, and I thought I would put that bee in your bonnet and see if you can pop up with any ideas."

"And why do you want to talk to them? … But of course you want to talk to them. It makes a lot of sense. I'll get back to you, dear." And, with that, her grandmother hung up.

Doreen bounced out of bed and raced into the shower. If nothing else she should get dressed and might get a better idea of what was going on by the end of the day. She also had something else to deal with today. And that was this lovely contact person whose name the inmate had given her. She'd written the name down last night. *Ella Hickman.*

Doreen took a look on the internet, as she let the coffee drip. That was somebody else Nan might know. But Doreen didn't want Nan to connect the dots just yet to any commotion going down at the cemetery.

By the time she had coffee and was sitting outside with her notes, writing down a list of questions to talk to Ella about, Nan called back.

"Desmond," she stated. "Everybody called him Dezy. He was a little tetched in the head and a veteran."

"Who is that?" Doreen asked curiously.

"He worked at the cemetery for a long time. I think that's why everybody thought he was a little tetched in the head."

"Why? Because he was comfortable with the dead?" she asked in a light tone.

"I think so," Nan agreed. "I don't think I ever knew him to say hi to anyone, but Dezy was certainly the guy who worked at the cemetery all the time. If you needed to arrange flowers or a new gravestone or something like that, you would talk to Dezy, and then he would talk to the bosses."

"In that case, he wasn't a little tetched in the head, was he?" Doreen decided. "Otherwise he wouldn't have been capable of making those decisions."

"You could be right," Nan said, "but people get funny when they talk about cemeteries."

"Yeah, they do," Doreen agreed. "Any idea where this person is?"

"He's got to be getting on now, not even sure he still works there."

"And he might still be there because he's always been there," Doreen suggested.

"Meaning?"

"Meaning, he could be volunteering. Maybe he wanders up and down the place," she suggested, thinking of the man that she had seen in the distance yesterday.

"It's possible," Nan replied. "I suppose, if you contact the cemetery, they might give you the information."

"I'll do that," Doreen stated impulsively. And, with that, she phoned the cemetery right away. When she got one of the receptionists, the woman confirmed, "Desmond, yes, but he doesn't work for us anymore. He got past the age of being able to do any of the work."

"Right, but I think he still hangs around the cemetery a fair bit, doesn't he?"

"Oh, absolutely. He would say it's his home, where his friends are."

"And I presume we're talking now about the dead?" Doreen asked gently.

"For him, I don't think they were ever dead," the receptionist clarified. "He always had an affinity for people here.

He was very good with the bereaved, and it made it that much easier to have him handle the ceremonies."

"And did he do much?"

"No, not for a long time. He didn't do any of the actual digging or anything like that. He oversaw some of the new plots being dug out. He was there to ensure the people didn't vandalize the place and stuff like that. He was part of the caretaking team, until it got to be too much for him. Then we contracted that out to a bigger company in town," she shared.

"And did he take those changes well?"

"I think he understood that he wasn't capable of doing it anymore," the woman replied cautiously. "May I ask why you're asking all these questions?"

"Oh, I'm looking into some issues," Doreen replied.

"As long as it has nothing to do with what they found in the cemetery the other day," the woman said. "For that, you should talk to the police."

"Not a problem," Doreen stated, and she quickly hung up. She figured that the best way to find this Dezy guy would be to go to the cemetery again and see if he was still wandering up and down around the trees, overseeing the gravesites. Sounded funny to put it that way, but it was almost as if he were staying because that's all he knew or staying because he figured he was next or something along that line—she didn't know.

But, if anybody would have any information on that weapons cache, he seemed like as good a place as any to start. And the receptionist would not like anybody contacting Dezy because, if any secrets were to be found, Dezy could be the one to tattle.

With an internet search to see if his name came up, it

did a couple times. She went to images and got a half image of him in a crowd. At least she thought it was him; she wasn't sure. She should ask Nan if she knew what he looked like. But this guy was small, wiry, had an almost cavernous look to him. As if he were one step in the grave anyway. She didn't mean it in a bad way; it looked as if life had been a little rough on him. In that picture, he looked as if he had just lost somebody important to him.

And, of course, just because you worked at a cemetery, that didn't save your own friends and family from the same fate as everybody else.

Determined to get to the bottom of it, Doreen quickly put her coffee in a thermos, packed up the animals, and headed to the cemetery. As soon as they got back out again, Mugs was happy to roll around and enjoy an outing. He was quietly content at her side. Meanwhile Goliath took off. Doreen just shook her head. Thaddeus rubbed his head against her cheek, as if soothing her.

They walked up and down the markers, as she kept looking around to see if Dezy was anywhere close by. When she caught sight of somebody working on a grave, she walked over and asked if they worked there. He looked up at her and nodded.

"Yeah, I'm one of the contracted lawn maintenance guys," he added. "So, if you need help, you should call the office."

"I get it. I was looking for Desmond."

"Oh, he's around here somewhere," the man said, standing up to look around. "I saw him over on the other side there a little earlier."

She smiled and nodded. "Thank you, I'll go look for him over there then."

"He's hard to miss," the man added. "I like the guy just fine, but he does look as if he's lost his best friend."

She winced at that and nodded. "Thanks. I'll go see if I can help him out then."

And, with that, he chuckled. "That will be a change. I think he's been the guy who's been there for everybody else all these years."

She pondered that, as she headed in the right direction. Because, if Dezy was an empathetic person, he would have held a lot of hands over the years, commiserating with a lot of people who had suffered losses. It took a special soul to do that. As she walked up, she saw somebody sitting on a bench off to the side. Wondering if it was him, she called out, "Desmond?"

He got up and turned around.

She smiled at him, as she walked closer. "Hey, I've been looking for you."

He looked at her closely and asked, "Do I know you?"

She shook her head. "No, and I haven't been in Kelowna all that long."

He frowned. "You look familiar though." He pondered her for a moment.

She tried to ease him into a conversation, "Well, my grandmother does live in town over at Rosemoor."

"Ah," he said, and then he noted the animals, and his face brightened. "You brought the animals too."

"I brought animals?"

"Now I know who you are."

She winced at that. If she ever wanted to go incognito, she had to remember that she needed to leave the animals behind. Mugs walked over and gave Dezy a nice greeting. She hesitated, before adding, "You've been here a long time."

He nodded. "I have."

"And I guess you weren't interested in really seeing the end of your job here, were you?"

"Well, I did and I didn't," he told her, with a shrug. "The passage of time isn't all that kind sometimes."

She winced. "No, you're right. I hear you there."

He looked at her. "You're a long way away from retiring yet."

"It's a good thing because I don't have a job to retire from."

For some reason he felt that was funny. He looked around and lowered his voice. "I suppose you're here about the guns."

"Yes." She nodded. "I was one of the ones who found the mausoleum vault broken into."

He frowned at that. "It's pretty terrible." But he didn't sound as if it were too terrible.

"Yeah, I'm sure it is. The question really is, why did you do it, and now that it's been opened up and found out, will you tell the police all about it?" He stared at her in shock. She shrugged. "I get it. You weren't expecting me to figure it out, to connect the mausoleum vault to the buried gun stash, with your help for both, but really there weren't many options."

He stared at her and then looked around, as if making sure that nobody heard them. "You don't know what you're talking about."

"But I think I do. You would have made arrangements, one way or another, for this to happen—to add the broken-down Uzi to the vault. To oversee the burial of the big gun stash in the ground. Or you did the digging and burying yourself. I don't know, but very few people are in a position to pull this off."

He stared at her and then slowly sagged onto the bench. "Oh, wow. … Somehow I didn't think that would come back on me."

"Why would it not?" she asked curiously. "Only so many people it can come back on." He stared at her, but she could see sweat breaking out and almost panic building in his eyes. "Look. I'm not trying to make your life difficult."

He grimaced. "I'm glad you're not trying," he replied in a hard voice, "because I hate to think that you could do that so easily, without even putting effort into it."

She winced, having heard the same sentiment a time or two before. "I just would like to know what happened."

"What happened was easy," Dezy admitted. "I was forced to assign a grave to a person who already had a mausoleum spot."

"I get that," she said. "If they bought a grave spot and a place for their urn, not a problem. I figure they wanted to leave their options open."

He nodded. "Right? I didn't think it was a problem, but then he wanted a midnight burial."

"Ah, did they give a religious reason for it?"

"No, they didn't really give any reason. However they were adamant that was how it had to be done. They didn't open the casket or anything like that. They wanted it all done … furtively."

"Right, of course they did. And now we know why." She eyed him closely. "Did you know what was in the casket?"

He shook his head. "No, I didn't."

"And what did you think when it was opened up?"

He shuddered. "I figured that the police would be on my doorstep, but instead it's you." He looked at her and frowned.

She shrugged. "They'll be coming. I'm just that first wave," she noted, with half a smile.

He nodded slowly. "I didn't do anything wrong. I followed instructions. I would have done the same for a lot of people. So many people prefer a quiet, if not secretive, burial. It's not as if we haven't dealt with some very unique scenarios before. We've had a UFO guy, who wanted to be buried in this makeshift spaceship." Dezy smiled shyly. "That had to be done at nighttime because he didn't want the aliens to find him."

Her jaw dropped. "You should write a book. I'm sure you have dozens of good stories to share."

He laughed. "Probably."

"So you didn't know what was in there, what was being buried?"

He shook his head. "No, I didn't. And honestly I don't remember too much about who was involved."

"Can anyone make the burial arrangements or does it need to be a family member?"

"No, a lot of times friends end up making the arrangements. Either the family is too overwrought or the person may have been designated as the person to help out. Or there is no family, and somebody else is taking care of things, even lawyers. Although lawyers are less common, but it does happen."

She pondered that for a moment. "I guess anybody can make arrangements for burial plots, as long as you guys are clear that they have the right to do so. I mean, lots of funeral homes have you organize and prepay for your funeral, so your loved ones don't have to."

He shrugged. "Things were getting stickier by the day

back then on that stuff," Dezy pointed out, "but I can't imagine that anybody is really looking for any confirmation that you're allowed to do this. It's never come up before."

"Yeah, and what does it say about the world we're in now that that's something that I'm even asking about?"

"For the record, I didn't break into that vault. I never did anything to mar my years here. This is the place where I myself found a lot of peace in the world. I didn't want anything to blemish that." He stared across the peaceful greens. "But now?" He shook his head. "Now to even think that everybody would be looking at me as being involved? Well, that's terrifying."

"I don't believe they'll be looking at you as being involved," she replied carefully. "I think it's more of a case of you obviously have information, and they need it."

He sighed heavily, then turned to look at her. "I didn't even think about it, not till you asked me. I understood that the fake grave had been opened, but I don't even know whose name it was."

"Are there any records? Stating who made the arrangements?"

"Sure, it would have been somebody representing the estate, handling the person's burial. Although I don't know if a person was buried for that matter."

"And you have access to those records?"

He shook his head. "Not now. If you'd asked me a year or so ago, before I lost my job, then I would."

"But you think the cemetery would still have those records?"

"Sure. Why not? As far as we knew, it was a good clean burial."

"And it was," she agreed, with a smile. "I guess you don't

have any idea how many years ago that coffin was buried, *huh?*" He frowned at her. She shrugged, then suggested, "Five years, ten years, thirty years?"

"Oh my." He nodded. "It was a long time ago. I don't know how many years ago. Again the records would show."

"Right. I'll get the police to look into the records then. They have more pull than I do."

He nodded. "Ever since the cemetery was taken over by a bigger company"—he shrugged—"it's lost some of that personal touch."

"Is that what happened? A new company got the maintenance contract, and they looked at the bottom line and decided you weren't part of it?"

He winced, and a sadness filled his gaze. "Yeah, that's the way it worked. I didn't really have much warning either."

"They didn't want to keep you on to keep everybody happy?"

"I don't think anybody realized it before I knew it, and I was already out. It's called streamlining and modernizing."

"Sorry. Do you have something else to do with your life?"

"I'm retirement age anyway," Dezy noted, "so it's not as if I'm supposed to still be working. However, money is tight, and some extra work would not be bad. I would love to stay on, … even if just as a caretaker or a greeter, like one of those people at Walmart."

She asked him, "You want to be a Walmart greeter?"

He nodded. "Yeah, but at the cemetery."

"So you want to be a grave greeter?"

He looked at her and smiled. "I guess that's not really a good thing, is it?"

"It's not a bad thing. People are obviously overwrought

and grieving when they come. So a compassionate caring face isn't a bad thing to see in their time of need."

"I know so many of the people here. I thought I'd always be here."

"Well, I wouldn't give up just yet," she suggested, with a gentle smile. "When did you lose your job?"

He replied, "A few months back, not quite a year yet."

She nodded. "So not everybody knows that you're not employed here any longer."

"No, they don't."

Chapter 17

HER MIND STILL agog with all the information from Dezy, Doreen wandered to Nan's later that afternoon.

When Nan saw her granddaughter, Nan jumped up. "You found out something," she cried out in delight.

Doreen slowly shook her head. "Nothing concrete. Matter of fact, nothing even close yet."

"Ah, but you're on it." Nan gave a nod of quiet satisfaction. "I knew you would."

Doreen laughed. "*You* might know I would, but I wasn't so sure. I'm still not."

"Of course not, it takes time. You need that wonderful brain of yours to tell you something."

Doreen frowned. "You think I just ask my brain," she asked with curiosity, "and the answers come?"

"As much as I wish it were that easy, I'm sure it's not. You need to let things run around in your head for a while, don't you?"

"I do," Doreen agreed. "That's not necessarily a problem."

"No, of course not," Nan concurred. "Not sure it's all that great a solution though either."

"Maybe not." Doreen considered it for a long time, as she sat here.

Finally Nan asked, "You want to share?"

Doreen gave her head a shake. "No, I can't do that now." Then she smiled at her. "I did talk to Dezy though."

Nan stared at her in surprise for a moment at the conversation shift and then asked, "Oh my, how is he?"

"He's a character, and he's doing fine," she replied. "He's a very surprising person. And I think a good-hearted one too."

"Oh?"

"I think he's happiest at the cemetery, talking to people both alive and dead. … I think he's lonely," Doreen added.

"When we get older, we can only do so much before people think that we have no value. It's one of the reasons that we all appreciate you so much because you appreciate us."

And those were such sad words that Doreen could only stare at her Nan. "I hope that never changes," she replied gently. "You have a magnificent brain yourself."

"Well, I used to, I don't know that it's all that great anymore"—Nan chuckled—"but we can always hope."

"I think you're doing just fine, and don't let anybody tell you otherwise."

Nan smiled at her. "You're such a sweetheart."

"I try, but I'm not so sure at times. Sometimes I think I'd be better off if I found something else to do for a hobby."

"Oh dear, are you having a crisis right now?"

At that term, Doreen burst out laughing. "No, I don't think so. Just one of those reevaluations about what I'm doing with my life."

"Right now, you don't need to do any evaluation because you have cases to deal with."

Nan wasn't wrong, yet it wasn't exactly the easiest thing for Doreen to turn on and off. "No, you're right there. And a case that has lots of juiciness to it."

"The guns definitely add to that juiciness." Nan smiled. "And believe me. Everybody is talking about it."

"I talked to Jerry, the owner of Big Guy. Took Thaddeus there for a playdate."

But Thaddeus—having heard his friend's name—jumped down, bobbing his head back and forth. "Big Guy, Big Guy, Big Guy." No stopping him now.

Doreen winced. "We're not going there today," she told him, but Thaddeus wasn't having anything to do with her.

"Big Guy, Big Guy, Big Guy."

Nan quickly got up, raced into the kitchen, and came back with some crackers. "Here, Thaddeus. Have a treat." Thaddeus said, "Thaddeus loves Nan. Thaddeus loves Nan."

She burst out laughing. "He's such a con artist," Nan noted affectionately.

Doreen noted, "I should admit sometimes that I wonder if he isn't doing this on purpose."

"I wouldn't be at all surprised honestly. He does have a bit of a manipulator inside him, doesn't he?" Nan asked.

"Yeah, ya think?" Doreen quipped, with a headshake. "Yet he does it so well."

At that, Nan chuckled. "He does, doesn't he? But still we love him dearly."

"Of course we do. That doesn't change anything." Doreen laughed. "He's still got the ability to pull things his way, when he wants them to."

"But he's not mean about it."

"Oh goodness no," Doreen replied. "Thaddeus is all

about opportunity, and again I don't think he's bad about it either."

"No, he isn't. He's just Thaddeus." Nan gently stroked his feathers. "And I do miss him some days."

Almost immediately Thaddeus walked closer to gently stroke his head down her cheek. "Thaddeus loves Nan. Thaddeus loves Nan."

Doreen watched as tears came to the older woman's eyes.

"See? How could anybody not love a pet that gives you this response," Nan murmured, as she gently cuddled him.

Doreen nodded. "He's pretty amazing, and he comes from the heart, and he really believes and means what he says."

"I sure hope so." Nan chuckled. "I'd hate to think this was just to get treats." At that, Thaddeus pulled back, seemingly looking at her in outrage. But then he went back to eating his treats, leaving both of them wondering if he did understand what they were saying. Nan looked over at Doreen. "If you could ever crack the code of this guy, you would make millions."

"I don't know," Doreen murmured. "That code is something else."

"I agree. These birds are definitely a world unto themselves, especially Thaddeus. He's so full of heart, and yet he's got so much going on in his world that you never really know where and what he's up to."

"True that." Doreen focused on her grandmother. "Are you doing okay right now?"

"I am. A lot is going on with you, child," she noted. "Anyway I've picked up some treats." And, with that, she beamed a bright smile and disappeared again.

Doreen groaned. When her grandmother reappeared,

Doreen gasped and stared. "And here I was about to tell you off for once again stealing stuff," she muttered. The plate held pastries even fancier than normal and a piece of delicious-looking cake—almost like a birthday cake. "Did this come from the kitchen?"

Nan nodded. "It's Nelly's birthday," she said, with a laugh.

"Nelly?"

She nodded. "Yes, Nelly. She's seventy-four. She's still a baby," Nan teased.

"Just like me," Doreen quipped.

"We're just barely kids." Nan nodded, with a great deal of satisfaction.

"You got that right."

"Nelly has a mind of her own. Everybody in here does, and they're not shy about letting you know it." Nan sighed. "Although Nelly is better off here than she was out in the world. Such a sad family."

"So many people have sad families," Doreen noted, "and, as I do this work, I realize just how sad some of those families are."

Nan gave her a gentle smile and noted, "Sometimes the things we find out about people aren't all that nice, are they?"

"No, we've had a few cases where the family circumstances were tough, as you well know."

Nan nodded. "You've grown up a lot since you've been out in the big bad world. Finding freedom has been good for you."

"*Freedom*," she repeated. "You mean, since I left Mathew?"

"Yes. Exactly. … You haven't been in touch with him,

right?"

"No, not today."

"Today?" Nan repeated.

"I'm trying not to be in touch with him at all," Doreen clarified, then realized that Nan didn't know about the previous visit. She quickly explained.

"Oh my." Nan's brows pinched together with worry. "Are you sure you're safe?"

"I think so. Mack did check that he flew home again."

"But it's a one-hour flight," Nan pointed out. "He could be up here anytime."

Doreen gazed at her grandmother steadily, willing her to stay calm and to not panic over what Mathew could do. "He could be, but we won't focus on that," Doreen replied gently, "because I won't spend my whole life wondering about where he is and if he'll pop up, like a bad penny."

"The thing is," Nan stated, "you *know* he'll pop up like a bad penny."

"That's part of who he is and what he does," Doreen replied crossly, knowing she was right.

"I should give that man a piece of my mind," Nan declared.

"Please don't," Doreen murmured. "That won't make my life any easier."

"And that's the only reason I wouldn't," Nan snapped, with a *harrumph*, "but that man needs a tune-up."

"Let's just say that a lot of people are working on giving him his comeuppance," Doreen added, "and I've been told very crossly to stay out of it."

Nan grinned at her. "I bet Mack wasn't happy, was he?"

"Nope, he sure wasn't, and neither was Nick," Doreen admitted. "Mathew caused all kinds of trouble that he had no right to."

"Sure, but, once you start talking money"—Nan shook her head—"you know how quickly that goes down the tube."

"I hadn't realized just how quickly it could," she noted, with a half laugh. "For some reason I thought that he would fight more in the courts, and the rest would go by the wayside."

Nan shook her head slowly. "Oh, dear, you're more naive than I thought."

Doreen gave an exasperated sigh. "No, I'm not, Nan. I know perfectly well that he's a mean person and that he'll make my life miserable, if he gets away with it anymore," she added. "So I'm not planning on letting him get away with it from now on."

Nan studied her granddaughter intently, as if trying to read the truth in her mind. Finally Nan nodded. "Oh, I hope not. You do deserve so much more." She smiled gently.

"And I'm getting it," Doreen declared. "Don't worry. I am getting it. No matter how much the settlement ends up being, I will get it, and he will be out of my life. What he really needs is another project, something to focus on, something away from me."

"That may be, but it needs to not be you who finds it for him."

Doreen shrugged. "I don't intend on having anything to do with him, so don't worry about that." But it was obvious that Nan wouldn't relax about it. Finally Doreen stood. "And now I will head home, spend some time relaxing, maybe sit by the creek. There are definitely some things on my mind to roll around."

"Anything else on Hinja and the Bob Small case?"

She winced. "I talked to the inmate who pinned Bob Small for these murders," she shared, "but he wants something before he'll talk to me."

"Interesting. You couldn't get anything out of him?"

"I did get one name." She turned toward Nan. "Do you know an Ella? Ella Hickman?"

Nan stared at her granddaughter. "Sure I do. Ella Maxine Hickman. Nasty woman."

Doreen groaned inwardly. "When you say, *nasty*, what do you mean by that?"

"She's Nelly's younger sister, the one whose birthday cake you were eating."

Doreen stared down at the cake plate and froze. "Ella is her sister?"

"Yes."

"So why is she a nasty woman?" Doreen asked again.

"Nelly is a sweetheart—she really is—but she pales in comparison to Ella's personality, which is very domineering, a very much *in your face and you can't ignore* type person."

"Is that good or bad?"

"For Nelly, it's bad, as her sister, Ella, dominates everything. Nelly doesn't have a coherent thought when her sister is around."

"*Ugh*. More ugly family dynamics."

"Are you telling me that Nelly and Ella are involved in this Bob Small case?" Nan peered at Doreen closely.

"Not so much that I know anything about it yet," she replied, feeling her way cautiously and not wanting to upset Nan. "It is the name that the convict gave me."

"And we can't trust anything he says," Nan declared, with a sniff.

"No, we sure can't."

"And what did this convict say?" Nan asked.

Doreen shrugged. "Possibly Ella was Bob Small's girlfriend, other than Hinja."

Nan stared at her, and then she started to laugh. "Oh, wouldn't that be rich. … I would love to think that Ella had a relationship with a serial killer. She's such an upstart. She's one of those women who knows everything and can do everything better than everyone," she explained, with a disgusted snort.

Doreen sat again and slumped back ever-so-slightly, wishing she hadn't even brought it up. "So obviously you do know her."

"Of course we do." Nan sniffed again. "Everybody here does."

"Do you see her at all?"

"Not if we can help it. Not if we see her first. Nelly doesn't like her sister, and we all like Nelly."

"So the enemy of your friend is your enemy too?"

"Something like that, child."

Doreen nodded. "At least you got my meaning."

"Hard not to, but, yes. You're right. Nelly is a lovely person. Ella is not."

"I guess she's not all that easy to get a hold of and talk to either, is she?"

"No, she wouldn't give you the time of day. So, if you're planning on interviewing her, good luck." Nan shook her head. "You might as well give it up right now."

"Interesting. I wonder how she feels about all this now."

"The same as she always did, I imagine. She put her sister in here because she thought Nelly wasn't capable of living out in the world. The thing is, by putting her in here, Nelly has blossomed. So it was a good move for her," Nan noted grudgingly.

"Because she's away from her sister," Doreen hazarded a guess.

Nan nodded. "Exactly. Ella is very domineering. Poor Nelly couldn't say or do anything right."

"Interesting," Doreen murmured.

"Ella was a politician, and you know how I feel about those," Nan stated, with an eye roll.

Doreen groaned. "Nan, we can't say *all* politicians are bad."

"Why not?" she asked, with immediate candor. "That's how we feel."

At that, Doreen gave up.

Nan glanced at her, and, when Doreen realized she was being teased, she burst into laughter.

"It's good to hear you laugh. You don't do enough of it."

"I do plenty of it," Doreen corrected, glaring at her grandmother. "Now you, on the other hand, I don't want you getting irate."

"Too late," Nan stated. "You brought up that woman."

At that, Doreen groaned. "I'm surprised she has the ability to make you this upset."

"Sure, but, it being Nelly's birthday and all, we just had a dose of Ella."

"She's here right now?" Doreen asked, bouncing to her feet.

Nan looked at her. "You really want to talk to her, don't you?"

"Considering she's likely connected to Bob Small, yes, I would love to."

"And I'm warning you that she won't talk to you," Nan declared. "She doesn't have a good bone in her body."

"Does she have a bad bone in her body?"

"Lots of them, a whole entire skeleton of them."

Doreen burst out laughing. "I don't think she can be quite that bad." Although she was not positive, when she'd had quite a few opportunities to see dysfunctional families time and time again.

"You have a lot of goodness in your heart, so you are projecting," Nan stated. "I'm not so sure that Ella has any of that." She looked at the door. "Let me go see if she's still here. She had been talking to her sister today, which had Nelly all in an uproar. She was worried she would be forced to leave the home."

"Ah"—Doreen nodded—"that will definitely cause some stress, wouldn't it?"

"You have no idea. Trouble is, most of us don't have enough money to pay for Nelly's care, if we were to take it on."

Doreen stared at her grandmother. "Hang on a minute. You're telling me that you don't have enough money?"

"I have enough money," Nan said, "but I'm not sure that I can take on Nelly's care as well."

"And you really think that Nelly needs somebody to help out like that?" she asked.

"I don't know what Nelly's financial needs are." Nan sniffed again. "Believe me. Her sister isn't talking."

"Of course not." She winced. "Doesn't mean all things are bad though."

"Doesn't mean anything is good either though." Nan frowned at Doreen. "Remember? This Ella woman is evil."

Doreen winced at that. "I don't want that prejudiced view in my head," she replied.

"That's good of you. I do appreciate the fact that you're

trying to keep an open mind, but it's already a lost cause," she stated in that dark tone.

"Nan, if I could get a chance to talk to her, that would be absolutely lovely."

Nan sighed. "Let's go to the common room and see if she's still here then."

With that, Doreen put the animals back on a leash as needed and asked, "Do you think that's a problem if I take them with me?"

"Not at all. Besides, they would make Nelly's day perfect. She does love your animals."

"She's never seen them."

"But she wants to."

Not sure exactly what her grandmother was getting at—and more than a little worried at the manipulativeness that she knew perfectly well her grandmother was capable of—Doreen followed her out into the main area.

Chapter 18

DOREEN WAS GREETED by several other people, as were Mugs and Goliath. Several people stopped to say hi, and a bunch of others stopped to pet the animals.

When one of the management people stepped in to see what the commotion was, she saw Doreen, and Doreen tensed, waiting for the get-those-animals-out-of-here rebuke, but instead she was greeted with a hug and *Hi, how lovely to see you here. I'm sure Nelly would be so happy to know that you came to visit for her birthday.*

Not wanting to disappoint the birthday girl, and not sure what Doreen had gotten herself into, she followed Nan through the throng, where a large get-together was. She saw the massive cake, with a seventy-four written on top of it. She walked closer and looked at it in delight. "This is beautiful," she noted, turning toward Marion, the manager. "Who on earth created this?"

"Our new chef did," Marion stated, with a pleased smile. "She's doing a heck of a job here."

"I'm so glad to hear that." Doreen wanted to avoid any conversation about the cooks here because of previous cases involving Rosemoor staff. "Everybody seems so happy here," she murmured. The cake itself was stunning. Marion quickly pushed a piece into Doreen's hand. She looked at it and frowned.

"No, please enjoy," Marion said, then lowered her voice. "I know Nan already came and got you one."

Doreen rolled her eyes. "I think Nan is intent on fattening me up."

Marion burst out laughing and then patted her very ample belly. To which she added, "Just make sure she doesn't succeed."

Doreen chuckled. "She seems to think I need more meat on me."

"You could stand a little more," she agreed, "but I wouldn't worry about it. You're looking great." And, with that, she set off to talk to the other guests. Cake in hand, Doreen noted several people standing and staring at her. She gave them all a bright smile. "Hi. Which one is the lovely birthday lady?"

At that, another woman snorted. "Really? You crashed a birthday party, and you don't even know who the birthday girl is?" She crossed her arms over her chest and glared at Doreen. "Good God, takes all kinds, doesn't it?"

Nan stepped up. "She was invited," she snapped. "Just because Nelly hasn't met her yet didn't mean Nelly didn't invite her."

A little birdlike woman rushed forward and, in an excited whisper, asked Nan, "Is this her?" She cast a sideways glance at Doreen and squeaked. "She brought the bird too. She brought all of them."

Nan stated, with a proud smile, "Of course she did. They go with her everywhere."

Doreen winced, as she realized that she was part of the

celebration apparently. Or maybe the entertainment. She stepped forward and asked, "Are you Nelly?"

Nelly beamed. "I am." She clapped her hands, similar to what Nan sometimes did. "I'm so glad you came," she said in delight.

Doreen smiled at her. "Happy birthday, and what a way to celebrate." She motioned to everybody around her.

At that, Thaddeus leaned forward to take a swipe at the cake.

"Oh no you don't," Doreen corrected him, keeping the rest of the cake out of his reach.

He shot her a mischievous look and cawed, "Thaddeus loves Nan," with a particular emphasis on the *Nan* part.

At that, Nelly giggled. "Oh my, what a delight to hear him talk."

"Who would want anything like that to talk," snapped the other woman. "Really, Nelly, that disgusting bird should not even be here." She shooed Doreen back. "Get away from the food, for God's sake. Have you guys all gone nuts?"

At that, Marion stepped forward and stated in a firm voice, "This is Doreen. She's welcome here, as are her animals."

Doreen appreciated the support; she was also more than willing to leave if she was causing trouble.

As she glanced over at Nan to see what the underlying issue here was, Nan rolled her eyes and whispered, "That's Ella."

Doreen stared at the critical woman and realized that somehow Doreen must get on Ella's good side, so Ella would talk to her, but, by the glare she gave Doreen, that didn't appear to be something that Ella was particularly amiable to.

Doreen gave her an apologetic smile. "Sorry. I do try

hard to keep the animals away from people who aren't comfortable around them."

Ella gave a toss of her hair, sending her long strands flying everywhere. "It's not that I'm uncomfortable around them," she clarified, "but you do need to think about other people here too."

A lot of older folks were around, munching on cake, but absolutely nobody stood for or against Doreen.

"I think most of them know me very well," Doreen suggested, as she looked around, smiling. "Of course some people here I haven't met yet." Doreen asked the crowd, "Is anybody upset if I'm here with the animals?"

Everybody shook their heads and called back, "No."

Then somebody lifted a piece of cake to Thaddeus. And, with his usual greed, he bent and took a huge mouthful.

Doreen gasped. "Oh no, no, no, no, he doesn't need cake."

The place erupted with laughter.

"Believe me. He gets hyper enough." But amid so much laughter, more and more plates of cake were held up for the bird. She stepped back and stated in a firm voice, "We don't want him sick."

At that, several people backed away. "No, no, we can't have the bird sick," they cried out. And things slowly returned to normal.

Ella stepped forward and whispered, "You really should watch it around here. They're just like children." And she looked around with a smirk of distaste.

"Maybe," she murmured. "Your sister does seem to be happy here though."

"Thank heavens for that." She gave an eye roll. "She's not the easiest to look after."

"I think it's the age."

Ella nodded. "I know, and she didn't seem to want to come, but now she seems happy. So, if it keeps her happy, then great—but it's not cheap," she muttered.

Doreen wasn't exactly sure how much it cost to be here, although the figure would probably shock her, but she nodded agreeably. "I don't think any of these places are cheap."

Ella looked at Doreen, and then her shoulders sagged. "No, you're right," she agreed. "We did look into it before, and this is one of the most respected ones for the price and was more reasonable than some of them. Still, it's an absolute worry to think that we should pay this much to look after our older family members."

"She's your sister, isn't she?"

"Yes," Ella replied, with a sigh, "and our parents are now long gone. Thankfully we didn't cover the cost of them in this place too." She shook her head. "My sister's expense is enough."

"And she probably doesn't like to be reminded of that either," Doreen noted. "Growing old is not for the faint of heart."

For some reason Ella thought that was a great statement. She now viewed Doreen, as if seeing her with new eyes. "No, you certainly got that right," Ella agreed. The two women stood in companionable silence for a few moments. And then Ella added, "Now I get it. I couldn't figure out what was familiar about you."

Doreen looked at her in surprise. "Pardon?"

"You're the one who investigates all those mystery cases around town, aren't you?" she asked.

At that, several people close by looked over and nodded.

"That's our Doreen," said one man, seated nearby, twisting to look up. "She's one of us," he declared, with pride.

It was all Doreen could do to keep her mouth shut at that because she wasn't even sure who he was. Yet this was the general consensus from everyone's attitude, even though Doreen didn't know all of them. However, she'd been adopted by Rosemoor, and she smiled at him gently. "How are you doing today?"

He gave her a gummy grin. "I will do just fine, as soon as I snag me a third piece of that cake." He took several hobbled steps toward the side table.

Besides her, Ella made a disgusted sound. "I hope I never get that old," she muttered.

Doreen didn't think that was a fair assessment, not after seeing how much Nan and all of Nan's friends here—outside of some down days—seemed to really enjoy the life that Rosemoor offered them. "I think he's happy here and doing just fine."

"Sure, as long as he hypes up on sugar, then he can make it to his bedroom," Ella muttered, with another eye roll.

"Did you put this party on for your sister?"

"No, the home did." She crossed her arms over her chest and frowned again.

"Your sister seems to be loving it."

"Good thing," she grumbled. "I shouldn't be complaining to you. However, today was one of those days when I had to deal with the accounts. Once you start looking at where all the money has gone, that you spent a lifetime earning, it never seems to be enough."

"I'm sorry." Doreen understood entirely. "Those days are never good for anybody."

"No, they sure aren't." Ella looked over at Doreen. "Do

you work?"

"No, not at the moment."

Ella snorted. "Good, don't even start. The minute you start, it's almost impossible to stop. You see that money coming in, and you need it because you've got bills to pay. So if you've found a way to not work and still pay all your bills, don't change. After that, it's a downward circle."

Doreen wasn't exactly sure what that meant, but she was more than willing to smile and agree. "I do have lots of hobbies that keep me busy," she replied. "Of course these cold cases are one of them."

"Right. Isn't that something," Ella muttered. "I was close to one many, many years ago. That was scary enough, and I don't have anything to do with any of that stuff anymore." Ella seemed lost in her thoughts. "I escaped relatively unscathed, and I sure don't want to go back into that field again."

"You mean, you're a cop?" Doreen asked in surprise.

Ella burst out laughing. "Lord, no, but there was a chance that I dated a serial killer once."

"Oh, now that," Doreen noted, "would not be much fun."

"Not much fun and you always look back and wonder if it was or wasn't."

"Ah, can't be too many serial killers around here," Doreen replied.

"Do you know the case I'm talking about?" Ella asked, frowning now, taking a step back, as though trying to put some distance between them.

"Hard to say. I do know that a notorious one apparently dated two women in Kelowna, or two from Kelowna."

Ella blanched. "Yeah, that would be him. If I could get

my hands on that guy one more time, I would have a field day with him."

"What would you do?" Doreen asked curiously.

Ella shrugged, deep in thought.

Doreen added, "In hindsight, we always talk about things like that—if you came up against somebody who hurt you or upset you—but I always wondered what I'd do." And, in her case, Doreen had already had several chances to find out.

Ella shook her head. "I don't know, but he messed up my life there for a while. It's all water under the bridge now. I sure don't want anybody bringing it back up." With that, she turned to look at Doreen, giving her a pointed look.

"Maybe not," Doreen replied, "but, with this gun cache that's been found in the cemetery, it might come back up anyway."

The other woman paled. "Good Lord, I hope not." She was quiet for a moment, then gave a decisive shake of her head. "That's not his style anyway."

"Yeah, what's his style?"

"Small. Silent. Stealthy. I think he preferred to strangle his victims."

Doreen filed that away. "Why *small*?"

"He was a trucker and had to keep everything hidden. He crossed borders. He crossed province lines. He was all over the place most of the time. This guy told me, at one point in time, that he kept a small weapon, but he didn't need it because his hands were the best things ever. He had huge monstrous hands. Strong too."

"Doesn't seem to be somebody you'd go out with," Doreen noted, studying her.

"No, I didn't think I would go out with him either," she

admitted in a gloomy tone of voice. "I guess back then I was into gorillas." Instead of laughter filling her voice, there was almost a somber despair in her words.

Doreen nodded, comparing Ella's relationship to Bob Small to Doreen's with Mathew. "I think one of the hardest things to do is to look back at the choices we made—supposedly when we were of sound mind and capable of making those decisions. Yet I look back, and I shake my head and wonder what drugs I was on."

Ella looked at her and then started to laugh. "Oh, goodness, that's exactly me. At the time I was going to be somebody. I was going to be somebody special, and yet something about this man just drew me in. I've regretted it ever since."

"And yet you got free and clear. He obviously didn't take you out, so why?" Doreen asked, eyeing Ella curiously.

"I don't know. I did ask him once, during pillow talk, what on earth would drive him to do something like that."

"He actually told you what he did?"

"He was more bragging about it, but I didn't really believe him. I thought we were just doing this *Ha, ha, ha, I'm a big tough guy* routine. *You don't know how many people I've dealt with in my life on a permanent basis.*"

Shocked, Doreen asked in a whisper, "Did he admit to killing all those people?"

"No, he didn't say that at all, but he did have an envelope, with pictures of all these girls. Only after he left did I look up some of them and realized that they were all missing and presumed dead."

Doreen's breath caught in the back of her throat. "Now that would have been scary."

"You're not kidding," the other woman stated, her voice

gruff. "The guilt though? Now that part was the hardest."

"You mean, the guilt about knowing and not saying anything?"

Ella frowned at her. "How do you know I didn't say anything?"

"Because, in a case like that," Doreen explained, "I would imagine fear kept you quiet."

"Fear of what though?" she asked, as if a test.

"Fear of him ever finding out that you turned him in," Doreen replied. "Right?"

Ella shuddered visibly, and then she nodded slowly. "You really do understand, don't you?"

"I do," Doreen confirmed. "And I'm telling you right now that there'll be an investigation, and it could be something that becomes public."

"That would kill me," Ella stated flatly. "I don't know how anybody can live with this stuff going on in their head. That guy was not somebody to fool around with. He was scary."

Doreen nodded. She'd found a lot of scary people in town but none like her ex.

Ella turned toward Doreen and asked her, "Are you investigating it?"

"To a certain extent, yes," she replied. "Did you know Hinja?"

Ella made a disgusted snort. "Yeah, that was his other girlfriend. Lord, it's really him who you're talking about."

"Yeah, sounds like it. Did you hear what happened to Hinja's niece?

With a headshake, Ella asked, "No. What?"

"She was suspected of being Bob Small's victim."

The color drained from Ella's face. She grabbed

Doreen's arm and quickly moved her off to the side, where they had more privacy. In a hushed voice she asked, "Are you telling me that Hinja thought her boyfriend Bob Small, this lovely serial killer between us, actually killed her own niece?"

"Yes, he had a fixation on young women with curly hair," she whispered. "Her niece disappeared, and Hinja started to worry, and that's when she noted her curling iron was missing too. She also saw an envelope, filled with photos of women's faces, and they all had curly hair."

Ella Hickman stared off into the distance for a moment and then nodded. "They did have curly hair." She shuddered again, wrapped her arms around herself, and whispered, "I can't imagine what she went through."

"She passed away recently," Doreen added, "and, of course, she never got any answers because the case has never been solved."

"Not even about her niece?"

Doreen shook her head and kept her voice low. "Not only that, no body has been found, no evidence of anything."

Ella nodded her head slowly. "Yeah, he told me that he would never get caught."

"So far he hasn't, until I spoke to an inmate recently."

Ella stared at her. "You do get around, don't you?"

"I sure do. Anyway, he said he had information about Bob Small. Of course the inmate wants something in return for this info."

"Of course he wants something," Ella muttered, with her characteristic eye roll. "And what will you do?"

"Not sure yet, but you need to know that he gave me your name."

She blanched. "Good God." Her bottom lip trembled,

panic appearing in her eyes. "I can't have people knowing."

"They might find out," Doreen shared, "so you need to be prepared for that. I won't pass it around obviously. That's not what I'm all about, but I want to try and help Hinja's family find out what happened to the niece. So you need to be on your guard."

"Even though she's gone and will never come back?"

"Even though she's gone and will never come back," Doreen confirmed. "Finding closure is important for families."

Ella sighed. "I knew this would come back to haunt me one day. … At times I worked so hard to put it behind me and to forget about it all. Until you've had something like that in your history, you don't realize how much it's made an impact and how much you look behind you ever after, wondering if he'll come after you next."

"And I think that was part of Hinja's problem," Doreen suggested. "And, for the same reason as you, she never told the police anything, until it was too late. She figured that he probably wouldn't come back around anymore, but she couldn't take the chance."

"No, of course not," Ella noted. "He made it very clear that, if we ever did anything that he didn't like, that we would be sorry."

"Did he ever threaten you? Abuse you?"

"No, he was a perfect gentleman while we were together," Ella stated. "That's what made it so strange. But, when he came out of the blue and said that the police were after him, and they had been for a long time, I didn't know what to think. I asked him what for, thinking he was trucking illegal goods, something along that line. He was kind of exciting, dangerous looking, a big man, and he was a heck of a lover too," she added, with a nod. "He was that big powerful presence. Yet, whenever I laughed at him, thinking these were teasing conversations, he gave me a half smile and said he liked to *take care* of people."

"Did he give you a reason?" Doreen asked.

Ella shook her head. "Honestly I thought he was joking for the longest time. Then, when I realized he was serious, it's not exactly something you can turn around and ask questions about. Once I understood that he might be serious, I shut up." She stared off into space. "I've only loved two men in my life. Both were bad boys. Both very dangerous." She returned her gaze to the room around them. "And, because of that, I'm alone and never feel safe."

"Did he ever give you any idea why he chose his victims or how he chose his victims or where he left them?"

"No, he just said that he knew places."

"Right, and that's the problem. Being a trucker, he probably had a lot of places."

"And I have no idea where those places would be—or how many victims he had."

Doreen faced Ella straight-on and declared, "Dozens and dozens are attributed to him."

"Oh, Lord," Ella whispered, her eyes closed. "When this gets out, it'll be big news, won't it?"

"It will be," Doreen agreed.

Then somebody squawked, and somebody else cried out.

Doreen turned to see Goliath jumping up onto the table and helping himself to a piece of cheese. When one of the cooks came after him, Goliath carried the cheese in his mouth and bolted along the table, knocking to the floor a piece of cake on a paper plate. "*Uh-oh.* I've got to deal with this fast." But it was too late.

Mugs was given an opportunity to put Goliath in his place and was already in full charge mode. Doreen snagged his leash, just as he skidded onto his butt and came to a sliding stop, hitting the table leg. She cried out, "No, Mugs, no."

He gave her a look, yet his tail wagged hard, and he woofed several times.

Doreen groaned. She quickly threw away the cheese and the cake left on the floor by her animals and told them, "Hey, guys, you know what that means. Time for me to take you away from this crowd and disappear."

She looked back to say something to Ella, but Ella had disappeared. Doreen looked around for a moment, not seeing her, and realized that Ella had escaped during the chaos. Having lost the opportunity to set up a future meeting, Doreen quickly raced out of the large room.

Nan followed behind her. She was laughing so hard. "Oh, that was priceless. I do like it when the animals get into trouble."

"You do?" Doreen asked Nan, shooting her a look. "I feel terrible."

"We saved the rest of the cake, so whatever."

"Yes, but you also know that it'll be a black mark against the animals again," she murmured. "Let's not try to get them into trouble."

But Nan was still chuckling as they made it back to her room. As they stepped inside, Nan asked, "Now what did you find out?"

"I found out a bunch," Doreen replied. "Did you see what happened to Ella at the end there?"

"Yeah, she slipped out the side door and disappeared."

"Interesting. I was thinking I could maybe talk to her

again."

"Did she talk?"

"She did, but then the commotion happened, and I didn't get much chance to follow up. I wanted to set up a second meeting."

"Well, she's pretty cagey. Also you can't believe a word she says."

Doreen looked over at Nan, wondering how much of it was hard feelings on her part.

But Nan was adamant. "Be careful, she's dangerous."

"Even now?" she asked.

"Once a snake, always a snake," Nan concluded, "and that one, my child, she's a viper."

Chapter 19

BACK HOME AGAIN, Doreen sat outside—tired, worn out, her mind fuzzy—as she reviewed everything that she had learned today. She should probably update Mack but wasn't sure what he was up to. She'd heard sirens earlier, wondering if it was something connected to him but hadn't even had a chance to ponder that.

When he rang before bedtime, she asked, "Hey, hard day?"

"A busy day," he noted, but the fatigue in his voice was evident.

"Nothing to do with any of these cases, I hope," she asked.

"No, not at all, just more chaos and crime."

"Seems as if there's no end to that right now."

"Yeah. What about you? Did you find out anything?"

In a wry tone, she asked, "How long do you have?"

Startled, he replied, "As long as you need."

She laughed. "No, you're pretty tired."

"I am," he agreed, "but, if you've got information, let's have it."

"It's nothing necessarily usable, but I spoke with Ella

Hickman today."

"Seriously?" he asked. "She talked to you?"

"It was a very strange set of circumstances." She explained about Nelly's birthday party held at Rosemoor.

"Oh, good Lord," Mack said. But, when she got to the reason why she had to leave, with the animals kicking up a fuss, he was laughing. "Thank you for putting that image in my mind," he said, when he finally calmed down. "I needed that."

She smiled into the phone. "See? Sometimes it's good knowing me."

"There are always good things to knowing you," he commented affectionately, "but also downsides too." He yawned then.

Doreen said in a quiet voice, "You, sir, need to grab some shut-eye."

"I do, but I wasn't even sure where we were at for meals and plans this week. With the weekend coming up, I was hoping we could do something."

"Sounds good to me," she replied cheerfully, "but it certainly doesn't need to be decided tonight."

"No, as long as we're on a schedule," he noted.

"As far as I'm concerned, we are. Is your brother coming up?"

"I think he is. I suppose we should do something with him, *huh?*"

She burst out laughing. "I think he would understand either way, but that's up to you."

"I'll see," he grumbled. "I guess I'll talk to him in the morning." And, with that, he said good night and rang off.

It was late. She was tired too. However, she was keyed up from that conversation with Ella.

Also Nan's warning played over and over again in Doreen's mind. Did Nan really have some serious problem with Ella or was it one of those many cases where people had problems with each other, while, to other people, it wasn't a problem. Doreen knew she wasn't even making sense in her own mind. She was that tired.

As she showered and headed to bed, Mugs got into bed beside her, barely giving her any room to stretch out. She groaned and muttered, "Come on, buddy. Move over." But he wasn't having anything to do with it. Thaddeus was already up on his roost, and the excitement of the day had apparently worn him out because he was already nodding off. Goliath studied everyone with disdain. Doreen smiled at all her animals. "You guys really are a godsend," she murmured.

At that, Goliath jumped up on the bed and stretched out right where she could lie down.

Doreen groaned. "But you really need to learn how to share," she muttered. Goliath didn't even raise his head or try to look at her. She picked him up, shifted him over, and he reached out and gently dug his paw into her arm, as if to say, *Hey, easy. I'm sleeping here.* Yet he didn't even open his eyes, just stretched out once again and collapsed beside her. She smiled at that.

"You guys are something," she muttered. She wasn't sure what that something was, but it was definitely special. They were all special in their own ways. She lay here in bed, desperately trying to fall asleep, but her mind kept going over and over what Ella had shared earlier. She'd been rather outspoken and conversant, when Doreen had expected her to be quite closed off about it all.

But then Doreen had surprised Ella. Doreen wondered,

when they spoke again, if Ella would act as if this conversation had never happened. Doreen had had that happen a time or two now, and it made her wonder how people could forget that fast.

She couldn't figure out exactly what it was that bothered her, but something did. And her mind just went around and around that conversation with Ella. Doreen finally took a dip into sleep. When she woke up in the middle of the night, she knew what it was that had bugged her. And maybe it was a judgment on her part. But how many people had pillow talk about killings that somebody had done and then continued to sleep with the man and didn't contact the police? Doreen pondered that for a long moment, before finally drifting off into a better, happier sleep.

Chapter 20

WHEN DOREEN WOKE the next morning, she was determined to get to the bottom of the Ella link to Bob Small.

She got up, had a quick shower, and headed downstairs to the kitchen. When she got there, the animals were all standing at the kitchen door to go out. Surprised, she opened the door, and Mugs went outside, barking like crazy, and yet he hadn't been barking until she opened the door.

"So what's going on with you?" she muttered to him. But he was off on his own, doing something at a pace that who knew what was going on. Maybe it was the deer again. Worried about Mugs—less about the deer because Mugs was not likely to attack—she raced behind him, calling, "Mugs, come back here. Mugs, come back."

But he wasn't having anything to do with it. He did come to a dead stop at the water's edge though. She came to his side and grabbed his collar.

"What was that all about?" she scolded, as she looked around. She couldn't see anything, and that in itself was a worry too. She pondered what was going on and what was going through Mugs's mind. Yet she trusted him. He'd saved her life many times already. To ignore his reaction would be foolish. Mugs appeared to be over whatever it was that had upset him, so Doreen let go of his collar and went back inside again.

She kept a cautious eye out the window, but she didn't see any sign that Mugs was upset about something. Still, he was on guard. Wary.

She took her coffee outside with her laptop, although it was probably too bright to see the screen. She glared at the sun and then gave it up, closing the lid on the laptop, and sat here for a long moment. When Mack phoned a few minutes later, she smiled and asked, "Hey, feeling better?"

"Yeah. Quite a bit better. You?"

"I'm okay. I didn't have a great night, but that's all right."

"Any reasons why not?"

"Just …" She stopped and then realized that she couldn't hide it from him. "Just this case and something that Ella mentioned last night."

"Like what?" he asked curiously.

"I don't even know that it's worth bringing up," she muttered. "Maybe it's a judgment on my part."

"I'd like to hear it. You don't say very much against other women."

"I'm not sure if I'm picking up Nan's judgment or what it is."

"Maybe you should tell me, and then we'll both know." A note of humor filling his voice let her know that he was feeling much better now.

"I'll think about it. It does feel wrong to talk about it."

"Ha, now you've really got me curious."

She laughed. "Didn't mean to. That's not part of what

this is all about."

"Are you sure? … Because it seems something's going on."

"Definitely something's going on. I'm not exactly sure what."

"Okay, we can talk about it later today."

"Are you coming by today?" she asked.

"I thought I would, depending on how my work schedule goes. If it gets crazy again, I'll cancel."

"I understand. I guess that must be tough on your love life, *huh?*"

After a moment of silence, he replied in a studied neutral tone of voice, "I didn't think it was a problem. Are you telling me it is now?"

She winced, blushed, then laughed. "That was one of those observations that make me look like an idiot."

"As long as you're not trying to tell me something. Is my job a problem for you?"

"Is my hobby a problem for you?" she asked.

"Yeah," he confirmed in exasperation. "It often is."

She chuckled again. "No, your job is not a problem. I'm sorry. I wasn't thinking about my being part of your love life."

"Maybe it's time you did," he suggested in a quiet voice, and, with that, he hung up.

Chapter 21

BY MIDMORNING SHE'D completed the little bit of housecleaning that she'd planned on doing and had written down what she could remember of Ella's conversation, when Nan called her. "Hey," Doreen answered. "How did the party go after I left?"

"Oh, it calmed down right away after you left," Nan told her, "but I really want to know about the conversation with Ella."

"I'm not sure I have much to say. I was wondering, however, about talking to her sister, Nelly."

"That's not a bad idea."

"I don't think that Nelly knows anything. We often look at people around us, and we assume that they don't get as much attention as they really should."

"In Nelly's case, Ella more or less treated her as if she were a piece of furniture."

"Exactly," Doreen agreed, "in which case then Nelly probably knows a whole lot more than her sister thought."

"I don't know if Nelly would be up for talking to you about her sister though. Ella's ingrained it into Nelly's head that family is family, privacy is privacy."

"I was really surprised that Ella said as much as she did yesterday in the first place. I think I surprised her. Now today, I'm afraid she'll have second thoughts and completely deny everything," Doreen mentioned.

"I told you that woman's evil," Nan repeated.

Doreen chuckled. "I don't know about evil, but there's definitely a problem."

"And what about the guns?" Nan asked.

"That's another story too." Doreen pondered that. "I should talk to somebody about that as well."

"Let me contact Nelly and see if she's up for a conversation about her sister. I'll get back to you." And, with that, Nan ended the call quickly.

As Doreen sat here, a knock came at her door. She was surprised, but, with the animals barking and racing around, creating bedlam out there in her living room, she headed to the front door and stared at her visitor. "Dezy?" She took a step back and said, "Come on in." He hesitated and looked around nervously before he entered. "I hope it's okay that I'm here?"

"It's fine that you're here," she stated. "I'm surprised that you knew where I lived."

He looked at her, and a small smile played at the corner of his lips. "Yeah, even the tourist buses have your place listed."

She winced at that, took a quick look over at Richard's front door, which was closed thankfully. "I'm having coffee out on the deck. You want one?"

"I'd love one," he said. And he proceeded to follow her out to the deck. She quickly poured him a cup and joined him. He sat down, looked at the place, and smiled. "This is lovely. You're really blessed to have it."

Doreen nodded. "Even more blessed because Nan went to all the trouble to set me up here."

"Lucky you. I guess that's how you manage to do all these cases, *huh?*"

"To a certain extent, yes." After a few minutes, where he sat in comfortable silence, she asked him, "So what can I help you with?"

He sighed. "I think I might know who the guns belong to."

She frowned but nodded. "Okay. Do you want to tell me about it?"

He nodded. "It'll take me a minute though."

"Is this a bad story or a good story?"

"I think it was somebody trying to do good, but that doesn't mean that it ended up being good for any of us."

"Okay," she replied, not exactly sure what that was all about. "You seem troubled, so relax."

He stopped, took another sip of coffee.

She added, "Take your time. We don't need to go anywhere soon."

He gave her a grateful smile. "I'm glad to hear that because it might take me a little bit."

She sat back and waited patiently.

"So you see? There was a gang, way back when it happened, and they kind of dispersed. They had a big fight, some internal struggle for power. The police broke them up, and it got bad there for a while."

"Then what?"

"And, next thing I knew, everybody was pretty well cleaned out of town, which was a good thing. But somebody who'd been on the outs of the whole thing didn't want to see it all revived."

"Okay," she said, trying to figure out where this was going. "And so those guns were his. His or the gang's?"

"That's a good distinction," he noted in appreciation. "I don't know how that worked within the gang, but I think it was probably a collection of the gangs' weapons. He also knew that it would cause all kinds of problems if anyone else grabbed them."

"Meaning that he had all the weapons himself?"

Dezy nodded. "You're allowed to have a gun, if you have a license," he explained, "but you're not allowed to stockpile at this level."

"Okay, and so who is this guy, and why did he leave them there?"

"Because he didn't know how else to dispose of them, and he didn't want the gang reforming, and he didn't want the kids getting into it, and he didn't want the next up-and-coming generation getting involved."

She sat back. "So this was somebody's attempt to hide what he considered a dangerous armory?"

"Yes, exactly." He stared at her again in appreciation. "You really do get it, don't you?"

"Well, I get lots of things, but I think there would have been other ways to deal with it."

"And I think he thought that too at the time, but don't forget how the gangs weren't friendly with the cops. He wouldn't exactly turn in his friends. He didn't want any of these weapons to be nailed to other crimes of the past," he explained. "So it's more or less a case of what else could he do?"

She pondered that for a moment. "It's a unique decision." And then she got it. "You knew this guy, didn't you?"

He nodded slowly.

"And you're the one who turned a blind eye, when he needed to bury it."

"I didn't need to turn a blind eye because he went through the standard burial process back then, which wasn't all that hard to do."

"How long ago?"

He pondered that. "Twenty-five years maybe."

She nodded. "And so this person actually existed?"

"Oh, he did, and he's the guy who buried them all. Later, when he died, he wanted his ashes to be interred in the same cemetery."

"Hang on a minute," she said. "So he had the grave for the guns, and he had the mausoleum spot for his ashes?"

He nodded. "Yes, that's correct."

"But the guns were buried in the grave, so why was the one Uzi put in with his urn?"

"Because it was his last piece, the one that he kept himself. He wanted it dismantled and kept with his ashes."

"But when his vault was smashed, we found the urn and the gun."

"Apparently," Dezy stated, with a shrug. "I honestly didn't think it would ever see the light of day again."

"Did you put the Uzi in there with his ashes?"

"No. I presume his attorney did that, as it was part of his will," Dezy confirmed. "And because it was given to us in pieces, I don't think anybody even knew how to put it back together again."

"Right." She sat here in silence, contemplating everything he'd shared. "So somebody was trying to do a good thing, keeping all these weapons out of the public's hand."

"Exactly. He was also trying to shield all his friends who may or may not have been incriminated by some of these weapons. Or so I think."

As the story went, it wasn't a bad way to look at this, but it was also open to an awful lot of other interpretations. "What is his name, and when did he die?" she asked.

Dezy smiled. "Joe Smith."

"That's his legal name, not an alias?" she asked, frowning.

Dezy shrugged. "As far as I know, his legal name is Joe Pillin."

"And Joe Pillin died already. How long ago?"

Dezy sighed. "I'm a little fuzzy on all the dates of death, and I can't go check the records now that I've been let go. However, I believe Joe died at least two years ago."

"Okay, so now you're saying, since this guy who buried the guns some twenty-five years ago is now recently dead, and nobody has—since Joe's death—tried to dig up the cache of guns, that maybe nobody else knew about the guns buried at the cemetery?"

"Exactly. But now that people do know, of course the gossip is rampant."

"Of course it is." She frowned. "So, why did somebody break into that particular vault in the mausoleum, and did they know that the weapon was there, and, if they did know, why didn't they come back?"

"That's what's got me worried."

"And I've got another question for you. Do you think that's the end of it? Or is there another weapons cache in that graveyard somewhere?"

Chapter 22

DEZY STARED AT her in shock and then shook his head. "I have no idea. I don't think so. It was a fairly unusual scenario to begin with, but I did understand it."

"Sure, I understand it too, what with all those weapons used as part of their gang territory fights, wars, whatever you want to call it. Now we have an otherwise typical case of somebody with a huge stockpile, knowing he would die eventually, living the gang life but his gang dispersed, so not wanting to see any of this hitting the streets. So, yeah, that's not a bad way to do it. I don't think it's necessarily 100 percent unique. I'm sure history has a few other records of this happening," she muttered. She pondered it for another long moment. "Of course the big question really is, who knew about it, who opened the vault, and did they know about the guns in the grave too?"

"Was a note left for somebody with Pillin's urn?"

She stared at him in shock. "Meaning, other guys, other people might know about this and maybe even a second stash."

He winced. "I didn't think there was another stash, not until you mentioned it, and now I don't know."

"Did Joe have any family?"

"No. He had no blood family. Once the cops busted up their gang, Joe had nobody at the end of his life."

"How about earlier on? Did he maybe have any kids he didn't know about or accept as his who might have just found out he was their biological father?"

"I don't know," Dezy replied. "Honestly I have no way of knowing any of that."

"So what was your relationship to this guy?" When he hesitated, she looked him straight in the eye. "What I'm asking you is nothing compared to what the cops will ask you."

His shoulders sagged. "I guess I was hoping that, if I told you, I wouldn't have to deal with the cops."

"You'll still deal with the cops, but, so far, you haven't done anything wrong."

"The cemetery owners won't think that way."

She pondered that. "I don't know. That was a long time ago, and you don't have any way to know who signed off on the paperwork, or was there any written record back then?"

He nodded. "There are records, and they were scanned in and went digital when computers and the internet came about."

She nodded. "So that would be one thing to check into, but that also doesn't mean it was anything criminal. As you've said before, you knew about the Uzi but not about all of what was in the coffin."

"Right. I just knew about the Uzi in the vault," he confirmed. "I didn't know about the contents in the grave for a long time. Not until I heard Joe Pillin was cremated and in the mausoleum. Yet people can change their minds, right? Anyway it all started to make more sense after you asked me about the stash."

"In that case, you shouldn't feel bad about telling the cops."

"You think?" he asked, looking at her hopefully.

She nodded. "Was a lawyer involved?"

He nodded. "Absolutely. And it was all done legally—as far as I know. The gun in the vault was in pieces, so maybe nobody knew if it was even complete, or nobody knew how to put it together or something," he suggested.

"I guess it was his favorite gun, and, if he wanted it there with his urn, that isn't exactly a problem," Doreen added.

"Some of these guys with their guns, I'm sure they all had their favorites too."

"Better than killing his cat and sticking it in there with him," she muttered.

He smiled at her. "We do have a lot of people buried with their pets too," he confirmed.

At that, Goliath decided to jump onto her lap, as if the idea of her dying or him dying or even the thought maybe of them being buried together was too much for him. He head-butted her heart, and she winced. "Be nice."

Dezy looked at her in fascination. "You do have a unique relationship with the animals," he noted in a hushed tone.

"Yes, I do, indeed." She smiled at Dezy. "I love them most of the time." Then she glared at Goliath, who insisted that she pet him more.

"You should love them all the time," Dezy suggested. "You only realize how lonely life is when everybody else is gone from your world, and nobody even knows that you're alive anymore."

She felt his loneliness, and it had to be hard. She nodded. "I've been lonely, but, right now, I am blessed to have my grandmother."

"That's a good thing." Dezy smiled. "She'll come my way soon enough."

She stared at him for a moment and then realized that Nan would be at the cemetery one day. She nodded slowly. "Not exactly something I want to think about."

"It never is," he replied, "and yet that is one end none of us can escape."

Doreen did not want to go down that pathway with Nan. Her grandmother was special and a huge part of her world.

"Anyway," Dezy added, "I don't know what to do now."

"You haven't told me who he was to you."

"I would if I could."

"Okay, so, if you don't mind, I guess I know what to do." She picked up her phone and texted Mack. **Where are you?**

At the office. The response was instantaneous, and then he phoned her. "Why?" But he seemed busy, with rustling papers heard from his end.

"I know you've had a pretty rough couple days, but any chance you can come by?"

He asked, "Is it important?"

"Yes, very much so."

He groaned. "I'll be right there."

And, with that, she faced Dezy and said, "We'll dump it all on his lap."

He frowned. "Do you trust him?"

She nodded. "Yes, I do. Absolutely I trust him."

He sighed with relief. "After all the years of bad press and whatnot, you tend to get worried that some of the cops aren't any good."

"I'm sure bad cops are everywhere." But, in a firm voice, she added, "That's not the case with Mack."

Dezy asked, "Is that the guy who was at the cemetery with you?"

"Depending on which time," she replied, "yeah, that would be him. He's a big guy, but he's also a good guy." Seeing the uncertainty in Dezy's eyes and realizing how the years have dealt with him, she continued. "I promise. Mack won't be hard on you."

Dezy shrugged. "I think you put too much faith in people."

"In certain people, yes." She smiled. "I believe in Mack and Nan."

"And all the good people I knew are back at the cemetery."

"So, even if you aren't employed by the cemetery anymore," she noted, "you can still spend a lot of your time there."

"Maybe. It feels more like I'm a trespasser now."

"I'm sorry," she murmured. "That's not fair."

"No, it's not, but what can you do?"

"I get it. Still, maybe we can do something about this. Maybe we can come up with a nice solution for you too."

He looked at her hopefully. "Do you think, if you talked to them, they would hire me back?"

"I have no idea," she admitted, studying him. "I don't think anything I say would remedy that." Then she shrugged. "But let's see what happens when we talk to them."

"That's fair. We don't really know how this will end up." He sat here nervously.

She refilled his coffee, as she waited for Mack, but she could see Dezy getting more and more nervous as time went on. "Tell me about your family."

He frowned at her and then shrugged. "I don't really have any."

There was almost a nonchalance about it that surprised her. "Interesting," she replied. "Nobody left alive?"

"No, nobody at all," he said, with one of those fatalistic shrugs. "I was raised in foster care. I don't know whatever happened to my family."

"I'm sorry. That can't have been easy."

"No, no, it wasn't," he agreed. "Sometimes you win in the family lottery. Sometimes you don't."

"And you never married?"

He smiled at her. "No. Everybody used to say I'm a bit tetched in the head. I'm not exactly sure what that means."

She winced because it was one thing to talk about somebody like that, but it was harder if he'd heard that gossip in relationship to himself too. "I'm so sorry. People aren't always the nicest."

"People are just people." He shrugged. "It's how you react that makes what they say okay or not okay in your world."

She stared at him, appreciating that outlook. "I'm glad you have such a great attitude in life."

He gave her another one of those odd smiles. "When you don't have any family, it almost feels as if you don't have anything to lose sometimes," he shared. "So I get that, for a lot of people, my situation was tough, but I didn't know what I'd lost. I didn't know what I didn't have. And, maybe because of whatever problems I do have learning things, maybe it didn't affect me the same way. Anyway, it's okay.

Maybe I would have liked to have had children at some point in time, but then I see them racing around out of control and realize that I probably didn't have the temperament to raise them anyway," he muttered. "So it's probably a godsend that I don't have any."

She looked at him for a long moment, and then she started to giggle. "I think an awful lot of people wish they hadn't had kids," she said, with a smile. "At least you were smart enough to know that ahead of time."

"And not everybody"—he grinned at her—"is willing to talk to me and to treat me like I'm a human being. Lots of people avoid me. Because of my job, I think, as much as anything."

"But, if you think about it, it's not even so much avoiding *you*," she clarified, "but maybe avoiding what you represent."

"What I represent?" he asked. "What do you mean?"

"Think about it. When they see you, they are reminded of who and what's lost to them in the graveyard. They are still dealing with their losses at the time that they see you. It's not as if they see you at a pub, I presume."

"No, I don't drink, and I don't go out much."

"Exactly," she said, "so, if you think about it from their perspective, you represent something that they're struggling hard to deal with, and they just want to avoid you because you bring back the bad memories for them."

"I hadn't considered that," he murmured.

"Well, you should," she encouraged. "I think it's not so much even that people are trying to be mean. Sometimes things are just so difficult, so complicated, that they don't know what to do with it."

He looked at her and nodded. "I think you're one of

those nice people."

She winced. "That always makes me feel as if I'm supposed to be somebody else."

"No," he declared. "You're not supposed to be anybody else. I can't be anybody else. You can't be anybody else. We are who we are."

She smiled and nodded. "I think that's quite true." Mugs started to bark, and she called him back, knowing it would be Mack, but still it made Dezy nervous. She reached out and gently patted his hand. "It's all right."

"Is it though?" he asked. "I don't know him, and I'm not all that good with strangers."

"Sure you are," she stated. "This is why you're so good with the people at the cemetery. Remember?"

He lowered his voice and replied, "Yes, but I greet the dead, not the living."

She didn't even have a chance to respond to that, when Mack walked in through the kitchen, saw the open kitchen door and came straight out to the deck.

"What's up?" he asked in exasperation. Only to stop when he saw Dezy.

She looked up at Mack and said, "This is Dezy. He worked at the cemetery."

Mack nodded slowly. "Yeah, I was trying to get a hold of you."

Dezy replied, "Well, I'm here now."

Mack looked over at Doreen for some explanation. She began, "He knows about the guns."

At that, Mack sat down with a hard *thump*. "Okay, so I guess we need to talk."

She explained what had happened. "I will put on some more coffee."

He nodded. "Thanks, I could use a cup."

She smiled at Mack. "Dezy's nervous, and he doesn't know you, so go easy."

He frowned at her. "I won't beat him up or anything."

"No, but that cop persona of yours is scary."

He stared at her. "I still have to do my job."

"You can do your job," she agreed, "but you just can't scare and upset Dezy in the process."

He rolled his eyes at that. "I got this. Go put on coffee."

She burst out laughing, patted Dezy on the shoulder, and said, "Dezy I'm putting on coffee but will be right back." He looked at her worriedly. She shook her head. "It's all good. I promise."

He looked over at Mack and then back at her. "I'd really prefer it if you, … I'd feel better if you stayed."

She hesitated, looked at Mack, and asked, "Do you mind waiting on coffee?"

He shook his head. "No, I can wait on coffee, but, man, it's been a long day." He looked over at Dezy. "So what's going on, Dezy?" And Mack's voice was casual, relaxed even. Dezy glanced at her, then back at Mack. Finally he replied, "I probably should have said something a long time ago. It just seemed like it wasn't hurting anybody."

"Not only that, he was trying to do the right thing," Doreen interrupted.

Mack looked at her, then returned his gaze to Dezy. "So tell me in your own words."

Dezy tried; it took him a couple attempts, a couple promptings from Doreen, and finally he got the whole story out.

Mack sat back, studying him. "Okay, I get why this all happened, and you're right. It definitely got all these weapons off the street. Of course there is the other side to that."

Doreen nodded and added for Dezy's benefit, "Who opened the vault now is what we're trying to figure out. Presumably someone knew the Uzi was in there. Plus, Mack, there was something else. Dezy wasn't sure if something else was in or with the urn."

"What do you mean?"

"Well, first, the Uzi was taken apart," Doreen replied. "I guess that's what all the metal pieces were."

Mack nodded. "We already knew it was an Uzi, so what do you mean about something else in there?"

"Remember how the urn was on its side?"

He nodded. "Yes."

"What if there was a note?" Doreen asked. "Presumably it wasn't a random smashing of just anybody's vault, right? I'm just guessing here, but somebody must have known about the Uzi, and I'm wondering if somebody got a letter, found a note, maybe a copy of the will? I don't know."

Mack pondered that. "Something must have changed, so obviously we should look for something somewhere, and this guy Pillin died when?"

"A little bit ago," Dezy replied. "before I lost my job, maybe a couple years ago now."

"That makes sense," Doreen said. "I'm thinking Pillin left instructions or a note about what he'd done."

Mack pulled out a notepad and added some notes. He looked over at Dezy. "And you say he had no family?"

"None that I know of." Dezy glanced over at Doreen apologetically. "He and I talked about the fact that we were both in that same boat, no family, nobody to leave anything to."

"Do you know what he was planning to do with this stuff, once he died, like sell it all and give the money to a charity or anything?" Mack asked Dezy.

"I don't know. I thought it would stay where it was all buried."

"And who would know about any will, if the dead man had no family?" Mack asked, a question that she hadn't even thought to ask. "Who was closest to him?"

Dezy pondered that and then shook his head. "Again I don't know."

Doreen looked over at him. "The cemetery would have a contact person in case of Pillin's death, shouldn't they? A girlfriend? The lawyer?"

"The lawyer?" Mack's eyebrows shot up. "A lawyer was involved?"

When Dezy gave the name of somebody she'd never heard of, Mack pinched his lips and nodded. He wrote it down, and she tried to commit it to memory, but then realized it was a poet's name, so it wasn't that hard to remember. *Robbie Burns.* "Is that even his real name?"

"It is," Mack confirmed. "He's still an active lawyer in town, right here in Kelowna."

Chapter 23

LONG AFTER DEZY left, Doreen and Mack sat over a simple dinner of sandwiches, made of whatever she had left in her fridge. She looked over at him. "Is this Robbie Burns lawyer bad news?"

"Not so much bad news, but he was known to have a lot of gang affiliations," he shared calmly.

"Well, it fits then, doesn't it?"

He nodded, took another bite of sandwich, but didn't answer her question.

She took another stab at this question, trying to get him to open up. "What do you think about Dezy's story?"

"It makes a lot of sense to me," he said, with a shrug. "When you think about it, that's an ingenious solution."

She beamed. "That's what I thought. Really, if you've got that cache of weapons, and you don't want it to hit the streets …"

"Obviously he didn't think those weapons would have been worth a lot. Ends up going to the grave, after spending all that money to buy them. So who got this Pillin guy's estate?"

"Oh, I see what you mean."

"So, if somebody inherited it, then what else did they inherit is the question," Mack clarified. "But they broke into the urn, so what does that mean? Maybe the urn gave directions? Instructions? Something else?" he asked.

"That's the real concern, isn't it? Just because we found one cache of weapons doesn't mean there's still another one, right?"

He nodded. "That casket was way heavy, and the minute the wood started to go, the weight dumped out. So that makes me wonder if they tried to put it all in one grave, but maybe they didn't have enough room, so needed a second grave."

"So either they jammed everything in it, in order to get it done once, or possibly there's a second one. Or," she added, "somebody was hoping to get it, but you got there first."

He nodded.

"Anything back from ballistics?"

He shook his head. "Not yet. The chances are that, if from a gang, then these weapons were probably used in all kinds of crimes. Remember too. Murders have no statute of limitations, but the rest do, which may have all expired over the last twentysomething years."

She winced. "I guess in this case there are a ton of ugly possibilities."

He nodded. But a glimmer of a smile crossed his face. "But this isn't your fault," he stated.

She looked at him in astonishment. "Good, I certainly wasn't thinking it was."

He burst out laughing. "That's good to know. And, by the way, we think Dezy was the anonymous caller with the tip to open up the grave with the same name as on the mausoleum vault."

She stared at him. "Really? I didn't know you got an anonymous tip."

"That'll be my assumption now. Somebody phoned and told us that the grave under the same name needed to be opened. And considering we found the Uzi in the mausoleum, it didn't take long to realize that likely other guns were there."

"And this Pillin person had a lot of gang affiliations?"

"Yes. Since then I've been questioned by other branches of law enforcement as well."

"Oh," she replied, sinking back into her chair again. "I guess that makes sense. Everyone wants to know about the weapons cache, don't they?"

"Everybody does," he confirmed. "We've also been contacted by multiple departments in Vancouver."

She again winced. "Okay, so this is big."

"It's very big, but we have to work our due diligence on our end, so other people can close cases on their ends."

She asked, "Are we sure this guy's dead?"

He looked at her. "The urn and the grave weren't enough for you?" he asked, with a note of humor.

She flashed him a smile and casually picked up a piece of fat she'd cut out of her sandwich and handed it to Mugs.

"You shouldn't feed him at the table," Mack said.

She nodded. "Yes, I know, but I think now I do it just because my ex used to say the same thing." She looked over to catch the sour look on Mack's face, and she burst out laughing. "I didn't mean to say that you sound like my ex. Just that I'm doing this because he wouldn't want me to—something I probably shouldn't do."

He relaxed at that and nodded. "Seems as if you're still

rebelling a lot because of him."

She nodded. "I am. Whether I should be or not, I don't know."

"Don't worry about the *shoulds* at this point. Be you, and the rest will fall into place."

She chuckled. "Being me has led me to all kinds of different cases. And this one is getting complicated."

"It is and it isn't, but, if we can resolve the guns, that would be good. The question is, who would know about it?"

"My vote is the lawyer," Doreen stated.

He gave her a dry look. "Why?"

She flashed that knowing smile again. "Because he's a lawyer, and that means he's a bad guy already."

Mack burst out laughing. "You can't make that blanket statement."

"I already did," she murmured.

"What about my brother?" he asked, giving her that flat stare.

She shrugged. "There's an exception to every rule."

He grinned at her. "Not a bad response."

"Your brother truly is an exception," she repeated, "but okay, I see your point. So, if it's not Pillin's lawyer, he at least should know who else inherited."

"Yeah, and that's where I'll start in the morning." He got up and carried his plate indoors.

She followed him with hers and asked, "Are you okay to head home, to grab some sleep?"

"I am, but first I suggest we go for a walk along the creek."

"Oh," she said in delight. "A *walk*, walk?"

He asked, "Versus what? Walk, jump, walk, skip?"

She rolled her eyes. "Versus having a destination in

mind. Is this just for fun?"

"Just for fun," he confirmed. And he held out his hand. "You up for it?"

"Sure, bring it on."

Chapter 24

DOREEN WOKE UP the next morning with a newfound sense of satisfaction and peace in her heart. She lay in bed for a long moment, remembering holding hands as she and Mack walked up and down the creek. They'd gone up well past Steve's place, with all the bodies he had buried there, almost trying to erase some of the traumatic memories that she and so many other people had for that man and his property.

Even as she and Mack walked back to her house, they had talked about easy things, stuff that didn't matter—not business, not cases, not even her animals—just the joy of being outside, the joy of being together.

And when she mentioned it to him, he smiled, squeezed her hand, and nodded. "That's how it should be." It made her realize how much she'd missed in life.

With her ex, she had never had that sense of joy, that sense of peace with being somebody you really cared about. Her marriage to Mathew had been pretty rough most the time, and she hadn't really understood just how much of a negative influence he had had on her. Of course he was still a bad influence.

Now it made her heart smile to even think about Mack. She hopped out of bed, pushing her ex out of her thoughts, and headed for the shower. Mack was a whole different story. He was nothing like Mathew. But she also knew that Mack wanted more from her, and she wasn't sure she had it yet to give.

No, that's not true. The voice inside her head was strong. She had it in her. However, she wasn't sure if she could give it to him. She was … and she winced to say it out loud. *Scared.* Her inner voice was *sooo* clear. And she knew it was right. She was scared. Scared of making a mistake again. Scared of losing herself again.

With a groan she snatched her phone and quickly sent Mack a text. **Good morning.** When she got a **Good morning** right back, she smiled. Her sense of equilibrium restored again, she dressed and headed down to the coffeepot, determined to focus on the good things in her life. And when her phone rang soon afterward, she snatched it up and sang out, "Good morning."

Only to realize it was the wrong person.

She winced to know that she would be in big trouble from everybody for having answered it. What was her problem? Except that she was distracted and had been thinking about Mack. Dang, when she heard Mathew's voice come through the phone, she snapped, "Why are you still calling me?"

"To ruin your day apparently," he replied on a jovial note.

"Yeah, that's true, and I'm tired of it."

"Good, then let me off the hook."

"See you in court." And she went to hang up.

"Wait, wait, wait," he yelled.

A note of almost desperation filled his tone. Curious, she asked, "Why, why should I?"

"Look. I didn't do you right back then," he began, "and my scenario with Robin was the wrong thing to do."

Her eyebrows shot up at that. She'd never, *ever* heard him apologize, and it made her even more suspicious. "This is a change," she noted. "What's the matter? You've got some leg breakers after you?"

First came a moment of silence, and then he replied, "And if I did?"

But there wasn't the same bravado; it was almost a curiosity to see what he would say. "I'm sure they were all good business friends of yours anyway, so just buy them off."

"What if it's more money than I have?"

She laughed at that. "I doubt it. You've been hoarding money since forever," she muttered. "Now, stop calling me." And she quickly hung up. Knowing that she would still be in trouble, she sent both Mack and Nick a text, letting them know that Mathew called, and, yes, she made the mistake of answering and had hung up again.

Mack called her almost immediately. "Are you okay?"

"Yeah, I'm okay." She winced. "I expected you to phone me, giving me the fifth degree for answering."

"I'm sure your lawyer will do that," Mack replied, with a note of humor. "And I guess I'm questioning why you answered."

She hesitated, and then shrugged. "Because I thought it was you," she snapped. "I was thinking about our walk last night and how good it was to have somebody I could relax around and not feel as if I had to be perfect all the time."

"That's good," Mack stated. "It's a little disturbing that you didn't look at the number first though."

"That'll get me in trouble with my lawyer again," she noted, "but I was making coffee, and I thought it was you, and I snatched it up, and I said, *Good morning*, and of course it was the wrong person. He also sounded odd."

Mack asked, "In what way?"

"Maybe a little desperate, but I'm not sure. It was a different tone than I've heard from him before. As if something else was going on in his world, and he needed this divorce to come to an end or needed me out of it or something. I don't know. Or he needed the money," she added.

"I wouldn't listen to that either," Mack stated. "According to what Nick said, Mathew's got loads."

"Oh, I know he does, but I wonder how much of that money was his legally and how much of that money he may have gotten from somebody else or is holding for somebody else."

"No matter what he's doing, it's not your problem, stay out of it, and don't feel sympathy for him."

"Fine, and, yes, it was a mistake. I didn't want to talk to him."

"Good," Mack noted calmly. "So the next time you'll look at the phone number, right?"

"Yes, yes, yes." She smiled now. "Have a good day."

Of course Nick phoned afterward.

"You talked to him?" he asked, disbelief in his voice.

"Look. I just finished talking to your brother, not the easiest of conversations," she added. "Yes, I talked to Mathew. I didn't mean to. I thought it was your brother calling me."

"And yet you keep telling me that, and so then I keep wondering why you aren't looking at the Caller ID display."

She mentally kicked herself. "Yeah, me too. Believe me. I

just got off the phone with Mack, explaining the same thing."

"That would have been fun too," he said, with a note of laughter.

"No, it wasn't, and, yes, it's my fault, but I got to tell you that Mathew didn't sound quite right."

"In what way?"

"I don't know. A little unnerved, worried? I don't know."

"I wouldn't listen to him, and, if he's in trouble, it's of his own making."

"True," she acknowledged.

And their words were in her mind long after she hung up the phone. It was easy for them to back off and to try to get her to behave, although she winced at that because that's not what they were trying to do. They were trying to protect her. Plus her soon-to-be ex was not exactly the easiest person to get along with, but still something had been off in his voice.

She didn't know how to explain it. But it hadn't had that same bravado that she was used to or that same sense of control. Maybe he understood that something was coming to an end, and it was an end that he didn't like and didn't have any control over.

Still, she had to continue to hope for the best. As long as she could remember to check out who was phoning, it would be fine. With her coffee in hand, she went outside and sat out on the deck and then remembered that Mack was supposed to contact the Pillin lawyer. She quickly sent Mack a text and asked if he'd made the contact yet. He responded with **No.**

She frowned at that, but of course he was busy, had an

awful lot of things on his plate, so whether it was a case of not having gotten through to the lawyer or not having had a chance to even call, that was a completely different thing. But she hated waiting. She sat here, drumming her fingers on the tabletop, trying to figure out what her role in this was, what she could do without pissing everybody else off more than she already had, when her ex phoned again.

She stared down at the number and refused to answer it. When he left a voice mail, she was surprised but listened to it.

"Hey, I know you don't believe me, but I really need this to come to an end, and I need it to come to an end fast."

She sent Nick the message and a text, saying that Mathew called back again. Nick sent her a thumbs-up and a little note saying he would take care of it.

She wasn't so sure about what Nick would take care of, but surely if Mathew wanted to deal with something and to get their divorce dealt with fast, the easiest thing was to sign the paperwork.

Chapter 25

DOREEN FOUND IT hard to get Mathew out of her mind. This went on throughout the day. She went to Millicent's, worked on her garden, did some shopping, came back home, then decided that she needed to get out again. The easiest place to get out to right now—which would make absolutely no sense to most people in the world, but to her it was almost like a draw—was to the cemetery with Mugs, Thaddeus, and Goliath in tow. She should take a quick trip to Wendy's consignment store and see if there was money waiting for her, but she could do that with a phone call and right now she wanted the serenity of the cemetery.

Once there, she wandered happily, glancing up, she caught sight of Dezy up on the side. She waved at him, but, instead of waving back, he disappeared into the trees. She frowned at that and then casually headed in his direction. He was no longer there. She frowned, studied the area, kept on walking, wondering if he had a bigger role in any of this than he'd let on. And, if he did, what repercussions would it bring for him?

Presumably, after Mack contacted the Pillin lawyer, the lawyer would contact Dezy, and that could cause him some trouble too. As she wandered through the cemetery, really enjoying the peace and the ambiance, her animals appeared calm and relaxed too.

Some names on the headstones she recognized, some family names she recognized, and still a lot of people she'd never heard of were buried here. With the animals quietly at her side, as if understanding her odd mood, she came around the corner to find Dezy, sitting on a nearby bench, almost waiting for her.

He looked up and gave her a nod.

"Hey," she greeted him, walking over to him. "Are you okay?"

He shrugged. "It feels very strange."

"Being here but not here?"

"I contacted the company to see if there was any way I could stay on the payroll," he shared abruptly, his gaze roaming the aisles around him.

"And what did they say?" she asked curiously, as she sat down on the bench beside him.

"They didn't say no," he began. "They didn't say very much at all. I was hoping I could get onto the payroll first, before all this mess was publicized." Then he looked at her and asked, "That won't work though, will it?"

"I don't know," she murmured. "People get upset when employees take things into their own hands."

He nodded. "I get that, but nobody was there to help support me back then either."

"Did you have another boss at the time?"

He nodded. "But he was killed in a car accident not too long afterward."

"Did he say no to all this?"

"I didn't tell him because I knew he wouldn't be supportive, … and I know that they'll say that I should have brought it up, that I should have talked to people, that I should have done more," he admitted. "But what do you do when the person you must talk to will just give you an absolute flat-out no on it?"

"I understand," she murmured. "And it's too easy for those other people to criticize after the fact. However, just because I feel this way doesn't mean a lot of other people will."

He didn't say anything for a long moment. "I need to find something else to do with my time," he added.

She smiled. "You are entitled to be here. It is a public place. You've made friends here. No reason you can't still be here."

"I wonder if I could work in one of the other cemeteries."

"I don't know. It's worth trying."

He sighed at that and nodded. "I'm sure they have their own staff," he muttered.

"But that doesn't mean that they don't need help with the gardens or something else," she suggested, "and then there's always volunteering."

He looked at her and then slowly nodded. "I always wondered about that, even if just to stay close."

"And maybe you should consider that here. This is where you want to be, and maybe that would be okay here."

"Maybe," he said, brightening. "I am okay for money. At least I hope so."

"I don't know what your situation is. If this is where you want to be, if this is where your heart is, then find a way to make it happen."

He looked over at her. "You think they've contacted

Pillin's lawyer yet?"

"I don't know," she replied honestly. "I'd like to think so, but I also know that things were pretty busy down at the station."

He snorted. "Aren't they always? Seems like every time you need the cops, they're too busy for anything."

"Did you take any of this to the cops before?"

He shook his head. "No, I didn't. Maybe I should have, but I was also pretty scared about the gangs at the time."

"And what about this Pillin, the man who buried all the guns?" she asked. "Were you scared of him?"

He pondered that and then shook his head. "Not really, and maybe I didn't know enough to be scared. The gang thing had blown up in the years before, and then it'd calmed down. So there wasn't a whole lot of news about it, and I didn't really have anybody affected by it. Therefore, I didn't really worry about it."

"And are you the one who phoned in a tip after the mausoleum was broken into, about checking into Pillin's grave?"

He looked at her, startled, and then slowly nodded. "How did you figure that out?" he asked. "It was supposed to be an anonymous call."

"I didn't figure it out. Mack did."

He shrunk down into himself. "Oh, that'll get me into more trouble too then."

"No, not necessarily. He didn't ask you about it yesterday, right? I'm the one who's asking you about it right now because I'd just as soon find out for sure."

He stared off into the distance. "It's a good thing to find out the truth sometimes," he noted, "but it's not all that easy when you can't explain your actions."

"You were no longer an employee, and you were a concerned citizen, and you had insider knowledge," she reminded him. "So it makes sense that you were the one who called."

"As long as nobody else finds out that I made that call."

"And when you say *nobody else*, I presume you mean the person who inherited the guns?"

"Yeah. That's my current concern."

"And you have no idea who it is?"

He shook his head. "No, I really don't know anybody else who was involved in it." He raised both hands, palms up. "That makes it sound even stupider, but, back then, it was a long time ago, and it happened so fast that most of us just were happy to move on."

"I think that's typical of life. When something like that happens, you bury it." Then she laughed. "In this case literally."

He grinned at her. "That's very true."

"And there was no ceremony, there was nothing, right?"

"No, the grave was dug, the box was put in, it was covered up, and the headstone went down."

She pondered that. "And Pillin never contacted you again?"

"No, I heard about it after his death. His lawyer contacted me to say that it was part of his wishes."

"And he contacted you, why?"

"Well, one, I was still working here," he replied, "and, two, I was connected to the original scenario."

"And that makes sense. At least then there was nobody else to explain things to."

"That's what I thought," he murmured, "but then it makes you wonder."

"Do you think the lawyer had anything to do with the break-in?"

"I don't know why he would. There was no need for it, and, if Pillin's attorney put the Uzi in there anyway, and nobody else knew about Pillin's wishes, why would somebody pick that vault in the mausoleum?"

"Was there any connection between the lawyer and Pillin, other than they both dealt with gangs?"

Dezy shrugged. "I don't know whether there was or not. That was well above my pay grade." He laughed at that. "But I would presume there was some connection because otherwise why wouldn't the attorney have turned it all over to the gang way back when?"

She pondered that. "I really want to talk to the lawyer."

He looked at her in alarm. "I wouldn't do that," he warned her.

She smiled. "Believe me. A lot of people wouldn't want me to do that either. When you get to a certain point where you need answers, that means going to the people who would have them."

"And yet this lawyer isn't necessarily anybody you want to get involved with either," Dezy added.

She studied Dezy's face. "Do you think he's dangerous?"

"I don't know that he's *not* dangerous. I do know that he's … got connections that can make life very difficult for people."

"Well, if he's been doing what he's been doing for a long time, he'll still have affiliations with anybody left from the original mess."

At that, Dezy nodded. "That's what I mean. So, if you happen to cross him, I don't know that he doesn't have people somewhere in his world who can come and take you out."

She stared at him. "That's disconcerting."

He nodded. "You do understand how these gangs work, right?"

She laughed. "I do. I really do. I'm not naïve. It's just frustrating when you hear some of this stuff and when you realize how much of it is going on around you."

He didn't say a whole lot to that, but Dezy nodded. "Always, always stuff is going on that you don't really see. It's funny, but, when you're one of those invisible people, like me, the information that flows around you is something that they never even stop to think about."

It sounded intriguing. "Meaning that you heard an awful lot of stuff going on that people didn't worry about you hearing because you were invisible?"

He nodded. "Something like that. People didn't pay me much attention because I was just staff."

"I've heard that more than a few times. It's funny how people are so blind, isn't it?"

"Funny and sad," he noted. "My life could have been enriched a lot more if I'd been able to communicate more easily with people."

"I think you communicate just fine," she stated, looking at him.

He frowned at that, looked at her animals, and said, "You're easy to talk to."

Considering it's not the first time she'd been told that, she stayed quiet and nodded.

"I think the animals help a lot," he murmured.

"I think they do too," she agreed gently. "They're good for people, and they're good for my soul."

He smiled at that. "They also know it. They're very

comfortable being with you, and I think that helps too."

She wouldn't argue that because, as far as she was concerned, the animals could do no wrong, much to Mack's dismay. She smiled at Dezy and asked, "Are there other things that you overheard that may be important?"

"Over the years, I've heard lots, but some of it is probably no longer of value, and, some of it, the time to do something about it is well past."

She stared at him in fascination. "Anything in particular?"

He looked over at her. "Maybe, I don't know, feels like tattling."

She chuckled. "I get that, but sometimes tattling is what we need to do in order to clear away some of this. Now if it's actually tattling, that's a different story. However, if it's information on a case or about somebody having done wrong, that's a whole different story."

"I'm not sure that people can easily make that differentiation."

"Easily? No," she agreed. "I don't think a lot of them can do it easily. Still, that doesn't mean that they can't do it or that they shouldn't do it."

"Ah." Dezy smiled. "That's a different story, isn't it?"

She waited peaceably at his side, the animals lying down, content. "So is someone else connected to these guns?"

"Maybe. I have heard a bunch of things over time. One guy stood over the grave, cursing and swearing at it."

"Oh, interesting, but then maybe some people were angry that their loved ones had gone and left them."

"Maybe, he sounded angry that they didn't leave him something."

"Now that I believe," she noted, with a headshake.

"People have expectations, and, when they don't get what they thought they would get, what they think they deserve, they get angry."

"Yeah, this guy was angry all right. He did say something about *I should have done this earlier.*"

"*Hmm*, as in?"

Dezy shrugged. "I took it to assume he meant *kill Pillin himself.*"

She sat back and stared. "Really? Why would you have thought that?"

"It was the way he said it. *I should have taken care of you earlier. I should have taken care of this a long time ago, before you had a chance to change anything. Now it's all for naught.*"

Her eyebrows shot up at that. "Interesting," she muttered. "Of course that doesn't prove this person is guilty, but it's intriguing."

"Oh, that's an example though." He gave her a wry look. "Again I'm just furniture to people."

She nodded. "Well, if anything was said that really bothers you, you should write it down, let me know, and I'll look into it."

He stared at her. "Do you really think you could look into it?"

"I would like to think so. Will it be easy? No. However, that doesn't mean it's impossible though."

He smiled at that. "I don't think that boyfriend of yours would like it."

"He doesn't like a whole lot that I do." She chuckled. "But, if I bring justice to some people, it's worth it to me."

"I hadn't ever considered it before, but so many people are out here, and I don't know how many of them got justice."

"Lots of them can't get justice. Sometimes it's car accidents. Sometimes it's plain poor decisions. People always do things that makes you cringe and ask why? *Why would you have thought that was a good idea?*"

Dezy nodded. "I've seen that too. People die from stupid stunts all the time."

"Anyway, as far as Pillin's lawyer goes, it will be interesting to see what happens."

Dezy stood, gave a self-conscious shrug, and added, "Pillin's lawyer has a son."

Her antenna popped up. "And is the son a good guy or a bad guy?"

Dezy pondered that. "I don't know. He was here a couple times. Recently. If he was looking for something, I don't think he found it."

"A couple times? What was he doing?"

"Weeding gravestones, working from one to the other. But all these graves are mapped out."

"Now that the one has been found with all the guns," she asked, "are you thinking there might be another one? That he might be looking for another one?"

"I don't know, but he *was* looking for something."

"And when was this exactly?"

"The last three days," Dezy replied. "Matter of fact he's here right now."

She slowly stood up. "Where is he?" When Dezy hesitated, she shook her head. "This isn't the time to hesitate."

"But it isn't the time to get you into a lot of trouble either."

"I'm always in trouble," she admitted. "That's an accepted thing between us." He stared at her, and she shrugged. "Come on. Where is he?" She glanced around the cemetery.

"I at least need to see who he is, so I can recognize him at a future time."

"In that case, come on." And he led the way down to a section that she had yet to see. As they approached the area, she asked in a low voice, "Are there any unmarked graves around here?"

He shook his head. "Not that I know of. I'm sure there are probably some from way back when, but not new burials."

"Right."

Then he nudged her hand gently and pointed, and there was a youngish man, midtwenties, wandering up and down a row. He was reading names and then going back down the other side and reading the names on the other side. She asked Dezy in a whisper, "Do you know his name?" At Dezy's headshake, she continued. "I'll look him up on the internet later."

"I'm not sure but it could be Stuart."

She pondered what the son was doing and turned to ask Dezy, only to find that she was alone. Somehow Dezy had melted away into the shadows. She stared around, wondering where he'd gone, but she saw no sign of him. Frowning at that, it showed a level of stealth that she wasn't used to, but it also said a lot about Dezy and how he managed to move around. She quickly pulled out her phone and looked up Stuart Burns and there it was – an article about his father. And as luck would have it, a photo of the two of them. Not a great one but still it was good enough to realize the family resemblance."

Even the pathway he'd taken her down to here wasn't one that she knew. It was probably not even marked on any of the cemetery maps. But then Dezy had been here for a lifetime, from what he had told her. She stepped closer to where the young man was. When he turned to look at her and frowned, she smiled suddenly. "Hey, beautiful day to come visit, isn't it?"

He stared at her, his frown deepening, and grumbled, "Not really."

She stopped. "I'm sorry. You're right. It's wrong of me to assume that it's a good day for anybody to be here. … I'm sorry for your loss."

He then realized what she was trying to say, and he shrugged. "I didn't lose anybody. I'm here looking for somebody."

"Oh," she said in a bright tone. "Can I help you?"

He glared at her and replied, "No, I'm fine."

Then he turned back to looking at the graves, but he was moving slower and looking over at her often, as if to keep an eye on what she was doing or when she'd be leaving. Except she was fascinated by the graves in this area. Most of them were buried among the long grass and shrubbery, and that in itself was kind of nice. Instead of big monuments or upright headstones, she much preferred the low-level horizontal individual stones, almost hidden within nature. Obviously a lot of people wanted a place to come and to care for and to look after their loved one, but that didn't mean it had to be something ostentatious. It could be something subtle and nice, as a quiet memento, while at the same time honoring Mother Nature.

Finally she stopped, looked down at one grave, glanced over to see him standing there, staring at her. She smiled at him. "Are you sure you don't want that help?"

He shook his head. "What are you doing here?" he asked, his tone tight.

She smiled. "I come here often, visit, and get my head in a better space. I feel closer to the people who are buried. I love to walk up and down and read the names. Some are really interesting."

He snorted. "That's it. I know your type. You're just a lookie-loo."

"A lookie-loo?" she asked.

"A window shopper." He snickered.

At that, she studied him a little closer. "I wouldn't have said that I'm shopping for a gravestone, if that's what you mean."

"How about a grave?" he asked, his voice hardening.

She looked down at Mugs, who was staring at the stranger, but his ears were half-mast, and his tail was not wagging. Mugs was not a happy camper, but, so far, he hadn't done anything terribly aggressive.

"Why are you bringing animals here?" the angry man asked. "Do you think that anybody buried here wants to get pissed on?"

His comment was so out of left field that she didn't even know what to say at first. "I don't think anybody here cares," she replied, as soon as she could get the words out.

He laughed at that. "That's true, and the ones who do care are always the living, and they are the ones left to sort out the mysteries of life."

By the way he said that, Doreen read between the lines that this man had some mystery that he was struggling with.

"Well, I'm here, if you want to talk or if you want help finding something," she offered, with a wave of her hand at the graves. "A lot are here, if you're looking for someone or something in particular. Who knows what else we could find in a grave, now that all those guns were uncovered recently."

She shook her head. "The whole town's agog with it."

He snorted at that. "As if anybody in the town cares."

"Oh, I don't know. Curiosity gets people going more than anything."

"That's because they're nosy," he declared, with an ugly snap of his voice.

"Wow, that's a judgment too."

He laughed. "What are you, some nosy do-gooder?"

She winced at that. It certainly wasn't the first time she'd been called that. She gave him a sunny smile. "And if there's one grave," she stated, treading cautiously, "full of weapons, who knows that maybe there is another one?"

He stared at her, and she saw something in his gaze, and it wasn't nice. She backed up ever-so-slightly.

He nodded. "Yeah. I don't think anybody wants you putting out insinuations like that. Graveyards would be at a disadvantage if people came through here looking for other marked graves to break into." His voice turned soft, yet deadly.

Yet she smiled a knowing smile at him. "You are Robbie Burns's son. And your father was the lawyer who arranged that grave full of weapons, wasn't he?"

He stared at her in shock. "Who the heck are you?" he asked. Then his voice deepened. "I don't even care about that, but what else do you know?"

"All kinds of things," she claimed. "It's what I do."

Stuart glared at her, looked at her animals.

Then Thaddeus popped his head out from under her hair and said, "Thaddeus is here, Thaddeus is here."

Startled, Stuart cried out in disgust, "Oh my God. You're that nosy do-gooder, aren't you? The one who goes around solving all these crimes?"

"Sure, if that's what you want to call me. I've been called worse, I guess, so whatever."

"I can imagine. Why are you even here?" Stuart asked, looking around frantically. "Did you find something?"

"No, sure didn't, but, hey, watch the news. Maybe I will yet."

At that, Stuart slowly turned to face her, and that darkening of his gaze was a threat when she saw it. "I figured that lawyer father of yours probably mentioned something to you, and that's why you're here."

"My father doesn't know anything," he spat, his voice deadly quiet. "You keep him out of this."

"Oh, he'll know something, whether he's prepared to tell you or not. Maybe that's why you're a little upset. Maybe you're afraid Daddy's keeping something from you. Something that you would like very much to have. The question is, what would that be, Stuart?"

He stared at her. "I don't know who you are or what you think you're doing here, but you're not welcome here, and you need to leave."

She stiffened. "People ordering me around, telling me what to do, tends to make me really angry," she muttered. "I've been working on it, therapy of a sort, trying to make sure I get a bit more of a backbone to tell people off." And, sure enough, she felt her spark of temper coming along. She glared at Stuart. "I don't care who you are. I'm allowed to be here, just as much as you."

"You might be allowed to be here," he snapped, "but I highly advise you to leave."

"Nope, not going to, and you can't make me." He stared at her in shock, as she crossed her arms over her chest. "Do you really think people don't know where I am and that they don't know that you're here, checking out the graves to see which one's next?"

"You don't know anything about it," Stuart cried out. "People like you make everything so difficult."

"I'm sorry if your father made life difficult for you with the job that he had. That couldn't have been easy. But you are not making anything easy on yourself either."

"You don't know anything about my father," he said again.

"I know Robbie Burns handled a lot of the gang deals, and his affiliations have always been in question. Of course he's got to be getting old by now too."

Stuart stared at her, as if she'd grown two heads. "You don't know anything," he snapped. "You need to shut up."

"I could, but talking to you is pretty fascinating." He glared at her, and she shrugged. "I mean, think about it. You're out here, looking for a grave. Of course everybody would assume that you know something. Maybe you're in Pillin's will."

He stared at her, all the color dropping from his face.

"Oh, did you think we didn't know that Pillin set this up?" She smiled. "Oh, yes, you must really think we're stupid."

"You are stupid to even talk to me." And, with that, Stuart turned and raced into the shadows. She headed over to the path where he had been walking. The animals turned around to see whether he'd really disappeared or not. However, she felt Stuart's gaze on the back of her head, knowing that he was watching her, waiting for her to leave.

She strolled up and down, making note of many names in her head and yet not exactly sure why. But, as she got closer and closer to where Stuart had been standing, she recognized something of importance, but she didn't stop. Instead she went to the end of the lane and then slowly walked past, glancing at both sides of the path, before mentally marking off one location in her head, counting tombstones to it, before slowly walking toward the exit.

As she left, she called out, "It's okay. It's all yours now, Stuart."

She couldn't hear whether he was there or not, but all of a sudden a stillness surrounded her. She laughed.

Besides, I already found it. She congratulated herself, and, with that, she took off.

Chapter 26

BACK HOME, DOREEN scrambled some eggs and had a piece of toast, as she sat here pondering what had happened. When Mack called a few moments later, she asked, "Hey, is this a social call?"

"Maybe. I just spoke to Pillin's lawyer."

"Oh, interesting. How did that go?"

"Pretty useless," he muttered, "but then we expected that, right?"

"Yeah, you need to look into the son, Stuart Burns," she suggested.

He froze. "Why?" he asked in frustration. "What's his son got to do with any of this?"

"I'm not exactly sure, but can you get the contents of Pillin's will released?"

"I need a warrant for it."

"I thought they became public after a while?"

"In this case, Burns has done something to stop that."

"Interesting," she murmured. "Well, something is in that will, and you probably want to keep an eye on it and the son too."

"What do you know about Stuart?" he asked, his voice

wary.

"I talked with him at the cemetery this morning. He's looking for another grave," she shared. "Been doing that for three days now, according to Dezy, and … the kid's pretty determined to get to it before anybody else."

Mack muttered a curse word. "Tell me exactly what happened."

She started with her conversation with Dezy and then continued to her conversation with Stuart. "The thing is, I'm not sure he knows exactly what he's looking for, but he knows there's something."

"Now the question is what."

"And does his father know anything about it? And, if his father does know anything about it, does the son, and does the father want his son involved?"

"And that's a lot of really good questions," Mack noted, "but I can tell you there won't be any answers from the father. He's already lawyered up, and we won't get anything out of him."

"You can't bring him in for questioning?"

"For what?" Mack asked. "A grave full of weapons?"

"Honestly, yes," she stated. "Surely that's a big enough issue to warrant an investigation."

"Absolutely is, if we connect the weapons to owners. And the captain's on it, but it's not that simple."

"It never is," she muttered. "But, if the father doesn't know anything, somebody does, and I think that somebody is the son."

"I'll talk to him."

"Good," she said, "and I think Dezy knows more than he's saying too. He also confirmed that he phoned in about where to check for the grave."

"I thought so," Mack confirmed. "I wish he hadn't done it anonymously."

"He was afraid it would get back to the gangs, and he was pretty upset that I knew too."

"Of course he was. When you do things anonymously, that's because you don't want anybody to know," Mack replied in exasperation.

She smiled. "Yeah, I get that, but it doesn't always work out that way, does it?"

"No, not when you're around," he noted, with a sigh.

She laughed. "Anyway, I did see something interesting, and I want to go back to the cemetery, but I figured that you probably want to go with me."

"Okay," he said cautiously. "You want to tell me why?"

"Because of one of the names I saw there," she shared. "I think we should go as soon as possible."

He muttered another curse word. "You want to go now?"

She looked down at her watch. "I just finished eating my scrambled eggs and toast, so I could."

"All right. I'll swing by and grab you."

"Good," she said, with a cheerful note. "The animals will be happy to get out again."

"You could leave them at home for once."

"No, I think in this case I'll take them with me."

He hesitated and then asked, "Did you have a problem with the attorney's son?"

She smiled. "Let's just say that Stuart has a problem with me."

Mack cursed again. "Okay, fine. I'll be there in about ten minutes." She ended the call, went back to the kitchen, and cleaned up the little bit of a mess she had made. As she got her shoes on again, she received a text from Nan.

Don't forget about Mack's birthday.

She stared at it and winced. Because, of course, she had forgotten about it. Matter of fact it was probably so close that she didn't have time anymore to do anything about it, not that she had any idea what to do in the first place.

She texted her grandmother. **When is it?**

And with that she got a reply. **One week.**

She stared at that and laughed. At least it wasn't in two days. But she had the animals leashed up and outside by the time Mack drove up. She hurried to his truck, loaded up the animals into the back seat, and, with, him at her side, they drove out of the cul-de-sac.

Chapter 27

As soon as Mack and Doreen drove into traffic, he asked, "What's this all about?"

"Maybe nothing," she muttered. "Now that I think about it, this could be a wasted trip." He frowned at her, and she shrugged. "Bear with me. … Are you off work?"

"I am at the moment, although I would classify this as work too," he noted, "particularly if you're involved." She glared at him, and he just smiled. "You do tend to make life interesting."

"I don't mean to be a problem though," she stated in a small voice.

"No, but you generally make things happen."

"Not sure that's a good thing either."

"It doesn't matter," he said. "We're too far gone to even worry about it at this point."

She wasn't exactly sure what that even meant, but figured that, as long as they were moving in one direction, they'd keep on moving.

As soon as they reached the cemetery, she got her animals out of the truck, leashed up and ready to go. "I'm not sure exactly how to get to where I was on foot or even if there's a way to drive closer, but it was up here." And she pointed on one of the big You Are Here maps nearby.

He nodded. "We can go on the side here." And, with that, he led the way up and around to the other section of the graveyard.

She smiled, as she and her animals got to walk now. "If nothing else, it's a beautiful time for a walk." He glanced at her and didn't say anything. "Well, it is," she muttered.

"If you say so."

She sighed. "Are you upset with me?"

"No, not at all," he replied. Yet gave her one of those long-suffering sighs that he did so well.

Hearing that, she stopped and glared at him. However, at the sight of his bright smile, she nodded. "Okay, good."

"Unless of course you've gotten yourself into a spot of trouble again."

"No, not at all," she stated, as they marched in the right direction. "It did feel as if Stuart was up to something."

"Is that what we're here for?"

She shrugged. "Maybe."

"Do I need backup?" he asked, with a note of humor.

"We've got backup," she declared and held up her dog leash.

He rolled his eyes at that. "*Great.*" Almost as if understanding what Mack had said, Mugs barked at him. Mack chuckled. "No, you're right, Mugs. You've done a heck of a job up until now. I'll take you as backup any day, buddy."

Mugs danced and pranced around Mack, not understanding the words but sure as heck understanding acceptance and love.

She smiled, as she walked closer to the area that she was looking for. "It really is beautiful out here." He gave her that sideways look. She groaned. "Besides, you haven't been getting any exercise lately." At that, his eyebrows shot up. She winced. "No, I'm not saying you need to exercise or anything else," she clarified, trying to backtrack.

He watched with interest as, instead of backtracking, she got herself further into trouble. Finally she fell quiet.

As they neared the spot, she grabbed his arm and pulled him back.

"What's the matter?" he asked in confusion.

She pointed. "There he is."

"And," Mack noted, watching the young man, "Stuart's allowed to be there."

"But what is he doing?"

Mack took a closer look at the man, and his eyebrows shot up. "What is he doing?"

"He's trying to lift the gravestone," she muttered.

Mack looked around. "You stay here." She glared at him. He gave her that hard warning look and said, "No. Stop. This isn't the time." And, with that, he quickly disappeared.

She looked down at Mugs. "See? We bring him all the action, and then he won't even let us partake," she muttered. "I'd go down there and ask Stuart exactly what he's doing." But, of course Mack was trying to be a whole lot more subtle. Although as Doreen watched Mack circle around the young man, she wasn't exactly sure how subtle that was.

When Mack came up casually alongside and called out to the man digging, Stuart stopped, frowned, straightened, and looked around. He saw Mack standing there, his hands on his hips, studying the young man carefully.

Stuart almost stuttered as he called out, "Hey, it was a little off-center. I was trying to fix it."

Mack studied him, without saying a word, and something about that look of Mack's made Stuart give another explanation, as if understanding no way Mack would accept what he had said earlier.

"Honest, I was trying to do a nice thing." And Stuart got up and tried to step back, but accidentally tripped and slipped down onto his knee. Swearing, he got up on his feet. "Besides, what is it to you anyway?" he asked, with some of his belligerence from earlier with Doreen returning.

Mack eyed him carefully. "I know who you are," he stated.

"That's nice. It's got nothing to do with anything."

"I wouldn't be so sure about that," Mack stated. "An awful lot of people keep an eye on this place."

"What do you mean, *keep an eye on it*?" Stuart asked, looking around, catching Mugs's movement, Pilling on Doreen. He glared. "You," he yelled at her.

She looked over at Mack, who glared at her as well. She shrugged, stepped forward, and asked, "What about me? I'm allowed to be here, if you are."

"You! You probably went and told somebody that I was here."

"You think too much of yourself, Stuart," she replied, with an airy wave of her hand. "What do I care if you are here? But now I'm curious about what you are doing."

"No, you're not curious. You are more than that."

She stared at him. "There's something more than that?"

"Yeah, you're a busybody."

She frowned at him. "I get a little upset with people who keep calling me that. It's not very nice."

"Nice? I'll give you nice," he muttered, taking a step toward her.

"I wouldn't do that if I were you," Mack stated in a conversational tone of voice.

Stuart turned and glared at him. "I don't know who you think you are, but the pair of you are a pain in my butt."

At that, Mack's eyebrows popped up. "Why? Because I'm standing here and asking you what you're doing?"

"Yeah, it's none of your business," Stuart snapped. "This grave was a friend of mine, and I'm fixing it up."

"If there's a problem with the stone, you're supposed to have somebody from the cemetery fix it."

"Yeah? And how long will that take?" he asked, with an eye roll. "Everybody here is so busy that nobody has any money or time to look after the graves," he complained. "Government contracts and all that BS."

"That's possible," Mack admitted, "but I highly doubt that what you're doing is anything to improve it."

"Says you," he argued, sticking his jaw out pugnaciously. "And it's got nothing to do with you anyway. If you're with her, you're even more of a problem."

At that, Mack stared at him. "You think so?"

"Yeah, I think so," Stuart declared. "You'll both get in trouble for this."

"Wow, more threats." Mack looked over at Doreen. "Is this the same guy who you were talking to earlier?"

She nodded. "Yeah, sure is. Stuart Burns. The lawyer's son."

Stuart turned and glowered at her. "*You* are nothing but trouble."

"Yeah, I've heard that a time or two as well." She nodded. "Still, I believe I understand what you're doing here." She walked closer and smiled when she saw the name on the headstone. "It is very, very interesting that you're looking into this grave."

"I am not looking into it," he snapped. "I was fixing it."

"And it's a friend of his apparently," Mack added, coming up beside her.

She pointed to the headstone. "Interesting name."

"What do you mean?" Stuart asked warily.

"Yeah, interesting name," Mack agreed, looking over at her. Yet his eyebrows were asking her what was interesting about it.

She smiled. "Obviously you guys know who this is, so I won't tell you. You'd get mad at me and make some comment about me being a busybody."

"You *are* a busybody, sticking your nose where it don't belong."

"Really? Seems you're the one sticking your nose where it doesn't belong," she declared. "You're trying to dig up a poor dead man's grave."

"I am not," Stuart cried out, looking around. "Don't say things like that out loud. People will get mad at me."

"Yeah, they sure will." Mack crossed his arms, as he studied the young man. "Probably for a lot of good reasons."

"You don't know anything about it," he snapped.

"Maybe, maybe not," Mack noted, "but you're sure giving me a lot of reasons to check into it further."

At that, Stuart frowned at him. "Why would you check into anything?" he asked in confusion.

At that, Doreen gave Stuart a fat smile. "Mack here is a cop, so there is that."

Thaddeus shouted, "Slow down, slow down, slow down." She tried to shush him up, but he was on a roll at the moment. He stared at her.

"You and those animals are disgusting."

At that, Mugs rumbled something deep in his throat and stepped forward, getting quite perturbed at Stuart's tone of voice.

She tried to calm him down. "It's all right, Mugs. Stuart didn't mean to insult you."

"Yes, I did," Stuart snapped. "You're all lunatics."

"I wouldn't say that," she argued, crossing her arms over her chest. "And I really, really don't like it when people treat me and my animals that way."

"Oh, back to that *ordering you around* thing? You don't like it when somebody tells you what to do?"

"No, I don't," she snapped. "And you're pissing me right off again."

Stuart snorted. "Like I care."

"No, you probably don't," she agreed, "and that's why you're here, trying to dig up a grave per the instructions that you've been given from Pillin's will."

The color drained from Stuart's face. "How do you know anything about that?"

"You think you're the only person who got that note?"

He stared at her. "What?"

"Yeah." She nodded. "So take that."

He stared, looked back at Mack. "Both of you? That's not fair. It was left to me," he cried out.

"And what will you do with it though, is the question," she stated in that tone of voice, almost of a confidante. "I mean, people could do lots with that."

"Of course but it's mine. It's not for you." And he looked as if he wanted to cry.

"Yes, it's tough growing up in that world," Doreen added, "where your dad's trying to tell you to stay away from anything to do with it. Yet that's how he made his money, isn't it?"

Stuart nodded. "He made a ton of money off the gangs."

"But he's also not old enough to die and to give it all to you yet, is he? And you don't want to wait for your inheritance, do you?"

"It was given to me," Stuart snapped, his expression morphing into an ugly look.

"At least part of it was. You had to figure the rest of it out though, didn't you?"

He nodded slowly. "So that means he's told other people too," he groused, his voice getting harder. "That means there will be more people …"

"He did something like that before, didn't he?"

"That was only within the actual gang itself though. I didn't think he'd do something like that when it was for me."

"Why, because you were his favorite?"

"I *was* his favorite," Stuart declared, almost ready to cry. "And I don't believe you. I don't think he left you anything."

"He may not have left me anything," Doreen acknowledged, "*but,* if I'm the first one to get it, well, of course, then it's mine."

"You can't have it," Stuart yelled, his face turning blotchy red, as he glared at her. He took a threatening step forward, and Mugs immediately backed up and then jumped forward against his leash, trying to get free. The angry young man stared down at the dog and then laughed. "Is that dog trying to protect you?"

"Yeah, I wouldn't laugh at him either," she shared. "That tends to upset him."

"You're pathetic," Stuart sneered.

"Yeah, so are you," she replied. "You are supposed to

make your own money in this world, not show up here, stealing dead people's stuff."

"They're dead. What do they care?" he asked. "Besides, what do you know about it?"

"I know a lot, at least I know enough to get into trouble," she replied, with half a smile.

"I think you always get into trouble," he guessed. "I can't imagine anybody trying to keep you out of trouble."

She glared at him. "Here we go with the insults again. I really don't need that right now."

The young man shook his head. "None of it matters anyway. He's gone. What difference does it make?"

"Well, Pillin's gone, but he's left a pretty twisted legacy behind, I presume," she replied.

"No, no, he hasn't." Stuart stared at her.

"But he had to leave it all to somebody."

"And did you know about the weapons?" Mack asked.

"No, of course I didn't know about the weapons," Stuart stated crossly. "If I did, I would have done something about them."

She nodded, looking over at Mack. "That makes perfect sense. I wondered why anybody would have left the gun stash there for so long."

"They left them there because they didn't know about them," Stuart snapped.

"And what would you have done with them?" she asked.

"Sold them to the highest bidder, but they are gone now." The young man glared at them and then shrugged, turning to leave. "Nothing to find here."

Mack asked, "So why were you digging?"

Stuart looked over at Doreen. "I didn't trust her not to come back, and obviously I was right."

"Yeah, and you didn't find anything?" Doreen asked.

The young man shook his head. "No, and that pisses me off even more."

"What did Pillin say in the will? I might help you sort it out."

He laughed at her. "If I can't figure it out, you really think you can?"

She nodded. "Yeah, sure do."

He glared at her. "You're too smarty-pants for your own good."

"I've heard that a time or two as well." She turned to Mack. "It's over to you now. I don't think defacing the grave is very much of a crime, at least not when something so much more serious is here."

"Nothing more serious at all," the angry young man declared, staring her down.

"No?" she asked Stuart. "You didn't get the guns, and you would have sold them if you could have, and I don't know that anybody—even outside of your dad—knew anything about it. Well, I mean, one other, two others, but other than that, I think they were sworn to secrecy."

"My dad didn't know anything about the weapons stash," Stuart declared.

"Sure, he did," she murmured. "He's the one who arranged the fake funeral to bury all those guns."

He stared at her and slowly shook his head. "No, no, he didn't."

She nodded equally slowly. "Yes, he did, and Pillin and the other person, who dug the grave and buried the heavy coffin at nighttime, away from prying eyes, knew too of course. But, for whatever reason—paybacks, fear, something—they left the gun stash where it was. And maybe it was a good thing to leave the guns there. Maybe because all kinds of incriminating evidence could hurt people and could hurt careers," she suggested. "And maybe that's why your dad doesn't want you digging up the rest."

"Doesn't matter what he wants. I can't stay in this hick town any longer."

Knowing that she was starting to get somewhere, she added, "And, of course, growing up in your dad's shadow, that wouldn't have been fun."

He stared at her. "You have no idea. Everything my father said and did was controlled by the gangs."

"Sure, but that was a long time ago," she noted. "Unless he's still active with the Vancouver ones."

"You never get out," Stuart replied, "never. If I want out, I need a payload of money."

"And do you really think that somebody else from the gangs isn't here, trying to do the same thing you are?"

He looked around nervously. "If that's the case, I wouldn't even be alive anymore."

Mack stepped forward. "You need to explain that," he said, his voice soft but with an edge to it. "Because, if any danger is here, we need to know about it."

"What do you guys care?" Stuart laughed. "The gangs have had the cops in their pockets for decades."

"There will always be one or two bad cops," she noted, "but that does not spoil the entire force."

"*Really?*" Stuart jeered in a scoffing tone. "You keep believing that, but, if anybody from those gangs still has any influence or knew about this cache of weapons, you can bet they'll all be up here in a heartbeat. And I don't want to be around when they find out."

"Find out what?" Mack asked.

He looked at him and laughed. "When they find out that some of them are missing."

"I don't know that any guns are missing," she stated, "Unless you think that somebody, one of the bad cops took something."

"No, but I'm pretty sure they all didn't go into that grave."

She pondered that for a moment and nodded. "Maybe that's what kept some people safe and clear all these years."

"Maybe," Stuart guessed. "I don't know, but there were more than weapons. I don't know if you guys found anything else or not, but more than just weapons were in that grave."

She looked over at Mack, who didn't even turn her way.

"What else was in there?" Mack asked Stuart.

"You think I will say anything? I don't even know what it is. I just know that something else is here, and I was looking for it. I thought for sure this would be it, but now I figure it must have been back in the original grave, and you guys missed it." The angry young man sneered at Mack. "And the grave is still open right now."

"And a big hole of nothingness," Mack declared.

Stuart added, "Maybe I'll go take another look." He glared at Mack. "But then you guys will take another look and will ruin it, like you do everything else."

Mack didn't say anything, giving Stuart a hard stare. When he finally looked over at Doreen, he asked her, "Do you know anything about it?"

"Nope," she admitted, "I don't, but it makes sense."

Mack shook his head. "Not a thing about this makes any sense."

"It all makes sense," she disagreed gently. "I'm not sure

anything else is in either of the graves. He's grasping at straws. I think he got a clue, but he doesn't know what to do about it. And he won't tell us, in case we'll be the ones who figure it out and take off with the prize." She looked back at Stuart. "Remember? Mack's a cop."

"Yeah, well, that's a guarantee he'll take off with it." Then Stuart scoffed.

She smiled. "I get it. You've had a pretty raw deal in some ways, and you're really hoping that this would be your ticket out of here. However, if the gang hears that you found this second stash, do you really think your life's worth anything?"

Stuart frowned at her. "Maybe I'll buy my way into the gang. I won't get accepted any other way."

She stared at him. "Is that what this is? Proving to Daddy that you can do it? Proving to Daddy that you've got what it takes to be part of this?"

He flushed. "No," Stuart yelled, "I don't care about proving anything to Daddy, so stop saying that."

She shrugged and looked at him. "Seems to me that there's an awful lot of *proving to Daddy* here."

At that, yelling erupted from the trees. "Don't you say another word," a man called out, as he limped his way to where the trio stood.

Mugs barked several times at him. The guy sent her a snake-like look and ordered, "Keep that dog in control, or I'll sue you for it."

"Oh, now I know who you are," Doreen replied. "You're the lawyer, Robbie Burns. The gang's pet. Father to Stuart."

Mack spoke up. "Were you aware your son's out here, defacing graves, trying to find the second stash to make his way out of this world, and apparently into your old world?"

Doreen added, "Your son wants to find acceptance with all your old cronies, by somehow solving this riddle."

Robbie glared at her, then at his son. "What are you doing here?" he snapped.

Stuart flushed and glared back at his father. "I'm allowed to be here. It's a public park."

He used the exact same phrase that Doreen had used on him earlier. She almost laughed out loud at that, but his father was having none of it.

"Get your butt home," Robbie snapped. "We'll talk later."

But Stuart shook his head. "Don't talk to me like that," he cried out.

Doreen felt sorry for him. She'd taken that kind of mental abuse all the time from Mathew, and she knew what it felt like. She turned to the lawyer and said, "You really should treat your son better."

He glared at her and asked, "Who are you anyway?"

"Somebody who cares," she replied, "which, obviously from your tone of voice, you don't."

He stared at her. "You don't know anything about me. You don't know anything about my son."

"Stuart is here trying to solve what happened to Pillin, not so much about how he died, but what he left behind," she explained. "Thinking that would be his ticket out of here or maybe his ticket into the gangs. If he solves the mystery, then you'll respect him—supposedly."

"He's not that stupid," Robbie snapped. He looked over at his son, saw the look on his face, and groaned. "Okay, so he is that stupid. Stuart, I told you that you don't want anything to do with the gangs. They would just as soon kill you as look at you."

"They have a code," Stuart cried out. "I can buy into it." When he saw his father's expression, he added, "Or I can take the money and run. I don't really care at this point. I want a life, and I don't want a life here."

Doreen faced him. "You can always try, … I don't know, for a job."

He glared at her. "You need to shut up."

She figured he probably had a right to say that, considering she didn't have a job either.

But his father was studying him. "You need to go home and stay out of this, before you say something that could get you into trouble."

"Too late for that," Doreen shared, with a laugh. "We already know everything at this point."

The lawyer stared at her in horror.

She shrugged. "What did you expect? Unhappy children want to make something of their lives, want to *be* something in life. They don't want to be pawns."

The attorney considered Mack, then turned to his son. "Please tell me, Stuart, that you didn't tell them anything."

"I didn't tell them anything," the son cried out.

Even his father couldn't find a way to believe his son, and Robbie sighed. "How much trouble is he in?" the lawyer asked Mack, probably sensing a cop standing before him.

Stuart turned to her, his bottom lip trembling.

She realized that the kid was now in a lot of trouble. "Stuart didn't tell us anything," she admitted.

The lawyer looked at her, back at his son, who shrugged.

She added, "Nothing important for now. His life is safe, as long as you give us a hand."

Robbie shook his head. "No way. The only way you stay alive in this is if you stay in."

"You can always get out. You're almost dead anyway," Doreen told the attorney, then winced. "I am sorry. I didn't mean that to sound as callous as it did."

Stuart frowned and asked her, "What are you talking about?"

"Your dad's obviously ill," she stated. "Didn't you notice?"

He turned to his father. "Dad?"

Robbie shrugged irritably. "It's nothing." He turned and gave Doreen a hard look. "Except for this snoopy busybody."

Mack stepped in at that point. "Yeah, she's all of those things, but she's also compassionate, full of heart, and has a really good head on her shoulders. So why don't you tell us what the heck's going on here, before we get overrun by gang members."

At that, the lawyer clammed his lips together as he studied the son. It was obvious he didn't know how much he'd revealed about how much they knew.

"I get it," Doreen stated. "There was a clue in either the will or something that Stuart received personally, and that clue would bring everybody up here."

At that Stuart turned and looked at her. "And you won't stop it."

"Is that what Pillin really wanted?" she asked Stuart.

But his father answered instead. "No, it's not what Pillin wanted at all. He wanted this over with. He wanted the weapons to be hidden forever, but somehow it was found out." He turned and gave Stuart a hard look.

She nodded. "That's what happens when you break into a mausoleum and not the grave."

Robbie's eyebrows raised, as he stared at his son, who flushed.

"It was you, wasn't it?" she asked Stuart. "You thought whatever was in there would lead to the riches that you're currently looking for."

Stuart stared at her. "How do you know this stuff?"

She gave him a small smile. "You'd be surprised."

He stared at her, then looked at his dad. "I didn't mean to deface it. I thought I'd open it. I came with tools, but it cracked and went to pieces. And there was something in it all right," he shared. "Bits and pieces of a gun but I didn't know that at the time, and then I heard two people talking, who came in out of nowhere, so I had no choice but to run. Now when I think about it, it was you two."

Mack looked at him. "You saw us there?"

"The animals are a dead giveaway, so if you were trying to steal everything," Stuart pointed out, "we know as much about your criminal activities as you know about ours."

She shook her head. "I'm so sorry." Doreen turned to Robbie. "I don't know if there's anything you can do."

"Not much," Robbie agreed, shaking his head.

"That's what happens when you keep secrets," Doreen noted. "They become bigger and bigger to the point that they have a life all their own. Pillin wanted this all to go away. He wanted the weapons out of commission, I presume."

Robbie nodded. "Yeah, it's not that Pillin had a change of mind, but he didn't like the leadership and the direction everything was going. So, after the big dustup in town, he was not in charge of the weapons. However, the gang wanted to ship them down to the coast. Pillin trusted one person, and they arranged to have everything buried instead."

"And so it went, the story of the lost cache. Apparently the vehicle was hijacked," Robbie shared, "and the weapons were never seen again."

"And nobody became suspicious?" Doreen asked the lawyer.

Robbie shook his head. "No, not until you guys opened up the grave. And now we fear the worst is about to happen. The gangs will all be here in a heartbeat, sorting it out, figuring out where the rest of the stash is."

"The rest of what?" Mack snapped.

Robbie turned to Mack. "Pillin also had the money, the loot—lots and lots of money, a lot of jewelry, a whole lot of stolen items to be fenced—which were supposed to go in the same truckload. All of it disappeared. The cops figured it was an inside job. And have been waiting for a break in the case.

"Trouble was, it was an inside job, but it was Pillin himself trying to take everything out of commission. He figured that, with the gangs being broken up, it was time. So, if he removed everything, then everybody would be free and clear, and they could go their own ways, and Pillin would get free of the gang too."

"Look at that," Doreen noted, "a gang member with a conscience."

Robbie glared at her. "You have no idea. He was a good man. He was a man in love."

"Yeah, he was probably a good man," Mack agreed, "but, just like you, there were decisions to be made."

The lawyer stiffened at that. "Nothing I can do," Robbie stated.

"Well, your life has already taken a turn for the worse. Is that what you want for your son?" Doreen asked the lawyer. He gave her a haunted look, and she nodded. "That's why you tried so hard to keep him out of it, isn't it?"

Robbie nodded slowly. "Once I knew what Pillin had

done, … I knew that there would always, always be eyes up here; but he didn't tell me at the time, so I made the arrangements for the midnight burial, not realizing what was going on here. And for that," the lawyer stated, "I'm sorry because I don't know what I would have done, but surely we could have come up with another solution."

"Maybe," Mack acknowledged, "but the problem is now, until we find the rest of that stolen loot, we'll have this town overrun with gang members."

Robbie gave a one-arm shrug. "It already is. The trouble is, they don't look like gang members anymore," he explained. "They are ordinary business people, and you won't know who stabs you in the back, not until it's too late."

Mack nodded slowly, his face grim. He looked over at Doreen and at Stuart. "And how will you protect your son?"

"I don't know if I can." Robbie gazed at his son with such sorrow that Doreen spoke up.

"We can help. Stuart's young. He deserves a second chance."

"I'm not that young," the man-child almost cried. "For God's sake, I'm thirty."

She stared at him. "You don't look it, and you sure don't act it."

The man-child glared, but the lawyer snapped, "She's right, you don't, and this stunt of yours has proven it."

"Not if I get all of the money," Stuart declared. "I can get out of town, and nobody will ever find me." He stared at his father.

Mack shook his head. "It doesn't work that way. It's not just getting out of town and getting away. There's so much more to it than that."

Robbie nodded at Mack. "You do understand."

"Sure, I've been a cop for a long time," Mack stated. "It would have been nice if I had some of that history to know where everything was hidden. Do you know where the second stash is?" he asked Robbie.

The lawyer shook his head. "No, it was all done in encrypted code, and the last was a riddle, and somehow it's supposed to make sense, but it never did to me. I racked my brain over it the whole time."

"I suppose then you would have taken the money yourself and run," his son called out.

Robbie glared back at Stuart. "I wouldn't have broken into the vault."

"I thought there might be more to the riddle," Stuart explained. "You told me a little about it when Pillin died and you got hammered, warning me that everything would break loose now. But not enough to solve it."

"Of course not. If it was that easy, I would have done so a long time. And I wouldn't have taken the haul and run. But I might have given it all back to the gang to have bought our freedom and silence," Robbie revealed. "I'm too old to fight now, and my history goes too far back with them, but you? You can have a life of your own, only if you keep your nose clean and get the heck out of here."

"I will," Stuart declared, "but I don't have any money."

Doreen glared at him. "You need a whole lot less money than you think you need to leave here. And if it came down to your life, you'll be just fine if you ran away now with nothing."

He stared at her. "Do you have any idea how much it costs to live?" he cried out.

She winced. "Yeah, I have a better idea than you might expect, and I know perfectly well how hard it is to start all over again."

Stuart shook his head. "I'm not doing it. Dad's got money, but he's still alive, and I won't get any of that for a long time."

"Oh, I think you'll get it a whole lot sooner than you think." She looked over at Robbie and asked, "What is it, six months, one year?"

He glared at her. "How the heck do you know that?"

"Because I can see the tremors," Doreen stated. "I can see how carefully you walked down that hill. I can see how much you're barely holding on and how much all of this is hurting you because your son is in trouble. Even though he's been a pain and somebody you struggled to keep in check all these years, you don't want to lose him. I can see that you love him and that you want him protected, and this will be your last chance."

"What's she talking about, Dad?" Stuart cried out, when his father wouldn't answer. The man-child looked at Mack.

Mack raised one eyebrow at the attorney, and Robbie nodded slowly. "Yeah, she's right, and I don't even know if I have that long."

She nodded. "Even if you did, it's pretty hard to get the maximum years that they give you. Sometimes you get to go way past it, but other times, when stress and worry and fear eats away at you? You end up with less time." She turned to look at the son. "Your dad is dying. He's got only a few months left to live."

Stuart stared at her and looked at his father and shook his head. "No, that's not possible."

But his father nodded and admitted, "Yeah it is. I've got cancer. I found it the hard way. And the treatment? Well, … I'm not doing any more treatments. I'm done. I've had a good life, a hard life, but one I was hoping to leave you free and clear of—and then you get into this? With Pillin's death, everything burst open," he said. "If Pillin had lived longer, it would have been so much easier. Even at that point, I would have been happy to have passed on my obligations to somebody else, so I could get free and clear too, but that won't happen now. I already know that some of them are in town, and, with the guns found, everybody is after that damn second cache."

Mack nodded. "And you don't know where it is, right?"

At that, Robbie shook his head. "No. I wish to God I did."

"So what's the riddle?" she asked.

He looked at her and then shrugged. "It doesn't matter if I tell you. Honestly you won't figure it out. Besides, it's not a riddle but something Pillin said."

"So tell me," Doreen said again. "I'm not stupid."

"I'm not either," Robbie replied, with a hard tone. "But Pillin had this thing for a woman, and it didn't make any sense back then, and it still doesn't make any sense now, but the only thing he would tell me is that she chose a serial killer over him."

Chapter 28

THE TUMBLERS IN Doreen's brain fell into place. She swallowed hard and murmured, "Interesting."

"See? It doesn't make any sense," Robbie stated.

Mack jumped in and asked, "Did he have a wife? Did he have kids, anything?"

"A girlfriend named Lucy, but that was a long time ago."

The name wasn't right, but Doreen already knew that. She didn't want to give anything away, as she looked at the surrounding area, wondering how she could do this covertly.

A shout came from behind them, and a shot rang out afterward. And just like that, the lawyer fell in front of them.

Before Doreen had a chance to say anything, Mack threw himself at her, dropping them both behind a vertical tombstone. Stuart was hiding behind another one. Mack peered around the corner of the gravestone. He had his phone out and was already calling for backup.

Doreen overhead him and frowned. "Do you really think they'll come in time?"

He stared at her. "They should."

"Okay, I'm good with that." She caught the lawyer trying to say something. She wobbled over on her elbows.

He whispered, "Pillin had one love and only one true love."

"Who was it?" Doreen asked.

Robbie shook his head, his breath coming in hard gasping tones. "He never told me, just something … about a serial killer."

She stared at him and whispered, "Did he name the serial killer?"

Robbie shook his head. "No, he didn't." With that, he took a deep breath, a sound that rattled up inside his chest.

Doreen watched as the life drained from his murky eyes.

Mack immediately pulled her backward, so she was hidden again behind the gravestone. She looked over to see Stuart, staring at his father's body, tears in his eyes. "What did he say?" Mack asked Doreen.

In a low voice she said, "I'll tell you later."

He sighed. "We should do something about you and this *getting into trouble* stuff all the time."

"I didn't do anything," she argued, looking at him.

She double-checked her animals. Thaddeus had crawled up tight against her neck, and Mugs was not terribly impressed with the gunfire, but he sat up against her, behind the gravestone. He was trembling, the noise upsetting him. She looked around for Goliath, and, when she couldn't see him, she murmured urgently, "Goliath's not here."

Mack looked around and pointed. Over there was Goliath, dragging his leash behind him, wandering between the gravestones. She was about to whistle for him, but Mack stopped her.

"Don't. We don't want anybody to find us here."

"Somebody already knows we're here," she muttered. "I can't have anybody going after Goliath."

Even then another shot was fired in the direction of the cat, and Goliath disappeared out of view.

"There," Mack said. "That should keep him out of sight."

She stared at Mack. "I don't think so. You don't understand Goliath."

He groaned. "And I can't have you getting hurt, even if it means Goliath getting hurt." She stared at him in horror. He wrapped an arm around her and held her close. "Look. We'll go after him, as soon as we get out of here."

At Mack's comment, she realized that all of them *would* get out of here, alive and well. She poked her head around the corner of the gravestone. "Doesn't seem anybody is still even here."

Another shot was fired, hitting the stone above her head. She let out a shriek. As she hit the ground again, Stuart yelled at her.

"Your cat's gone around behind whoever is shooting at us."

She stared at Mack. "Oh no, no, no, no. You don't understand. That's bad."

Stuart looked at her in confusion. "What?"

And, out of the woods, came a yelp and a scream. Mack was up on his feet and bolting to the trees. She stared from behind and then called out, "Goliath, Goliath, come," but the cat wasn't having anything to do with her. Mugs was now Pilling on his leash, trying to get free too. She tried to hold him back.

Stuart looked at her and asked, "What is with those animals?"

She glared at him. "You have no idea." And then the leash broke, and Mugs took off. Doreen was up on her feet as fast as lightning and raced behind him. “Goliath, come to me. And get back here, Mugs,” she cried out. Even Thaddeus at her shoulder squawked. She groaned. “This is not the time.”

At that, another shot rang out, but it wasn’t heading toward her. Terrified that the shooter was after Mugs or after Goliath, she raced to the trees up ahead from Mack.

He glared at her.

She frowned. “Hey, I won’t let anybody hurt any of mine.”

He shook his head. “This is *not* the time.”

And she could tell he was mad. Of course he was mad. She had, once again, disobeyed his orders. Now, as she stood here, figuring out what to do next, something was pressed against her back. It was hard and cold.

“Well, look who’s here,” he said. “What the heck are you doing?”

She turned and said, “Mathew?”

Chapter 29

DOREEN STARED AT her ex-husband in shock. "What are you doing here?" she cried out. "Don't you know it's dangerous?"

He stared at her and then shook his head. "Good God." He caught Mack staring at him, with a thunderous expression on his face, but Mathew ignored him. "Oh, I heard about the money. Everybody's heard about that. At least everybody with any connections. So I figured I would come up and see what all the fuss was about. See for myself if you'd had any luck with it, and, of course, you're right smack in the middle of this chaos."

"But you're the one pointing the gun at me," she snapped, glaring at him.

He pocketed the gun. "I'm not coming up to a place like this without one."

She asked him, "Were you firing those shots?"

He shook his head. "No, the shooter is off to the side over there." He pointed to the trees on the right. "I'm not trying to kill you."

She studied him, then added, "But, if you did kill me, all your troubles would be over, wouldn't they?" He gave her such an innocent smile that she was immediately suspicious.

"Good Lord," Mack yelled. "When did you arrive?"

"I came up in the first flight. You were probably too busy to check." He gave him a cocky grin.

"Yeah, that could be," Mack snarled. "What are you doing with these guys?"

"Anybody who does deals, as I do …" he said, with that knowing smile of his, "you get to know people."

She asked him, "You deal with this gang lawyer?"

"No, I don't know anything about the lawyer here," Mathew replied, "but I do property deals with some people down on the coast."

"So how did you hear?"

"The grapevine is buzzing, how a group was coming to look for a stash of stolen cash, jewelry, and other valuables. And I wouldn't sit back and do nothing, not when I need a chunk of money to pay you off," he muttered in disgust.

She stared at him, not sure if she believed him or not. Something was going on in the back of his brain.

Then he shared sweetly, "But you did have a good point."

She winced. "Meaning?"

"If something happens to you up here, during all this, then that makes my life easier, doesn't it?" he repeated, with a sick smile.

She glared at him. "And, of course, you don't want to be the one who kills me yourself, right?"

"I wouldn't mind," he noted in a conversational tone. "There would be a sense of satisfaction in doing that. But, no, I'm not signing up for that because I won't spend twenty years in jail."

"Glad to hear that," she replied, "not that it makes me

feel any better."

He chuckled. "That's your problem. Anything you're doing here, this is all on you. It's got nothing to do with me."

"And you won't help me get out of here either, will you?" she accused.

He gave her a lazy smile. "No, I'll see you later—if you're still alive." And, with that, he turned and disappeared into the trees. She looked back at Mack, who was staring at her with a grim look on his face. She told him what Mathew had just said. "It really would suit Mathew if I didn't make it out of this," she murmured. "Then he would be free."

"Yeah, it sure would." Mack rubbed his face.

"How did this get so complicated?" she asked in bewilderment.

"I don't know," Mack admitted.

"I came to show you the name on the grave."

In the distance sirens sounded. "Good," Mack said. "We can get out of this now."

"This time," Doreen noted, "and yet what's to stop them from coming back?"

"Oh, they'll be back."

"I only heard one shooter though," she murmured. "Did you hear any more?"

He shook his head. "No, I just heard the one."

"And do you really think it wasn't Mathew?"

"No, I don't think it was Mathew," Mack confirmed. "The gun sounded heavier than the one he had."

Then another shot rang out, and she winced. "That's not cool," she snapped, and, before they realized—amid the commotion of sirens, shouts, and shots—somebody stood in front of them, holding a gun on them.

"Well, well, well," the gunman said, "this is the person I'm looking for."

She stared at him, shook her head, and stated, "I don't even know you."

"Nope, you don't," he agreed, "but I paid good money in order to find out all about you. You are the one who solves all these mysteries, aren't you?"

She nodded slowly and then realized this was some gang member, here to claim the stash as all his. "I'm really sorry, but you made the trip for nothing."

"I don't think so," he disagreed. "You and I, we need to talk."

She sighed. "Meaning that you'll shoot me if I don't tell you what you want to know?"

"Or I'll shoot that guy standing beside you," he said, with a laugh. "I don't mind either way."

"I'm getting really tired of people telling me what to do, and I'm getting *really* tired of people shoving guns in my face." She took a step toward him. Immediately the gun came up, and Mack tried to grab her and pull her back. She shrugged off Mack and looked at the gunman. "I'm not telling you anything," she snapped. "Absolutely not telling you and your friends out there."

"No, no friend of mine is here. I came alone."

"Is that you who's been shooting everywhere?"

"Yeah, sure is."

"Did you shoot my dog?" she asked, her eyes wide.

"Is that the dog running around here with a leash?"

"Yeah," she snapped, "that's mine."

"You really should take better care of your animals," he said, staring at her. "The terrible way people treat animals makes me angry."

"You're angry? Does that mean you didn't shoot him?"

she asked hopefully. And there in the distance she heard Mugs barking.

"No, I didn't. He was chasing a cat though." And he laughed at that. "Such a classic."

She groaned and then whistled. "Mugs, come back here."

"You think he'll come at that?" the gunman asked with a smile. "Maybe then I'll shoot the dog to keep you in order."

"You think so?" she asked, with a smirk. In the distance, she saw both Goliath and Mugs racing down the hill toward her. "On the other hand," she shared with a deceptive smile, "both of them might surprise you."

"Yeah, I doubt it," the gunman stated, "and you're just looking for a way to distract me."

She smiled. "Why would I need to distract you?"

"Because otherwise I might shoot you." And then he chuckled. "Besides, once Pillin was gone, he knew that this would happen. Everybody would come out of the woodwork. Pillin was the only one who could have done this, but nobody wanted to brace him. It was a certain death sentence. He was a force unto himself. Nobody could believe it when that cache of guns was found."

"Especially in his grave?"

"Dang, that was smart on his part and not good for us." His smile twisted, as he slowly raised the gun, "Now tell me where the loot is at."

"I have no idea," she declared.

He smiled, turned the gun toward Mack, and, as he did, Mugs took a flying leap, sinking his teeth into the gunman's hand, as Goliath jumped on the gunman's back. The gunman cried out and crumpled to his knees and went down, the gun firing harmlessly into the ground.

And Mack was all over him in a flash.

Chapter 30

DOREEN SAT, HER arms wrapped around her knees, all the animals curled up close and tight, and even Stuart sat beside her, the goings-on around them putting them in shock.

"Jesus," Stuart finally said. "Is it always this crazy in your life?"

She beamed a smile at him. "Yeah, unfortunately it is."

"Well, I'm giving up on the idea of detective work then," he admitted. "Honestly I don't know what I want to do. I wanted to feel as if I had some purpose. As if I wasn't a failure."

"I'm really not the best person for that discussion because it's one of the reasons why I do what I do. I want to help people," she shared, "and it's hard. Sometimes it's *really* hard. Sometimes you think what you're doing is a help, and the rest of the time it's not."

"Is he angry at you?" Stuart asked, motioning at Mack, who was studiously ignoring her.

"Yeah, I'm sure he is," she said. "He usually is."

"Are you guys an item or something?"

She looked over at Mack and laughed. "Yeah, or something."

Mack had obviously heard because he turned, considered her words, and then smiled, going back to what he was doing.

"He doesn't look like he's all that mad at you now," Stuart noted.

"He's mad because I put myself in jeopardy again," she explained, keeping her eye on Mack's back. "He's mad because I tried to save him, and he's mad because I always end up in situations like this."

"You've been shot at before?" Stuart asked.

"A couple times," she confirmed, with a nod, "and, of course, he has too."

"Wow, sounds as if you guys need each other."

"Maybe," she murmured. "You could be right on that point." After a moment, she faced him. "And you. What are the changes you will make now that your father's gone? Now that you don't need to leave to prove you can?"

"I don't know," Stuart replied sadly. "I didn't know about him being sick. I wish I'd known."

"Well, now you do," she pointed out, "so you can understand some of what he was trying to do, what he was trying to save you from."

"But why couldn't he have just said so?"

"I think he was afraid that maybe his place was bugged or somebody would find out, or possibly he knew it would be a major problem, once that gun cache was found," she suggested. "So I think he was doing everything he could to be a good father and to keep you safe."

Stuart sighed. "And now I don't even know what happens to his stuff."

"The law practice is a whole different story," she noted,

"but, with any luck, you'd inherit at least his personal assets."

"I hope so," Stuart said, "but I feel as if I don't deserve it."

"I don't think you're the only person who's ever felt that way either," she acknowledged. "It'll take a bit to sort out your life now, but maybe make better decisions after that, *huh?*"

He stared at her and nodded slowly. "Yeah, I think I will," he muttered. "At least I won't be trying to get away quite so hard anymore." He stared out at his father's body, still nearby. "It seems wrong to leave him lying here like this."

"It is, but it's up to the cops and the coroner to deal with this now," she told him. "It's a murder scene."

Stuart winced. "In a way my dad might have preferred this."

"Absolutely he would have," she agreed, with a smile. "He was heading for a very painful end of life with his cancer," she murmured. "This way he got to go out in a blaze of glory. I'm pretty sure that's every guy's favorite wish."

Stuart cracked a smile at that. "I think that's quite true, and, for that, I'm grateful." He looked over at her. "Thank you."

"Thank me for what?"

"I don't know," Stuart answered honestly, "but somehow I feel as if you turned this around."

She laughed. "I don't know about that. I *really* don't know about that, but … I'm sorry you lost your dad. Still, it could have been so much worse today."

"Yeah, and, if you were my girlfriend—which you're obviously too old," he said, with a wave of his hand, "but I wouldn't be very happy if you continued to put yourself into situations like this either."

She stared at him dumbfounded, as he got up on his feet.

"I need to take a walk, and I'll talk to you in a bit. And, no, I won't go too far way, and, yes, I know I should answer questions and give a statement." With that, Stuart turned and headed off.

Mack sat down beside her. "So you're too old for Stuart, *huh?*" he asked, with a snicker.

She smiled at him. "Besides, I'm already taken."

He looked at her, then nodded, and, with a note of satisfaction, declared, "You absolutely are." He wrapped his arms around her and pulled her up for a hug. Mugs jumped up to greet him.

"Did you know that's what your animals were doing?" Mack asked. "That they were coming down that hill to attack our gunman?"

"I saw them coming"—she nodded—"but you never know what they're up to. So, as much as I'd like to say that I had an idea, I truly didn't know what they were up to."

"That makes me feel better," Mack stated, "because sometimes you're a little too uncanny in the things that you get involved in. And sometimes I wonder how much you do know."

"Not very much," she said, "and certainly not as much as I should." He frowned at her, and she shrugged. "Seems there's more to know every time I turn around."

He nodded. "So we should find where that second stash is," Mack noted, "and that'll be the only way to stop the gold-rush hunters. Once it's been taken into police custody, the gang members will stop looking for it."

She nodded and looked around to see the captain even now joining everybody else—the coroner was here, and various other police officers were huddled about—trying to figure out what was next.

The captain walked over and asked Doreen, "Are you okay?"

She smiled and nodded. "Yeah, I am, thanks to Mack here. He threw me behind the gravestone."

Mack rolled his eyes at that. "Yeah, that was about the only thing I could think of to keep you safe."

"It worked," she said cheerfully. She looked up at the captain and asked, "Did you guys bring shovels?"

He frowned at her. "No. Do we need them?"

She nodded. "If you want to bring up that second stash so that nobody else comes after it anymore, then, yeah, we'll need shovels." She looked at him apologetically. "I could do it myself, but it would take me forever."

He let out his breath and asked, "I suppose you know where it is too, don't you?"

She gave him a small smile. "Maybe."

He nodded. "Give me five." And he disappeared.

Mack turned to her and asked, "Seriously?"

She shrugged. "Maybe, of course until it happens, I don't really know, but I think so."

"Will you tell me?"

She sighed. "I don't know whether it'll upset you or not."

He stared at her. "Why would it upset me?"

She burst out laughing. "Because it's a little too easy. If this was supposed to be difficult, I don't know in what way it was."

He stared at her in shock. "What do you mean?"

She pointed. "Come here." And, with that, she walked past several more gravestones and then stopped, and the captain joined them quickly afterward, plus several cops with shovels. She nodded. "This is the one that Stuart was working on."

"Why this one?" the captain asked.

"Because Pillin had a lady friend in his life by the name of Lucy," she explained, "and this person's name is Lucy."

The captain stepped back and said, "Okay, let's dig this up."

"It won't be here," Doreen said.

He stopped, looked at her, and frowned, "But …"

She shook her head. "Stuart was trying to dig in here, and he flipped the headstone and took a look, but it's not here."

At that, Stuart joined them. "That's right. I thought it would have been here too. It's close to where Pillin had paid for a second grave. Then, according to some old records I dug up of my father's, he let that spot go and found a new one. Are you saying this isn't the right spot?"

She shook her head, moved over three gravestones, and stated, "It'll be here."

At that, all three of the men walked over, took a look, and Mack whistled. "Good Lord, somehow you managed to connect this and bring it right back around."

She nodded. "And there's somebody else we should talk to again," she added, "but, for right now, for this moment, this is where your second stash is." And, as one, they all looked down at the gravestone.

The captain read the name out loud. "Maxine Small."

Doreen looked back at Mack to see if he understood.

"*Small*? This has something to do with Bob Small?"

Mack asked.

"Yep, Bob Small, the serial killer, boyfriend of ..."

"Ella Hickman?" He stared at the grave, back at Doreen, confused.

"Ella *Maxine* Hickman," she clarified, with a bright smile.

He closed his eyes in understanding. "So, whether legally married or not, in Bob Small's mind, Ella Hickman was Ella Maxine Small. Got it."

Seeing a sea of confused faces around her, she explained further, "Ella Maxine Hickman was one of two of Bob Small's girlfriends, and apparently, according to what we've heard, she may have also been the love of Pillin's life. Not to mention Ella told me something about her only choosing bad boys in life. Two of them in fact."

The captain looked at her, then frowned at the gravestone, and finally turned to the uniformed cops standing behind him and barked, "What the heck you waiting for? Let's go."

She stepped back at their request, and, with the animals and Stuart at her side, it took only a few minutes before she heard a hard *click*.

The captain looked at her, but she shrugged, while the cops peeled back the grass and the dirt. They lifted up a metal plate and sure enough underneath were metal boxes and more metal boxes. Most were closed, but a few showed deterioration from time and Mother Nature.

Slowly bringing up the metal boxes to stack around the grave, the captain pried open the first, then several others. Whistles of shock and astonishment filled the air. She leaned over to see the metal boxes were filled with silver, jewelry, and cash, plus a huge collection of gold coins. And that's just what she could see of a few open boxes. She grinned and held up her hand, the captain gloating at her side, who then high five'd her back. Cheers broke out.

Stuart beside her whistled. "Good God, I was so damn close."

Mack looked at him and nodded. "Yeah, welcome to my life, so damn close and yet so far away." He looked over at Doreen and grinned. She wasn't sure how he meant it, but she glared at him for good measure. He chuckled. "She's got a brain that none of us really understands," he admitted, with a shake of his head. "But well done, Doreen, well done."

The captain gave her a big fat grin and said, "You know something?"

"What?" she asked, looking at him.

"I think there's a reward or a least a finder's fee for recovering all this. In fact some of these pieces likely have rewards for their safe return. You, my dear, are about to get another payday."

She looked at him in delight, and then she crowed, "Does that mean I get to eat for another month?"

He burst out laughing. "I think by the time we're done with all this, you can eat for the rest of your life."

She threw her arms around him and gave him a very big hug. "Now that sounds perfect for once."

He added, trying to make it as clear as possible, "But it'll take time."

She rolled her eyes. "Yeah, doesn't everything," she muttered. But she stepped back again, as everybody hauled out the hoard. And she grinned, as she faced Stuart. "You might have thought that you could deal with this, but you wouldn't have had a clue how to. It's much better that law enforcement handles it all, so no one gets killed."

He nodded slowly. "Still, to know that I was so close."

She smiled. "*Close* only counts in horseshoes and hand grenades," she murmured.

He looked at her and added, "And in love."

"Only if it's the right ending," she noted. "Otherwise it can be painful." She looked down at Pillin's stash and felt sorry for him. A man who spent the end of his life hiding things and trying to do right, and yet, at the same time, never found the same peace and joy in his own life that he'd wanted for the world.

Epilogue

THE NEXT DAY, Doreen was lying by the creek, a cup of tea and a mystery book in her hand, dozing, resting, dozing, until Mugs barked. She looked up to see Mack coming toward her, a big box of pizza in his hand. She beamed as she recognized the crest of the eatery, one of her favorites.

He chuckled. "I didn't call to say I was bringing dinner, in case maybe you were still resting."

"I am, been here most of the day …" She motioned at the creek that trickled gently beside her.

"It is a beautiful place," he noted, as he sat down and opened the box, offering her a piece.

She frowned. "Do you eat anything other than pizza when you're busy?"

He nodded. "I do, but this is fast, easy, and it holds me."

"Right. Well, I won't argue because you brought it."

"Good thing," he said, then gave her a grin. "Everybody was so curious about this find that all our officers—even those off duty—worked in shifts, straight through yesterday, all night, and throughout today. So everything's already been itemized and set up in a locker," he noted. "They'll do a big press release, and the captain wants you to attend."

She rolled her eyes at that. "I can attend, just keep me out of the news."

He burst out laughing at that. "I think that's a little hard to do at this point. Of course the press was there soon after its discovery, so they already know that you're involved."

She smiled. "That's why I'm at the back of the house because the Japanese tour buses had come by with some extra runs, starting yesterday." She sighed. "Richard's barely even talking to me."

"That may be a blessing in disguise," Mack noted, with a chuckle.

"Yeah, I don't know. I may need a secret way in and out of my house now."

Mack frowned and asked, "Is it that bad?"

She shrugged. "It is, but whatever. It's all good."

"What about Stuart?"

She nodded. "I talked to him several times."

"Good. What about?"

"Well, now that he has some money coming to him, he's thinking about maybe going back to school."

"Oh, wow, that's not what I expected."

"No, but I think he's starting to understand how much that job and criminal lifestyle crippled his father."

"And that's a good thing," Mack agreed. "At least if he understands that, Stuart can do something better for himself."

"I think he will. At least I think he is trying hard to find a way forward. Losing his dad suddenly like that was hard."

"Of course it was, but he's done pretty well."

"He has, indeed," she murmured.

"Grab a piece of pizza."

She snatched a slice of pizza, sat up, and washed it down with water from her bottle. "And has work calmed down for you now?" When he glared at her, she apologized. "I know. It's my fault again."

"No, not in this case," Mack explained, "we needed to find that second hoard before everybody looted the graveyard. The fact that you found it is really no surprise."

"I think you would have found it too, if you'd gotten that far," she said, "but it was fun to see it uncovered. Buried treasures are everybody's childhood dream."

He chuckled. "It is, indeed, and it's still the talk of the cop shop."

"And will be for a while," she noted, with a smile, and he nodded. She added, "As long as no other cases come to light, you should be doing okay now."

"We were doing fine *before* this case," he stated, giving her a hard look. "It's just *somebody* keeps giving us more cases. Including one of an ex-husband who pulled a gun on someone—namely you."

She winced. "True I suppose, and I'm sure all those cases are a pain, but just think—between all the guns and now the loot—how many cases you guys could solve."

"Oh, don't worry. The captain's gloating all over that." Mack let out a big belly laugh. "He did say something about making sure that I treat you right, so that you never leave town."

She looked at him and then started to chuckle. "That's nice for a change. I figured he would offer you a bribe to get me out of town, so that you guys wouldn't work so hard."

He laughed even harder at that. "No, it's all good. And the fact that you've taken off a day or two and rested," he noted, "that's seriously good news."

"Of course I haven't done much of anything. That Mathew returned home without contacting me is even better. I could actually relax."

"And you only took these couple days off because Ella Hickman is away on a trip, isn't that right?"

She nodded. "I'll talk to her when she gets back."

"The police want to talk to her too. She's coming back today."

"Right, well, that would be good," Doreen noted. "More things to tie up."

"But you're hoping for more information on Bob Small, aren't you?"

"Yeah, sure am." Doreen smiled. "I won't rest until that one's dealt with."

He winced and nodded slowly. "It won't be an easy thing to deal with though, right?"

"I know," she murmured. "I was hoping it would be easier, but I don't think it will be."

"No, probably not, but still I trust that you'll take whatever precautions you can take and do a decent job."

She leaned over, kissed him gently on his cheek, and said, "Thanks for the vote of confidence."

He grinned, kissed her on the lips, and murmured, "You're welcome."

"And you're sure there are no other cases now?" she asked. "I could use something easy."

"*Easy*?" he repeated. "If that were the case, we would have solved them already."

"Good point," she muttered.

"But, no, I don't think there will be anything for a while," Mack guessed. "You rattled up this town pretty well."

She glared at him.

But he just grinned, then his phone went off. He sighed as he looked down at it and then answered. "Yeah, Cap. What's up? … Yeah, I'm sitting here, having some pizza with her. … Okay, I'll tell her. … Yeah, I'm coming." He got up, frowned.

"*Uh-oh*, what's the matter?" she asked.

He sighed. "Let's just say, things will get more difficult now."

"Why is that?" she asked, standing up with him.

"Because they found a body at the airport."

"A body?"

He nodded.

"At the airport?" she asked, her voice rising.

He nodded again.

She shook her head. "Please, not Ella."

He nodded again. "It's Ella. She was found in a patch of violets in the front of the airport, in one of the big garden beds, waiting for her ride."

She stared at him in shock. "Oh no," she whispered, somewhat sad and a whole lot of angry because all her dreams of getting answers on her Bob Small file were flying out the window. "Poor Nelly." The thought brought tears to Doreen's eyes.

"Stay here," he said, his tone grim. "I'll let you know what I can, when I can." And, with that, he strolled toward the kitchen.

She sank back down onto the ground, and then it hit her. "Violets." That was *V*. She snickered. She called out to Mack, "Are you still there?"

But there was no answer.

She picked up her phone and called him. "You did say

violets, right?"

"Yeah, I did. Why?" he asked.

She heard his engine start, as he got into his vehicle. "How about *Vanquish*?" she asked. "How does *Vanquished in the Violets* sound?"

He snorted. "I think you're grasping at straws."

"Nope, I don't think so," she stated. "However, *victim* is better. *Victim* is perfect."

"No," Mack declared, "not at all because this is my case, not a cold case."

"Ah," she argued, "but it'll be connected to one of the biggest cold cases you ever saw."

He groaned. "Fine, *Victim in the Violets* it is." And then he chuckled and added, "That's a good one." He ended the call, still laughing.

She put down her phone and laughed out loud. She reached over, gave Mugs a big hug, snatched Goliath and danced around with him in her arms, and then scooped up Thaddeus and plunked him on her shoulder. "We have another case," she exclaimed, noting the pizza Mack had left behind.

"Pizza *and* a case," she proudly proclaimed. "All we need now is coffee." And she raced into the kitchen to put it on.

Life is good. Life is very good.

This concludes Book 21 of Lovely Lethal Gardens:
Uzi in the Urn.

Read about Victim in the Violets: Lovely Lethal Gardens,
Book 22

Lovely Lethal Gardens: Victim in the Violets (Book #22)

Riches to rags. ... Old cases never die. ... Love spans decades, ... even if unrequited!

With her estranged husband still pestering her, Doreen is looking for a new case to keep her interest and to help her dodge Mack and his brother's scoldings. So she decides to delve deeper into the Bob Small case, especially since it pertains to Nan's now-deceased friend.

Only to have the case suddenly connect to a current friend and Rosemoor resident. When this woman's sister ends up murdered, and there's a connection to Bob Small, Doreen and her animals are off on the trail, ... much to Corporal Mack Moreau's disgust.

Anything to do with Bob Small is big. He was linked to dozens of unsolved murder cases, and no way will Doreen do anything private on this case. However, even she isn't prepared for the ending that suddenly shows up—with gun in hand and a story for the ages …

Find Book 22 here!

To find out more visit Dale Mayer's website.

https://geni.us/DMSVictim

Get Your Free Book Now!

Have you met Charmin Marvin?

If you're ready for a new world to explore, and love ill-mannered cats, I have a series that might be your next binge read. It's called Broken Protocols, and it's a series that takes you through time-travel, mysteries, romance… and a talking cat named Charmin Marvin.

Go here and tell me where to send it!
https://dl.bookfunnel.com/s3ds5a0w8n

Author's Note

Thank you for reading Uzi in the Urn: Lovely Lethal Gardens, Book 21! If you enjoyed the book, please take a moment and leave a short review.

Dear reader,

I love to hear from readers, and you can contact me at my website: www.dalemayer.com or at my Facebook author page. To be informed of new releases and special offers, sign up for my newsletter or follow me on BookBub. And if you are interested in joining Dale Mayer's Reader Group, here is the Facebook sign up page.
http://geni.us/DaleMayerFBGroup

Cheers,
Dale Mayer

About the Author

Dale Mayer is a *USA Today* best-selling author, best known for her SEALs military romances, her Psychic Visions series, and her Lovely Lethal Garden cozy series. Her contemporary romances are raw and full of passion and emotion (Broken But … Mending, Hathaway House series). Her thrillers will keep you guessing (Kate Morgan, By Death series), and her romantic comedies will keep you giggling (*It's a Dog's Life*, a stand-alone novella; and the Broken Protocols series, starring Charming Marvin, the cat).

Dale honors the stories that come to her—and some of them are crazy, break all the rules and cross multiple genres!

To go with her fiction, she also writes nonfiction in many different fields, with books available on résumé writing, companion gardening, and the US mortgage system. All her books are available in print and ebook format.

Connect with Dale Mayer Online

Dale's Website – www.dalemayer.com

Twitter – @DaleMayer

Facebook Page – geni.us/DaleMayerFBFanPage

Facebook Group – geni.us/DaleMayerFBGroup

BookBub – geni.us/DaleMayerBookbub

Instagram – geni.us/DaleMayerInstagram

Goodreads – geni.us/DaleMayerGoodreads

Newsletter – geni.us/DaleNews

Also by Dale Mayer

Published Adult Books:

Shadow Recon

Magnus, Book 1

Rogan, Book 2

Egan, Book 3

Bullard's Battle

Ryland's Reach, Book 1

Cain's Cross, Book 2

Eton's Escape, Book 3

Garret's Gambit, Book 4

Kano's Keep, Book 5

Fallon's Flaw, Book 6

Quinn's Quest, Book 7

Bullard's Beauty, Book 8

Bullard's Best, Book 9

Bullard's Battle, Books 1–2

Bullard's Battle, Books 3–4

Bullard's Battle, Books 5–6

Bullard's Battle, Books 7–8

Terkel's Team

Damon's Deal, Book 1

Wade's War, Book 2

Gage's Goal, Book 3

Calum's Contact, Book 4
Rick's Road, Book 5
Scott's Summit, Book 6
Brody's Beast, Book 7
Terkel's Twist, Book 8
Terkel's Triumph, Book 9

Terkel's Guardian

Radar, Book 1

Kate Morgan

Simon Says… Hide, Book 1
Simon Says… Jump, Book 2
Simon Says… Ride, Book 3
Simon Says… Scream, Book 4
Simon Says… Run, Book 5
Simon Says… Walk, Book 6
Simon Says… Forgive, Book 7

Hathaway House

Aaron, Book 1
Brock, Book 2
Cole, Book 3
Denton, Book 4
Elliot, Book 5
Finn, Book 6
Gregory, Book 7
Heath, Book 8
Iain, Book 9
Jaden, Book 10
Keith, Book 11
Lance, Book 12

Melissa, Book 13
Nash, Book 14
Owen, Book 15
Percy, Book 16
Quinton, Book 17
Ryatt, Book 18
Spencer, Book 19
Timothy, Book 20
Hathaway House, Books 1–3
Hathaway House, Books 4–6
Hathaway House, Books 7–9

The K9 Files

Ethan, Book 1
Pierce, Book 2
Zane, Book 3
Blaze, Book 4
Lucas, Book 5
Parker, Book 6
Carter, Book 7
Weston, Book 8
Greyson, Book 9
Rowan, Book 10
Caleb, Book 11
Kurt, Book 12
Tucker, Book 13
Harley, Book 14
Kyron, Book 15
Jenner, Book 16
Rhys, Book 17
Landon, Book 18
Harper, Book 19

Kascius, Book 20
The K9 Files, Books 1–2
The K9 Files, Books 3–4
The K9 Files, Books 5–6
The K9 Files, Books 7–8
The K9 Files, Books 9–10
The K9 Files, Books 11–12

Lovely Lethal Gardens

Arsenic in the Azaleas, Book 1
Bones in the Begonias, Book 2
Corpse in the Carnations, Book 3
Daggers in the Dahlias, Book 4
Evidence in the Echinacea, Book 5
Footprints in the Ferns, Book 6
Gun in the Gardenias, Book 7
Handcuffs in the Heather, Book 8
Ice Pick in the Ivy, Book 9
Jewels in the Juniper, Book 10
Killer in the Kiwis, Book 11
Lifeless in the Lilies, Book 12
Murder in the Marigolds, Book 13
Nabbed in the Nasturtiums, Book 14
Offed in the Orchids, Book 15
Poison in the Pansies, Book 16
Quarry in the Quince, Book 17
Revenge in the Roses, Book 18
Silenced in the Sunflowers, Book 19
Toes up in the Tulips, Book 20
Uzi in the Urn, Book 21
Victim in the Violets, Book 22
Lovely Lethal Gardens, Books 1–2

Lovely Lethal Gardens, Books 3–4
Lovely Lethal Gardens, Books 5–6
Lovely Lethal Gardens, Books 7–8
Lovely Lethal Gardens, Books 9–10

Psychic Visions Series

Tuesday's Child
Hide 'n Go Seek
Maddy's Floor
Garden of Sorrow
Knock Knock…
Rare Find
Eyes to the Soul
Now You See Her
Shattered
Into the Abyss
Seeds of Malice
Eye of the Falcon
Itsy-Bitsy Spider
Unmasked
Deep Beneath
From the Ashes
Stroke of Death
Ice Maiden
Snap, Crackle…
What If…
Talking Bones
String of Tears
Inked Forever
Psychic Visions Books 1–3
Psychic Visions Books 4–6
Psychic Visions Books 7–9

By Death Series

Touched by Death

Haunted by Death

Chilled by Death

By Death Books 1–3

Broken Protocols – Romantic Comedy Series

Cat's Meow

Cat's Pajamas

Cat's Cradle

Cat's Claus

Broken Protocols 1-4

Broken and… Mending

Skin

Scars

Scales (of Justice)

Broken but… Mending 1-3

Glory

Genesis

Tori

Celeste

Glory Trilogy

Biker Blues

Morgan: Biker Blues, Volume 1

Cash: Biker Blues, Volume 2

SEALs of Honor

Mason: SEALs of Honor, Book 1

Hawk: SEALs of Honor, Book 2

Dane: SEALs of Honor, Book 3
Swede: SEALs of Honor, Book 4
Shadow: SEALs of Honor, Book 5
Cooper: SEALs of Honor, Book 6
Markus: SEALs of Honor, Book 7
Evan: SEALs of Honor, Book 8
Mason's Wish: SEALs of Honor, Book 9
Chase: SEALs of Honor, Book 10
Brett: SEALs of Honor, Book 11
Devlin: SEALs of Honor, Book 12
Easton: SEALs of Honor, Book 13
Ryder: SEALs of Honor, Book 14
Macklin: SEALs of Honor, Book 15
Corey: SEALs of Honor, Book 16
Warrick: SEALs of Honor, Book 17
Tanner: SEALs of Honor, Book 18
Jackson: SEALs of Honor, Book 19
Kanen: SEALs of Honor, Book 20
Nelson: SEALs of Honor, Book 21
Taylor: SEALs of Honor, Book 22
Colton: SEALs of Honor, Book 23
Troy: SEALs of Honor, Book 24
Axel: SEALs of Honor, Book 25
Baylor: SEALs of Honor, Book 26
Hudson: SEALs of Honor, Book 27
Lachlan: SEALs of Honor, Book 28
Paxton: SEALs of Honor, Book 29
Bronson: SEALs of Honor, Book 30
Hale: SEALs of Honor, Book 31
SEALs of Honor, Books 1–3
SEALs of Honor, Books 4–6
SEALs of Honor, Books 7–10

SEALs of Honor, Books 11–13
SEALs of Honor, Books 14–16
SEALs of Honor, Books 17–19
SEALs of Honor, Books 20–22
SEALs of Honor, Books 23–25

Heroes for Hire

Levi's Legend: Heroes for Hire, Book 1
Stone's Surrender: Heroes for Hire, Book 2
Merk's Mistake: Heroes for Hire, Book 3
Rhodes's Reward: Heroes for Hire, Book 4
Flynn's Firecracker: Heroes for Hire, Book 5
Logan's Light: Heroes for Hire, Book 6
Harrison's Heart: Heroes for Hire, Book 7
Saul's Sweetheart: Heroes for Hire, Book 8
Dakota's Delight: Heroes for Hire, Book 9
Tyson's Treasure: Heroes for Hire, Book 10
Jace's Jewel: Heroes for Hire, Book 11
Rory's Rose: Heroes for Hire, Book 12
Brandon's Bliss: Heroes for Hire, Book 13
Liam's Lily: Heroes for Hire, Book 14
North's Nikki: Heroes for Hire, Book 15
Anders's Angel: Heroes for Hire, Book 16
Reyes's Raina: Heroes for Hire, Book 17
Dezi's Diamond: Heroes for Hire, Book 18
Vince's Vixen: Heroes for Hire, Book 19
Ice's Icing: Heroes for Hire, Book 20
Johan's Joy: Heroes for Hire, Book 21
Galen's Gemma: Heroes for Hire, Book 22
Zack's Zest: Heroes for Hire, Book 23
Bonaparte's Belle: Heroes for Hire, Book 24
Noah's Nemesis: Heroes for Hire, Book 25

Tomas's Trials: Heroes for Hire, Book 26
Carson's Choice: Heroes for Hire, Book 27
Dante's Decision: Heroes for Hire, Book 28
Steve's Solace: Heroes for Hire, Book 29
Heroes for Hire, Books 1–3
Heroes for Hire, Books 4–6
Heroes for Hire, Books 7–9
Heroes for Hire, Books 10–12
Heroes for Hire, Books 13–15
Heroes for Hire, Books 16–18
Heroes for Hire, Books 19–21
Heroes for Hire, Books 22–24

SEALs of Steel

Badger: SEALs of Steel, Book 1
Erick: SEALs of Steel, Book 2
Cade: SEALs of Steel, Book 3
Talon: SEALs of Steel, Book 4
Laszlo: SEALs of Steel, Book 5
Geir: SEALs of Steel, Book 6
Jager: SEALs of Steel, Book 7
The Final Reveal: SEALs of Steel, Book 8
SEALs of Steel, Books 1–4
SEALs of Steel, Books 5–8
SEALs of Steel, Books 1–8

The Mavericks

Kerrick, Book 1
Griffin, Book 2
Jax, Book 3
Beau, Book 4
Asher, Book 5

Ryker, Book 6
Miles, Book 7
Nico, Book 8
Keane, Book 9
Lennox, Book 10
Gavin, Book 11
Shane, Book 12
Diesel, Book 13
Jerricho, Book 14
Killian, Book 15
Hatch, Book 16
Corbin, Book 17
Aiden, Book 18
The Mavericks, Books 1–2
The Mavericks, Books 3–4
The Mavericks, Books 5–6
The Mavericks, Books 7–8
The Mavericks, Books 9–10
The Mavericks, Books 11–12

Standalone Novellas

It's a Dog's Life
Riana's Revenge
Second Chances

Published Young Adult Books:

Family Blood Ties Series

Vampire in Denial
Vampire in Distress
Vampire in Design
Vampire in Deceit

Vampire in Defiance
Vampire in Conflict
Vampire in Chaos
Vampire in Crisis
Vampire in Control
Vampire in Charge
Family Blood Ties Set 1–3
Family Blood Ties Set 1–5
Family Blood Ties Set 4–6
Family Blood Ties Set 7–9
Sian's Solution, A Family Blood Ties Series Prequel Novelette

Design series

Dangerous Designs
Deadly Designs
Darkest Designs
Design Series Trilogy

Standalone

In Cassie's Corner
Gem Stone (a Gemma Stone Mystery)
Time Thieves

Published Non-Fiction Books:

Career Essentials

Career Essentials: The Résumé
Career Essentials: The Cover Letter
Career Essentials: The Interview
Career Essentials: 3 in 1

Printed in Great Britain
by Amazon